Sweetbriar Summer

Also by Brenda Wilbee
  Sweetbriar
  The Sweetbriar Bride
  Sweetbriar Spring
  Shipwreck!
  Taming the Dragons
  Thetis Island

Sweetbriar Summer

Brenda Wilbee

Brenda Wilbee

Fleming H. Revell
A Division of Baker Book House
Grand Rapids, Michigan 49516

Published by Fleming H. Revell
a division of Baker Book House Company
P.O. Box 6287, Grand Rapids, MI 49516-6287

Printed in the United States of America

Library of Congress Cataloging-in-Publication Data

Wilbee, Brenda.
    Sweetbriar summer / Brenda Wilbee.
      p. cm.
    ISBN 0-8007-5619-3
    1. Denny, Louisa Boren—Fiction. 2. Frontier and pioneer life—Washington (State)—Fiction. 3. Women pioneers—Washington (State)—Fiction. 4. Denny, David Thomas—Fiction. 5. Seattle (Wash.)—History—Fiction. I. Title
PS3573.I3877S945 1997
813'.54—dc20
                                      96-43379

For current information about all releases from Baker Book House, visit our web site:

            http://www.bakerbooks.com

Dedicated to my
FATHER and MOTHER,
Roy and Betty Wilbee

For Everything

Acknowledgments

I first and foremost thank FLEMING H. REVELL for taking me on midstream. I'd written three earlier Sweetbriar books, published by a different house and now out of print. Nevertheless, Revell felt the series had merit and wanted to relaunch the line by producing three new books.

Second, I thank my mother and father, BETTY and ROY WILBEE, for their many contributions. One, their unrelenting confidence that I'd be able to pick up where I'd left off. Two, their financial underwriting of the project. And three, their comprehensive editing. Dad did the substantive work; it is he who is responsible for eliminating confusion in my narrative. Mum did the copy, and is responsible for the many detailed and picturesque word choices that made the narrative a more compelling read.

I thank CARLA RICHARDSON in Special Collections, Suzallo Library, University of Washington. Her suggestions and her own detective work always make research a rewarding and triumphant experience.

I am in debt to PHILLIPA STAIRS of the Puget Sound branch of Washington State Archives. Phillipa unearthed for me the historical journals of Seattle's third district court proceedings, 1854. *Merci beaucoup!*

I am very much in debt to WENDY ZHORNE, literary agent, for introducing me to Bill Petersen at Baker/Revell. And to ROY CARLISLE, former literary agent, for overseeing our early negotiations. As always, Roy, mercy *et merci.*

A heartfelt thank you goes to JACK WATT, Arthur Denny's great-grandson, for his unfailing support, his detailed comments written into the margins of my manuscript, his amazing memory of the facts, and his willingness not only to correct my mistakes, but to share details only family would know! For instance, Rolland was called Rollie, which I had gotten right. But Orion was *not* Orrie, which I had gotten wrong! Orion was Orion, says Jack. It's Jack who told me about Katy's chair. It's Jack who did Mr. Maurer's Dutch accent. It's Jack who keeps me on my toes! *Merci beaucoup, mon amie!*

I want to also thank Jack's brothers. I've come to count all three brothers—Bob, Jack, and Dick—for their support. And their unhesitating and unqualified permission to let me quote freely, sometimes extensively, from their mother's book, *Four Wagons West.*

Finally, I am grateful to my granny, LEONA BAGLEY GOOD-FELLOW BENT, a grandmother I'd never known. Due to a painful past shrouded in mystery, she nevertheless, last summer, allowed information to be relayed that she enjoyed my writing and dearly loved *Sweetbriar.* And *would I?* she wanted to know, *be writing any more?* This endorsement came at a discouraging time, and I was grateful for the acknowledgment. Also, this was my first indication she knew I existed, and gave me hope I'd yet be able to meet her. That day came only a short time ago. We trusted each other, I think, to make the connection and to guard it carefully because we both held the same love of history and because we both took such pleasure in reading of events that preceded our own disconnected lives. We had common ground on which to stand. And so it came to pass that my grandmother at ninety-two years of age let me into her life, trusting *Sweetbriar* and our shared historical interests to bridge nearly seventy years of unspoken time. Thank you, Granny, for first loving my books, and then me.

P.S. My grandmother tells me that Seattle's Bagleys are my cousins!

Contents

The growth of Seattle in '53, '54, and '55 was steady and strong, and the atmosphere of those years was happy. New people arrived. The mill hummed. Gardens of the pioneers' own planting were beginning to produce. White fences enclosed flower gardens, and kept the children in and the cows out. The Indians were friendly, some working in the mill, others peddling clams, salmon, and berries. To be sure, there were rumors of discontent among some of the tribes but these were not alarming, for Governor Stevens, superintendent of Indian affairs, would settle all of them.

—Roberta Frye Watt, Katy Denny's daughter*
in *Four Wagons West*

Part 1   **District Court**   19
Part 2   **Treaty Making**   69
Part 3   **The Swale**   113
Part 4   **James**   151
Part 5   **Gold**   201
Part 6   **War Drums**   245

* All references to Roberta Frye Watt come from her book *Four Wagons West* and are used by permission of Katy's grandchildren, Robert, Jack, and Richard Watt.

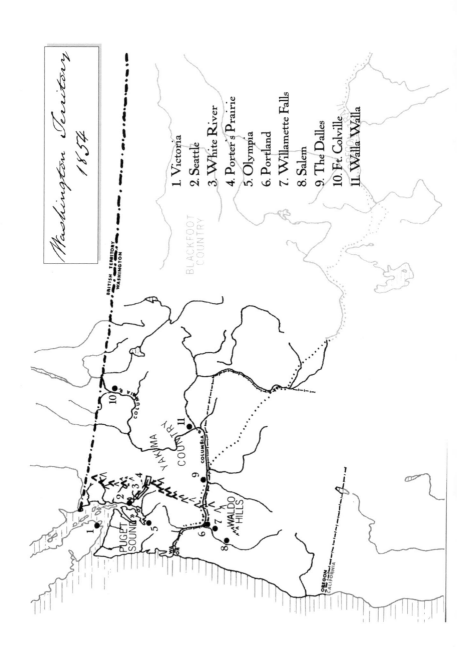

Washington Territory
1854

1. Victoria
2. Seattle
3. White River
4. Porter's Prairie
5. Olympia
6. Portland
7. Willamette Falls
8. Salem
9. The Dalles
10. Ft. Colville
11. Walla Walla

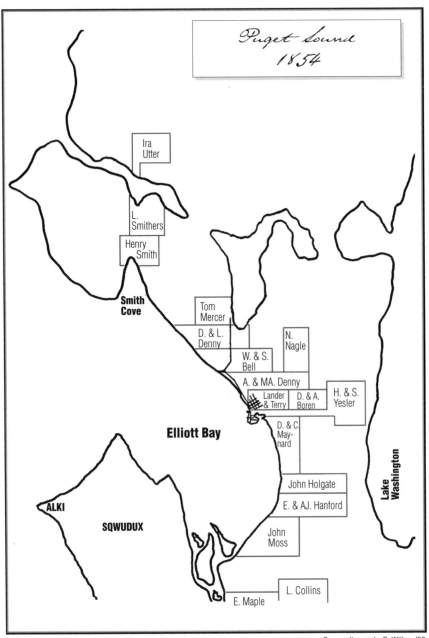

Puget Sound
1854

Ira
Utter

L.
Smithers

Henry
Smith

**Smith
Cove**

Tom
Mercer

D. & L.
Denny

N.
Nagle

W. & S.
Bell

A. & MA. Denny

Lander
& Terry

D. & A.
Boren

H. & S.
Yesler

D. & C.
May-
nard

Elliott Bay

ALKI

SQWUDUX

**Lake
Washington**

John Holgate

E. & AJ. Hanford

John
Moss

L. Collins

E. Maple

Composite map by B. Wilbee '96

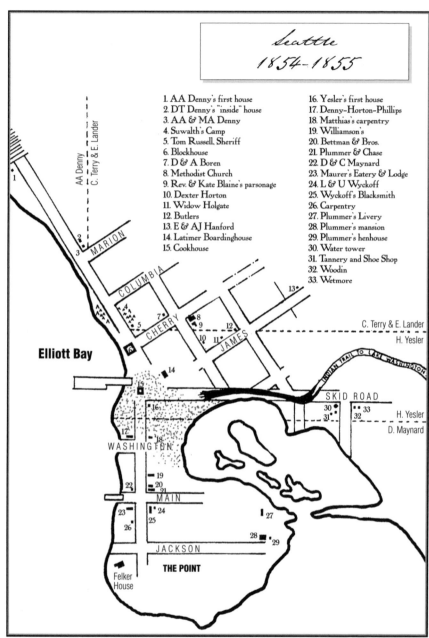

Seattle
1854–1855

1. AA Denny's first house
2. DT Denny's "inside" house
3. AA & MA Denny
4. Suwalth's Camp
5. Tom Russell, Sheriff
6. Blockhouse
7. D & A Boren
8. Methodist Church
9. Rev. & Kate Blaine's parsonage
10. Dexter Horton
11. Widow Holgate
12. Butlers
13. E & AJ Hanford
14. Latimer Boardinghouse
15. Cookhouse

16. Yesler's first house
17. Denny-Horton-Phillips
18. Matthias's carpentry
19. Williamson's
20. Bettman & Bros.
21. Plummer & Chase
22. D & C Maynard
23. Maurer's Eatery & Lodge
24. L & U Wyckoff
25. Wyckoff's Blacksmith
26. Carpentry
27. Plummer's Livery
28. Plummer's mansion
29. Plummer's henhouse
30. Water tower
31. Tannery and Shoe Shop
32. Woodin
33. Wetmore

AA Denny

C. Terry & E. Lander

MARION

COLUMBIA

CHERRY

JAMES

C. Terry & E. Lander

H. Yesler

Elliott Bay

INDIAN TRAIL TO LAKE WASHINGTON

SKID ROAD

H. Yesler

D. Maynard

WASHINGTON

MAIN

JACKSON

THE POINT

Felker
House

Composite map by B. Wilbee '96

THE BORENS AND DENNYS

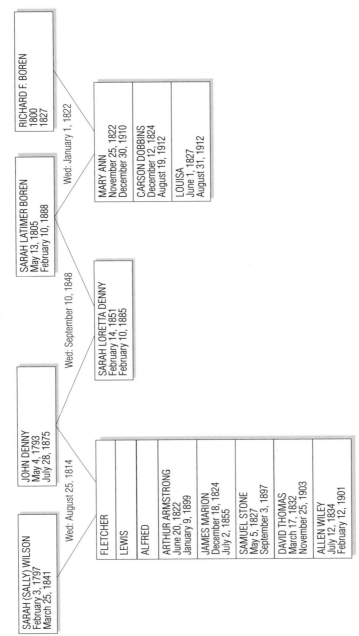

RICHARD F. BOREN
1800
1827

SARAH LATIMER BOREN
May 13, 1805
February 10, 1888

Wed: January 1, 1822

JOHN DENNY
May 4, 1793
July 28, 1875

Wed: September 10, 1848

SARAH (SALLY) WILSON
February 3, 1797
March 25, 1841

Wed: August 25, 1814

MARY ANN
November 25, 1822
December 30, 1910

CARSON DOBBINS
December 12, 1824
August 19, 1912

LOUISA
June 1, 1827
August 31, 1912

SARAH LORETTA DENNY
February 14, 1851
February 10, 1885

FLETCHER

LEWIS

ALFRED

ARTHUR ARMSTRONG
June 20, 1822
January 9, 1899

JAMES MARION
December 18, 1824
July 2, 1855

SAMUEL STONE
May 5, 1827
September 3, 1897

DAVID THOMAS
March 17, 1832
November 25, 1903

ALLEN WILEY
July 12, 1834
February 12, 1901

Top family group

DAVID THOMAS DENNY
March 17, 1832
November 25, 1903

LOUISA BOREN
June 1, 1827
August 31, 1912

Wed: January 23, 1853

EMILY INEZ
December 23, 1853
Unknown

ANNA LOUISA
November 26, 1864
May 5, 1888

MADGE DECATUR
March 16, 1856
January 17, 1889

DAVID THOMAS JR.
May 6, 1867
October 4, 1939

ABBIE LUCINDA
August 25, 1858
June 25, 1913

JONATHON
May 6, 1867
May 6, 1867

JOHN BUNYON
January 30, 1862
Unknown

VICTOR W. S.
August 9, 1869
August 15, 1921

Bottom family group

ARTHUR A. DENNY
June 20, 1822
January 9, 1899

MARY ANN BOREN
November 25, 1822
December 30, 1910

Wed: November 23, 1843

LOUISA CATHERINE
October 20, 1844
March 22, 1924

ORION ORVIL
July 17, 1853
February 26, 1916

MARGARET LENORA
August 14, 1847
March 30, 1915

ARTHUR WILSON
August 18, 1859
November 14, 1919

ROLAND HERSCHEL
September 2, 1851
June 13, 1939

CHARLES LATIMER
May 21, 1861
May 13, 1919

CARSON DOBBINS BOREN
December 12, 1824
August 19, 1912

MARY ANN KAYS (ANNA)
November 6, 1831
June 21, 1906

Wed: February 18, 1849

LEVINIA GERTRUDE
December 12, 1850
June 3, 1912

WILLIAM RICHARD
October 4, 1854
January 19, 1899

MARY LOUISA
1858
1926

From the Author

Sweetbriar Summer is the fourth novel in an eventual series of six Sweetbriar books—the ongoing story of David and Louisa Denny and Seattle history. This particular book opens upon the controversial trials of Seattle's Third District Court. The remaining story is the consequence of what happened at those trials.

Because I've been so exacting in my study of the Boren and Denny families and feel like I know their characters well, it's been a longtime puzzle for me as to why contemporary texts like to point out that during the 1854 trials Arthur and David—for the one and only time in their lives—voted against their consciences.

In the mid-1970s David's grandson, Victor Denny Jr., commissioned a well-known historian to write the story of his grandparents. Gordon Newell wrote in *Westward to Alki* the following in regard to those particular trials: "Even men like David Denny and Doc Maynard, compassionate friends of the Indians though they were, in the end found it impossible to sacrifice their friends and neighbors to the principles of abstract justice."[*] Where did Newell get the idea that David Denny had betrayed his Christian conscience? This was not

[*]Newell, Gordon. *Westward to Alki: The Story of David and Louisa Denny.* Seattle: Superior Publishing Company, 1977.

15

something the David Denny I know would ever consider. Had I misinterpreted David's character? Bill Speidel, Seattle's most humorous historian, wrote in his *Sons of the Profits* a similar indictment.

Where *was* this supposition of guilt coming from? In my research of untold documents and manuscripts and published texts, I'd not come across anything that even remotely suggested that David and Arthur had *ever* ignored their consciences. The closest reference came from Arthur Denny's granddaughter, Roberta Frye Watt. In her very accurate history, *Four Wagons West,* Ms. Watt reported that Arthur and David had both served on the trial juries. Yet she did *not* make any statement as to which of those juries David and Arthur might have sat on. Had Newell and Speidel simply jumped to conclusions? And subsequent writers, taking the wrong cues, now perpetuated a myth?

Sweetbriar Summer is cornerstoned on these trials and the consequences. I, therefore, could not begin writing the story until I'd resolved once and for all whether David and Arthur— both of whom I'd learned to trust in regard to their integrity— had, indeed, been guilty of ignoring truth. My suspicion was that they had not. But if they had, and Newell and Speidel were right, I wanted to know why. I wanted to know what internal struggle led these men into making a decision that was so uncharacteristic of their personalities and faith.

My search took me many interesting places. I finally found help at the Puget Sound branch of the Washington State Archives in Seattle, Washington, housed in a few back rooms of a terribly dilapidated and abandoned junior high school. There, the librarian unearthed for me the King County Court Journals of 1854. And there, written in antiquated script and faded ink, were the jury lists. Everyone's names, and the trials under which they served.

It is my hope and dream that with the publication of *Sweetbriar Summer* the truth of those trials—and the men involved—can now be made clear.

Preface

By her contemporaries who survived the hardships and deadly perils of the covered wagon migration of the 1850s to the last Frontier, Louisa Boren Denny was conceded to be the very epitome of everything that was best in the American pioneer woman . . . and for good reason.

—Louisa Boren Denny file,
Museum of History and Industry, Seattle

Many years ago, in 1851, Louisa Boren and Pamelia Dunlap kissed each other good-bye in a sweetbriar garden of Cherry Grove, Illinois. They wept as if their hearts would break for they knew they would never see one another again.

"The sweetbriar!" whispered Louisa to her dearest friend on earth. "It's God's promise of spring! I'll take some seeds to the Promised Land, and you keep some. That way we will never be parted! Not ever!"

"A tryst between us," answered Pamelia. "Spring will come, we will meet again. If not in this world, in the one to come, where we shall never be called to part! Remember God's promise, dear friend. Spring will always come!"

A tryst it was. Louisa Boren dried her eyes and pioneered west. In 1853 she married David Denny, Seattle's young founder, and all around the door of her log cabin she planted her seeds. In time the seeds scattered and grew and Louisa Boren Denny became known as Seattle's Sweetbriar Bride.

Today, in Seattle, Louisa is "conceded to be the very epitome of everything that was best in the American pioneer woman . . . and for good reason."

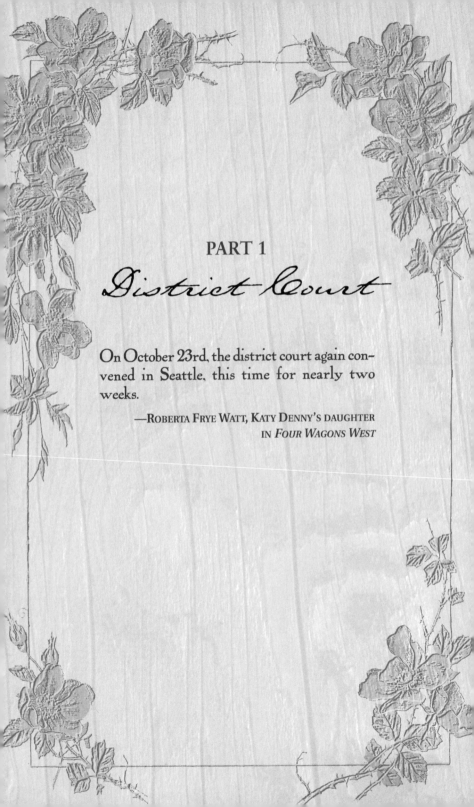

PART 1

District Court

On October 23rd, the district court again convened in Seattle, this time for nearly two
weeks.

—ROBERTA FRYE WATT, KATY DENNY'S DAUGHTER
IN *FOUR WAGONS WEST*

1

Monday Morning, October 23, 1854

"Oh what a book the story of my life would make!" Louisa Boren Denny exclaimed in a retrospective mood.

—Emily Inez Denny, David and Louisa's daughter
in *Blazing the Way*

Louisa Boren Denny opened her eyes to see the color and shape of things in her log cabin, then luxuriously rolled over and closed her eyes. The crowing of Good Morning and Peek-A-Boo had woken her in the gray light of dawn, but she left them to greet the morning alone and went away to sleep again.

When she opened her eyes next, a strip of yellow sunlight danced in scalloped wedges along the logs beside her bed. Under her scratchy Hudson's Bay blanket and shabby old quilt, one she and her sister Mary Ann had pieced together as children in Illinois, her bed was cozy with the warmth of her husband's body next to her own. A morning chill hung in the air, yet the world was a nice place to be in, she thought, with its layers of warmth and chill and promise of further warmth.

Summer in Seattle, 1854, had passed swiftly in a kaleidoscope of color and forward movement. New people had moved in; gardens had burgeoned; Captain Webster had bought the coal mine and was making it produce. Ships now plied the waters so regularly it wasn't uncommon to see one anchored offshore while waiting for another to finish loading at Yesler's wharf. And now Indian summer was upon them with all its attendant colors and abundant harvests... day after day of rich golden sunshine, frosty clear nights, and these crisp cold mornings. The scalloped wedges, she saw, came from a shaft of amber light streaming in through the unshuttered window of her cabin. *If I don't get up now,* she realized with a start, *I'll miss the fog patches lifting off the sea!*

Unwilling to disturb her husband or waken her ten-month-old baby girl, Louisa eased out of bed, pulled on a pair of socks—tucked beneath her pillow to keep warm!—and her doeskin moccasins, then tiptoed across the earthen floor. She slipped into her husband's bulky jacket and let herself outdoors.

The autumn air greeted her with the sharp scent of sea salt and kelp, a pungent seasoning that gave a gentle sting to the early morning stillness... stirring within some half-remembered pain, or old sorrow that no longer hurt. She passed her sweetbriar, growing beside the door, to hurry along the path to a short cliff and beach below. Along the trail, bush dahlias still in bloom gave further lift to her wakening spirits—as did the splendid view. She and David had built their cabin two miles north of Seattle, overlooking Elliott Bay of Puget Sound, Territory of Washington. Across the water, nearly thirty miles away, she could see the high jagged mountain range of Washington's Olympic Peninsula. These snowy mountains framed the western shore of the

Sound, and Louisa, her light brown eyes focused on the pristine beauty, breathed deeply into her lungs the tangy salt air.

She was a diminutive woman. Flawless skin, rosy cheeks, lively happy eyes, perfectly sculptured features, glossy black hair that put one in mind of a Dresden doll. But those who knew Louisa Boren Denny knew she was not made of fragile china. Hers was a character born of physical strength and forceful moral fiber. And as she surveyed the wakening world around her, so far from home and isolated by these mountains and sea, she thought of all that had happened to bring her here—to Puget Sound, the Promised Land of her dreams.

She thought of the long, arduous trek from Illinois, the heartbreaking separations from loved ones, the unceasing toil, the many dangers. She recalled their early days on the Sound, the struggle for survival, the curiously helpful Indians, the decision of David's brother to relocate their city on the inside of the Bay. *Better shelter and deeper water for a seaport,* Arthur had argued. She remembered, too, the exciting arrival of Doc Maynard, the timely appearance of Mr. Yesler with his sawmill, the quickening of spring, the many new faces arriving almost weekly. Now here they were three years later with nearly 250 settlers living in and around the Bay, with scores more scattered along the rivers reaching far back to the Cascade Mountains in the east. Truly this was the Promised Land, the paradise for which she'd left Illinois and the friends she loved. For in this new land she and David had at last married. Here they would plant and build and cultivate, here they would raise their family, here they would nurture all the beginnings of Christian civilization.

She was not naive, however. Last winter had been dark and, at times, terrifying, with murders and escalating tension between the Indians and whites. Luther Collins, one of their county commissioners, had inflamed matters by lynching Masachie Jim (who'd killed his wife in a drunken rage) and then lynching two other Indians arraigned on murder charges of one Mr. McCormick, a white man. The governor, before leaving in the spring for Washington City with the many pressing duties of their new territory, had ordered that Collins be tried for murder—as soon as Seattle's district court convened in the fall. *Today.* The Indians were to be assured, Governor Stevens had decreed, that what was good for the goose was good for the gander.

But was it? Louisa wondered. Would a white man convict another white man for lynching an Indian? Particularly an Indian who'd murdered his wife in cold blood? Yet if Luther Collins was not convicted, would the Indians retaliate? Because that's how they were. An eye for an eye.

She would not dwell on this. The local Indians were friendly. Many of them were engaged at the mill, others peddled their clams and salmon and berries. True, there were rumors of discontent, but these came from distant tribes from far over the mountains, and soon Governor Stevens would return from Washington City to settle whatever was troubling them. Besides, she reasoned confidently, hasn't Providence guided us in all our paths so far?

Low-lying fog patches hovered lightly over the surface of the water like wisps of breath. How she loved watching these vaporous clouds kissing the water before vanishing into nothing. On the beach, below the short cliff upon which she stood, the mist gathered in tighter clumps amongst the wild rose bushes. Behind her, where the forest resisted the sun, the fog held thickly, wreathing the three-hundred-foot Douglas firs, cedar, and hemlock trees like smoke rings.

"Where have you been?" she exclaimed suddenly, bending to pat Watch, their black Labrador hound who appeared out of the misty woods. But she recoiled quickly when she saw the dead squirrel he offered. "Oh, put that down! Goodness!"

They went back to the cabin and sat on the splintery front stoop, where she could more comfortably observe the thinning fog. Warm inside her husband's coat, she scratched Watch's silky ears and listened to the seagulls swooping and soaring overhead in the early morning sky—cawing, crying. She listened, too, to the chickens fuss and cluck in their coop out back. The domestic and the wild. Truly they had found the best of two worlds. She could not imagine a more perfect life.

Soon she heard her beloved husband stirring inside. He was lighting a fire; she could hear the familiar clang of the stove, the thump of wood. Would he wake Emily Inez? She hoped not. It would be nice to have their coffee alone, before going into Seattle to hear today's indictments.

The door creaked open. She felt the soft give of the stoop beneath her as her husband stepped outside. She scooted over to make room. Watch reluctantly gave up his spot and settled down between David's boots on the bottom step. "Thank you," she whispered, smiling up at her husband's still-sleepy face, the coffee cup he offered wondrously warm in her hands.

"You're welcome." He grinned and gave her a kiss.

"You're freezing—you have goose bumps on your arms," Louisa scolded.

David sat in his shirtsleeves, elbows on his knees, his own coffee cup pressed between the tips of his fingers. He leaned forward to take a sip and—without looking at her—said, "Someone stole my jacket."

She laughed.

They sat in companionable silence, drinking their coffee, watching the world take on brighter hues in the strengthening sun. Presently he asked, "How soon can you be ready to go?"

"What time do you have to be in town?"

He shrugged. "No special time. I'm just curious as to what the grand jury is up to. Rumor is they'll indict more than Mr. Collins."

"I wonder who," she mused. "Half the town was in on it."

"Well, we can't hang half the town, can we?"

"Nope." She thought about this for a moment. "David?"
He glanced at her obliquely.

"What will you do if the new sheriff puts *you* on Mr. Collins's jury? Will you convict him?"

He returned his gaze to the mountains across the water. "I don't know, Liza. I don't like thinking about it."

"What if you *had* to think about it?"

"No one wants more hangings."

"But if he isn't convicted, the Indians will retaliate against someone."

He didn't answer.

"We'd better wake up Emily Inez," she said with a sudden, weary sigh. "And get started."

"Liza, try not to worry so." He put an arm around her and kissed her hair. "We'll make out. We always do."

"I know."

2

Monday Afternoon, October 23, 1854

[District court] was held in the Felker House, which was more commodious than the cookhouse. Again, distinguished guests arrived, and King County pioneers from the farms along the riverways gathered in the village.

—Roberta Frye Watt, Katy Denny's daughter
in *Four Wagons West*

*D*avid and Louisa pointed their polished black Indian dugout southward, sliding noiselessly over the mirror of water that reflected the high dark bluff to their left. David glanced up at the dense green woods sitting atop the cliff. This wooded bluff ran from their claim on the north end of Elliott Bay all the way down to Seattle near the south. At its highest point the bank pushed up a hundred feet; at its lowest level, David realized, a child could easily scramble up the slope and get lost in the woods above. Frequent ravines cut the bluff and he knew by experience that numerous springs trickled laboriously through the hidden, stumpy seams to drain onto the beach, into the sea.

Emily Inez, tucked into her modified cradleboard and strapped to David's back, cooed and flapped her arms while he maneuvered the wobbly but well-designed dugout into deeper water. Fish skittered beneath them. The water grew dark. Along the beach twenty feet away Watch scampered across the gravel, sniffing at the tossed-up seaweed, yet keeping pace.

Half kneeling, half sitting in the stern, David gazed ahead to the surrounding islands and headlands which stood rugged and forested with tremendous trees. The water ran cold and deep. Nowhere did he notice harshness. Cold water and warm sun balanced each other; everything lay in a soft yellow haze that touched the world with Indian summer gentleness. Such a day made it easy to forget their man-made concerns.

His ear suddenly caught the tuneless chant of an Indian song drifting across the water—punctuated by the hollow drumming of paddles striking at intervals against the sides of a canoe. He turned to look. There, coming around Sqwudux, the peninsula that framed Elliott Bay's western shore, was a large Indian canoe.

Louisa laid her paddle across the crude gunwales of their own little dugout. "I love that sound," she sighed, turning around in the bow to give him a smile that never failed to warm his soul. "When we first moved here," she told him, "I couldn't hear the music. I wonder why? I think it's so beautiful now."

He knew exactly what she meant. Three years ago, when he'd first sailed into this bay as a nineteen-year-old kid, "canoe-singing" had sounded so foreign, a meaningless dirge. But after a while he had come to appreciate the nuances of native sound and rhythm.

Louisa started to paddle again. David matched his strokes to hers, and soon they passed the Bell cabin, a little log house

28

tucked up in the woods on their left, halfway to town. Another mile and Seattle's first house hove into view, all but hidden in the dark forest skirt. Here the embankment began a slow descent. The trees thinned, more cabins appeared—some log, a few frame, with split rail or smart picket fences guarding the spent gardens. In one final surge the bank pushed to a height of ten or fifteen feet, a sorry-looking hill denuded of trees and raw with ragged stumps. The Latimer Building popped into view, a two-story boardinghouse built by Louisa's uncle and set just off the summit. On the beach below the hillock was the campground of Chief Suwalth's small band of Duwamish, with their tipped-over canoes and rough shelters made of split-cedar planking.

Another ten yards, the bank gave way entirely, dropping to sea level and the triangle of flatland that housed Henry Yesler's sawmill—the very heart of Seattle.

David could smell Seattle before they came to it. The scent of sawdust, mixing and wafting with the breeze, came sweet to his nose. Thrusting his paddle deeply into the water, he shot past the denuded hill, and it took his breath away to see the busy triangle where the mill and cookhouse stood. Everyone was here; they must have come from miles around to hear today's indictments!

For a moment his concerns overtook him. What if he *was* put on Collins's jury? he wondered, Louisa's question flying at him and setting off a familiar conflict between his head and heart. Yet he'd learned not to ask the "what if" questions. Far better to take one day at a time. *Therefore do not be anxious about tomorrow, tomorrow will be anxious for itself,* he reminded himself, reciting from memory a verse from Scripture. *Let the day's own trouble—*

"David," called out Louisa, easing up from her cramped position to better see the excitement that surrounded the busy wharf and beach. "Did you say Will Brannan is on the grand jury?"

"Yes."

"I wonder if Elizabeth came in with him."

"White River is a long way away," he told her, angling his paddle backward and using their momentum to swing alongside Henry Yesler's wharf and up to the beach.

Henry Yesler's mill dominated and defined Seattle. It sat on an open platform straight ahead—the giant circular, steam-fed saw sheltered beneath a high tin roof. He ran his mill twenty-four hours a day to meet San Francisco's insatiable need for lumber, with two twelve-hour shifts, midnight to noon and back again, the fires never letting up. Everyone from around the Bay was needed to run it, or supply it, and David—no longer working in the mill himself— did his part by selling trees from his claim. Yesler paid him seven dollars for every thousand feet of raw timber. It sold in San Francisco for thirty-five dollars per thousand feet of finished board.

To the north, interspersed in the woods they'd just passed, lay the residential area. Close to thirty log and frame houses lined narrow stumpy trails, an invisible grid of streets his brother Arthur had platted and filed on paper a year ago May.

To the south was the Point, Doc Maynard's claim, a spit of land that eased out of the tideflats, gawky, ugly—but the very core of the business district. For a couple of years Hillory Butler and William Gilliam had been clearing the thick firs for Maynard, and Maynard had been selling the lots faster than the trees could come down. The newest construction going on was Arthur's commissary. David ducked under Yesler's wharf and came up on the other side to gaze southward at his brother's new store—across the narrow spit of sawdust and landfill that connected the Point to the mainland.

Yes, there was Arthur's store, all right. Twenty by thirty feet, he guessed. A stone's throw from the mill and opposite the carpenter shop, all but sitting in the sawdust and landfill that held back the tide and made the Point accessible.

"David," said Louisa, stepping up beside him, "why's Arthur building so close to the spit? If an extra high tide comes in he'll flood and float away!"

"He says Yesler's put in enough sawdust."

"He's not worried about the tide?"

"No."

Her expression told him she wasn't all that sure of Arthur's judgment. He wasn't either. The other stores were safe enough; the Point climbed as it went south. But where Arthur was building?

"Well, he ought to know," Louisa said with an amused shrug. "He always does, or at least he always *thinks* he does."

David affectionately shook his head.

She grinned. "Well, he does!"

He just laughed, though he wanted to hold her face with both his hands and kiss her soundly, for he loved the gaiety in her eyes whenever she was on to Arthur. "Come on, Mrs. Denny," he said instead, looping an arm over her willing shoulders and whistling for Watch. "Let's go see what's happening at the cookhouse."

"I thought Court was to be held at the Felker House."

He squinted again across the Sawdust, beyond Arthur's commissary and the short row of stores, to where Seattle's fancy hotel, built by Captain Felker for an outrageous four thousand dollars, sat atop the Point's crown, overlooking Elliott Bay. Two stories high, with a second-floor porch running across the front of it, the gleaming white Felker House gave the rest of Seattle something to live up to. "It is," he said, "but everyone's collected at the cookhouse. Come on, something's afoot."

They skirted the mill's south side. Louisa proudly watched her husband snatch off his knitted toque to wave at his many friends straining over the huge Douglas fir being fed into the circling saw. They glanced up, sweat dripping off their brows.

"Hey there, Horton!" David hollered above the high whine of the whirling blade as it bit into the wood.

31

"Hey there, Denny!" Dexter Horton hollered back.

"Hey there, Frye!" David shouted.

"Denny!" greeted young George Frye, a German immigrant, short on words but always big on smiles.

Suddenly David veered over to where one of the Indians was stacking boards, calling out a Snoqualmie greeting. He'd already learned Duwamish and Suquamish, now he was tackling Snoqualmie. Louisa gave him a moment while Yoke-Yakeman patiently corrected his pronunciation.

"How many of their languages are you going to learn?" she asked proudly when they were on their way again.

He shrugged. "I don't know. Why?"

"Just wondering."

She didn't recognize most of the people milling around the cookhouse—men and women from miles out, pioneers who preferred farming the fertile riverlands to chopping down the nearby forests. Still, she scanned their faces for someone she might know and thought again of Elizabeth Brannan, the English bride from White River. How lonely it must be to live sixteen miles from nowhere. Suddenly she spotted Ursula McConaha Wyckoff, another new bride—married to Seattle's blacksmith last July.

Ursula saw her at the same time. "Why, Louisa, I declare!" she greeted, hurrying over with her two-year-old daughter slung across her hip.

"Hello!" said Louisa. "And where's George Junior?" she asked, looking around for Ursula's rambunctious ten-year-old son.

"Down at the smithy. David. How are you?"

"Wondering what's going on in the cookhouse."

Ursula rolled her eyes and flipped her long, golden-brown braid over a shoulder. "The grand jury just finished handing down their indictments."

"That was fast," said David with a low whistle.

"Doc Maynard is trying to drum up some donations to pay an attorney for David Maurer. You know how Mr. Maurer is—he needs all the help he can get," said Ursula, laughing and pointing to her ear and waggling her finger around and around.

"David Maurer?" There was a sharp edge to David's voice.

"Him and Mr. Heebner. And Mr. Collins, of course."

David reached up to grab Emily Inez's mittened hands; she had begun to box his ears. "Heebner makes a little sense," he mused, "he got the block and tackle from the *Jefferson Davis.* But Maurer—"

"Isn't Mr. Maurer the one who punched you?" Louisa interrupted, looking up at her husband's puzzled face. "When you tried to cut down Masachie Jim?"

"Yes," he said, shifting his eyes between her and Ursula. "But you can't hang a man for punching a guy."

"Which is why Doc Maynard is madder than a hornet," Ursula explained. "You know how fond he is of Mr. Maurer! He let Mr. Maurer start his restaurant in the old Seattle Exchange, then he got Mr. Maurer into the building across the street. He's taking in lodgers now, Mr. Maurer is. Maurer's Eatery and Guest House, he calls it. Anyway," Ursula rattled on, "sewing circle is at my house. Did you bring your square for the quilt, Louisa?"

"Yes."

"If you see anyone, tell them they're invited, though I'm sure I don't have enough teacups."

"Maybe I can borrow one from Mary Ann."

"Oh, could you? Dear me, but there's Mrs. Bell and her girls. And that wee son of hers! I wonder how she's getting on? She should never have had that baby. Her consumption . . . *One o'clock!*" Ursula hollered over her shoulder. "*Don't forget!*"

"Goodness," said Louisa, watching her friend dash off.

"She's happy," said David.

"Yes," agreed Louisa, remembering. Last winter Ursula's six-year-old daughter had been killed by a cougar and in May, when coming home from the territorial legislature, her husband had been drowned. The two deaths, so close to each other, had nearly driven Ursula mad with grief—made all the worse by a rash statement she'd made just days before George's death. Hearing he'd be delayed in getting home, she'd saucily snapped, "Well I'm sure I don't care if he ever comes home!" When he *didn't* come home—when only his hat had washed ashore . . . Well, thank God for Lewis Wyckoff, thought Louisa now, slipping her hand into David's and giving her husband's fingers a warm squeeze. The blacksmith had somehow saved Ursula's sanity and turned her life around.

"She *is* happy," repeated Louisa, "and I'm glad. She deserves to be. But who would have thought," she sighed, leaning her head onto David's shoulder, "that she and Mr. Wyckoff would fall in love and get married?"

"Mm . . . You staying with me? Or going up to Arthur and Mary Ann's?" He jiggled her hand to prompt her answer. "Well?" he insisted, forcing her to leave aside the unpleasant, sad memories.

"I'd like to see what's going on in the cookhouse."

Doc Maynard was standing on a table when they entered, his octagonal glasses, as usual, pushed up on his forehead. Black hair tufted off the top of his head like meringue on lemon pie. "That's right! Sign your name, name your dollar! We need attorneys for our comrades, good Democrats every one of 'em! Hey, Dave! I'm heading up a subscription for Maurer's defense! What can I put you down for? I'm down for a hundred and fifty dollars!"

"A hundred and fifty dollars!" shrieked Louisa, forgetting herself, she was so thunderstruck.

"Dave, you going to let your wife henpeck you like that?" howled Maynard, winking at Louisa.

Louisa flushed a furious red, but David grabbed her elbow.

"Ten dollars will do!" Maynard shouted. "So will twenty! But fifty's better!"

"Let me figure this out, Doc!" David hollered back. "What's the going rate these days? What do *we* get paid when we work for someone else?" He threw the question out to the crowd and there was some disgruntled discussion. His question had put things into perspective. "Hey, Butler!" he hollered, spying the huge lumberman from Virginia. "Doesn't Maynard pay you about three dollars a day to chop down those trees and haul them off the Point?"

"Pays me two-fifty!" shouted the gigantic Virginian, and everyone laughed.

"I pay you three-fifty, and you know it!" shouted Maynard, his turn to flush a deep red.

"Ah, I was just pulling your leg, Doc! He pays me three-fifty, sure!" But the way the huge, burly man said it made everyone laugh even more.

"Now see here," insisted Maynard, "you get paid three-fifty and no fooling. And you don't have expenses! We don't have George McConaha anymore, which means we have to import attorneys from Olympia, and they don't come cheap. Plus we got to get them boat tickets—"

"Boat tickets, when you can catch a boat, are only ten dollars round trip!" snorted Arthur Denny, David's brother, pulling his tall, lean frame away from the squared-off logs of the cookhouse wall. He was older than David by ten years, as blond as David was dark. "The three men accused of murder are entitled to their defense; I'm the last to quibble that, and their attorneys are entitled to get paid. But paying an attorney . . . What's the total now? Six hundred dollars? Not counting that fifty you're trying to weasel out of Dave? Why, I'd say paying an attorney $600 is paying an attorney about $597 too much!"

The laughter exploded, yet when the last snicker subsided Maynard cleared his throat and said, "Arthur Denny, I hear you're on a jury."

"Yes, sir."

This was news to Louisa and she looked sharply over at David. Had the new sheriff drawn up the jury lists, then? Was David on one?

"Which means," bawled Maynard, "things ain't exactly going to get wrapped up in a day!"

"Meaning . . . ?" snapped Arthur.

"Meaning it's going to take more than three dollars!"

"State your point, Doc. If you're implying—"

"I'm implying nothing, I'm saying it! I'm saying you'll hold for a guilty verdict! I'm saying it'll take a high hat of cash to pay our attorneys—for each day you sit around on your high horse!"

Arthur eased back against the wall, jaw clenched. It was then that Louisa noticed he'd shaved his sandy beard.

"What's gotten into Maynard anyway?" she whispered to David. "That was pretty low-down!"

"I don't know."

Just then Dr. Henry Smith, one of Seattle's early pioneers, popped in. "Jury lists are posted for all three trials! Notices on the front door of the Felker House!"

Doc Maynard tugged on his raccoon-tailed cap and jumped off the table. He pushed through the crowd, but stopped short when he got to David and Louisa. He said nothing, though, and stormed on out.

"Well, Dave," said Arthur when the crowd dispersed, "guess we know which way the wind blows. Hello, Louisa."

"Hello, Arthur. Nice chin." She pointed.

"Thanks." They headed outside. "I've been put on Heebner's jury," Arthur grumbled. "Sure wish it was Maurer's. I could sleep nights acquitting him. He meant no harm—no more than anyone else who stood around watching."

"My name anywhere on a list?" David asked.

"Maybe you're on for Collins. Only Maurer and Heebner were posted when I was down there."

David groaned, and Louisa's heart skipped a little. She hardly dared imagine what was going through her husband's mind.

"Guess there's only one way to find out for sure," said Arthur. He poked his chin in the general direction of the Point where the Felker House sat high on the crown of the hill. "Want me to go with you?"

"How 'bout you, Liza?" David asked. "Do you want to go?"

"No, I'll take Emily Inez and find Mary Ann—No, no," she told him when he went to unfasten the straps across his chest. "You keep the cradleboard. It's heavy, and I don't need it."

He turned his back so she could loosen the leather thongs and ease Emily Inez out of her restraint. Arthur waited with obvious impatience while they said good-bye.

"Remember," she whispered, juggling Emily Inez on her hip and taking the smaller bag of diapers that David handed her, "if the new sheriff has you down for Mr. Collins, it's because he knows he can trust *you* to do what's best."

"Maybe." He gave her a quick kiss and was gone.

3

Monday Afternoon,
October 23, 1854

The "Maj Tompkins" looks well, and gives every indication of a worthy sea going craft, capable, at least, of performing between this place and Victoria. Captain John H. Scranton deserves, and we hope will receive, material assurance that the project of ocean steam navigation on the Sound will be duly appreciated, with the hope that he will receive from Government the contract of transmitting the mails regularly to all the county seats of the counties along the Sound, and be amply rewarded . . .

The Steamship "Major Tompkins" under the command of Capt. James Hunt, the first to ply regularly upon the waters of Puget Sound.

—*Pioneer & Democrat,* September 23, 1854

The sewing bee was for Louisa's newest nephew, William Richard Boren, born three weeks earlier to Louisa's brother Dobbins and his wife, Anna. The ladies of

Seattle crowded into Ursula's cozy new home on the Point, next to the blacksmith shop. The sound of happy chatter and occasional peals of laughter drifted through the double-hung windows of the front room as they stitched together the soft quilt they were sewing for the baby.

"Did you ladies hear about the poor fugitive slave they caught in Boston last month?" asked Kate Blaine, the preacher's wife, quite suddenly. She sat by the fire, her skirts hemmed a little too short in order to show off her fancy morocco boots.

"I did! A disgrace too!" huffed Mrs. Butler from Virginia, looking up from her sewing. "All that rioting! Thank God law prevailed and the upstart darkie was shipped back to his master!"

"Oh, how can you say that?" wailed Abbie Jane Hanford, a young mother of three little boys and expecting another child. "Slavery is such a terrible abomination. To think that the—"

"Quite so," agreed the minister's wife. "And if—"

"If Congress had *not* passed the Kansas-Nebraska Act," interrupted Catherine Maynard firmly, "where would we be?"

They all looked at Doc Maynard's wife blankly.

"Last spring," said Catherine, "Jefferson Davis, Secretary of War, tried to squash all the transcontinental railroad surveys—except, of course, for his southern route. And you know how our husbands are counting on the northern route terminating here in Seattle."

"Bee's knees!" snorted Mrs. Butler. "What's slavery got to do with the railroad?"

"Everything," said Catherine.

"Mmph."

"The North agreed to the Kansas-Nebraska Act—allowing for the expansion of slavery," Catherine explained, sewing as she spoke. "In exchange, Jeff Davis had to put the other railroad surveys before Congress. Including ours."

39

Kate Blaine rocked forward. "Catherine Maynard, you mean to tell me that we sold out to slavery, for a chance at the railroad? Oh!" she wailed, punching her knees with her fists. "If *women* could only vote we would wipe slavery off the face of this earth! I've just read *Uncle Tom's Cabin*—it's terrible what the poor slaves endure!"

Mrs. Butler peered over her glasses at the preacher's wife, stopping her. "I suppose you believe everything you read, Mrs. Blaine?"

Louisa tuned them out, her mind no longer on slavery, but on the railroad. For three years everyone in the country had been waging bets as to where the much-talked-about transcontinental would someday go. The person to peg it right stood to make a lot of money, for the railroad would instantly become the economic backbone of the nation. Seattle, of course, had been hoping for the northern route; they wanted the terminus. The terminus would make some waterfront pioneer a millionaire literally overnight, the rest of them not far behind. Louisa knew David thought *they'd* be the lucky pioneers. He'd already named an imaginary road Depot Way, and had it figured out where the train would someday come in and at what point on the beach the depot would stand. This was nothing different, though, than half the men in town. To Louisa it was a pipe dream. The political ups and downs were enough to discourage anyone from taking anything seriously. Like last summer, when the governor wrote Arthur from Washington City to say that Jefferson Davis had decried four of the five surveys in favor of his own—even though *his* train would detour through Mexico, south of the Rio Grande for six hundred miles, before reentering the States! And now? Because of the Kansas-Nebraska Act, everything was back on again? *Politics is a dirty game,* she thought.

"No one in Seattle is going to line their pockets with railroad money," Louisa heard. *Ursula,* she realized, looking up and paying attention.

"Jeff Davis," said Ursula scornfully while passing around a plate of maple sugar candies, "was only making a show of sending around that surveying steamer. In the end, he'll discredit the findings the same way he pooh-poohed Governor Stevens's report."

"What surveying steamer?" asked the very stout wife of Luther Collins, speaking up for the first time.

"Yes, what steamer?" Louisa asked. Had Captain Scranton's new steamer, which he'd purchased to service the Sound, arrived and no one told her? Had he gotten the mail contract? Was the mail here?

Her sister, Mary Ann, saw what was in her mind, and laughed. "No, Louisa, not Captain Scranton's steamer, not yet. Who knows when that will get here. This was a government boat." Mary Ann, five years older than Louisa, was married to Arthur, David's older brother. She set her sewing onto her lap. "Last month," she said, "a government boat put into Seattle. Commissioned by Jeff Davis himself, to survey the Pacific coast for the best harbor. The best harbor," Mary Ann quickly explained to Mrs. Collins who had a perplexed look on her face, "means the best spot for the railroad terminus."

"Seattle's still in the running, then?" asked Mrs. Collins. "The South ain't won yet?"

"That's what the captain told my husband," said Mary Ann proudly. "Furthermore, Captain Alden said Elliott Bay is the deepest harbor—and we're closest to China by two hundred miles."

"That's what my brother keeps saying!" burst out Ellender Smith, a pretty girl who was newly engaged to Mr. Plummer, one of the most prominent men in town.

"Now why don't Mr. Collins tell me these things!" huffed Mrs. Collins, embarrassed by her lack of information.

"I'm sure he's had a lot on his mind lately," said Abbie Jane graciously, quickly. Just as quickly she blushed. All afternoon the ladies, upon seeing Mrs. Collins at the bee, had been careful not to bring up the *real* reason they were in town.

Mrs. Collins blushed too. But then she pursed her lips and laughed. "Landsakes, you think I don't know my man ain't no saint? Begory, he'd o' lynched *me* afore now—if I weren't bigger'n him!"

"Oh, dear," said Ursula.

Louisa concentrated on her sewing. Imagine! Saying something like that about one's husband!

Having decided to help his brother put the roof on his new commissary, David worked with a vengeance. He liked hard physical labor, particularly when he had something to mull over, like getting stuck on jury duty for Luther Collins's trial.

A half dozen other men had decided to help as well, everyone waiting for the sewing bee to let out. Men like his brother-in-law Dobbins Boren, waiting for Anna. Henry Smith, for his widowed mother and pretty sister Ellender. And Hillory Butler, whose wife wasn't so pretty but who could play a pretty mean tune on the piano. And Ed Hanford for Abbie Jane. No point in going home, Ed had joked, when there's no supper on the table. A couple of loggers from Salmon Bay had stopped by, too. Two of their partners were on the grand jury, still in session, lining up indictments against some of the sea captains for dumping ballast into the harbor.

"Did I ever tell you about getting lost last summer?" Henry asked when David leaned back on his heels to ease the stiffness in his knees and back, and to draw a deep breath. Behind them lay the steep slant of the high roof covered with tidy, straight rows of sweet-smelling cedar shakes. Ahead, the wide-open roof boards.

"Nope," said David, taking in the view with an appreciative eye. The tide behind and below him was at its brim, flooding the beach. The shoreline nosed up abruptly, capped by immense evergreens. The land pushed up from there, up, up, swell after swell, hill after hill, piling itself into another great mountain range fifty miles inland—reflective of the

Olympics across the Sound—and through which the railroad, they hoped, would someday come. Excluding the small patch of ground out of which Seattle would grow, David could see no sign of earth or rock. Only the great forests billowing up and out, stretching green and gold-green to meet the snow-washed mountains ahead.

"Did I, Dave?" Henry repeated.

"No, Henry, you didn't tell me," said David, picturing Henry Smith's newly planted orchard on the north cove. A regular botanist, the young medical doctor had just been telling him how he'd grafted two different kinds of apples onto one tree.

They had a system. David would hand Henry the shakes like cards off a deck. Henry would lay them flat and hammer them down. After a while they'd trade off, crab-walking over to a new pile of shakes that either Dobbins or Ed had laid out for them.

"You'd remember if I did," said Henry, chuckling to himself. He hefted his hammer and pulled a nail from his canvas apron. "I took it into my head one day last summer to blaze a trail to Seattle. August, I think. Took a compass and started for town on as nearly a straight line as possible." He laid out the shake and let fly with his hammer, pounding in the short, squatty shingle nails with two hard blows. WHAM-WHAM. "But after about an hour or so the sun crawled behind the clouds. I had to rely on my compass. Tedious business."

David handed him another shake.

"Then about noon, to my astonishment—" WHAM-WHAM "—the compass reversed its poles. One minute it was pointing southeast, next thing I knew it had swung right around and was pointing northwest!"

"Is that so?"

"Would I lie? Now I knew that beds of mineral can sometimes cause a variation of the needle, so—" WHAM-WHAM

"—I was delighted at the thought of maybe discovering a *valuable iron mine* so near the water!"

David laughed and tossed off a defective shake.

"Hey, watch it!" someone hollered up at them.

"Sorry!"

"A good deal of time was spent, I can assure you, in marking the spot so there'd be no difficulty in finding it again! From that point on—" WHAM-WHAM "—I broke branches as I walked, so I could easily retrace my steps. I followed my compass *reversed,* calculating, as I walked, the number of ships that would load annually at Seattle with pig iron, the amount of ground that would eventually be covered at Smith Cove with furnaces—" WHAM-WHAM-WHAM "—and all the rolling mills, the foundries, all the tool-manufacturing establishments—" WHAM-WHAM "—etc!" WHAM!

David passed another shake.

"But night started coming on. I concluded I'd traveled too far east, that I'd passed Seattle. The prospect of spending a night in the woods, I can tell you, knocked my iron calculations right into pi!"

David grinned. "What'd you do?"

"Stumbled into a clearing . . . and a shake-built shanty—" WHAM "—which I figured was the ranch Mr. Nagle had filed on and was proving up. And which, as I understood," he added, pausing to squint northeast in the general direction of John Nagle's homestead, "lay somewhere between Seattle and Lake Washington. Howdy, boys," he said to the men who'd scrambled up on the roof to hear his story and were grinning—to David's way of thinking—like a row of Cheshire cats.

"So when I reached the fence surrounding Mr. Nagle's improvements," Henry continued with his own grin, "I sat myself up on the top rail for a seat and to ponder the advisability of remaining with my new neighbor overnight, or going into town. Sitting there, I couldn't help but contrast Nagle's improvements with my own. The size of his clearing was the

44

same, his house was a good deal like mine. The only seeming difference was that the front of his faced west, whereas the front of mine faced east. I was puzzling over this strange and amazing coincidence when my own mother came out of the house to feed the poultry that had commenced going to roost, in a rookery for all the world like my own, only facing the wrong way!"

Chuckles passed down the roofline.

"'In the name of all that's wonderful!' I said to myself, 'What is she doing here? and how did she get here ahead of me?' Just then the world took a spin around, my ranch wheeled into line, and, lo! I was sitting on my own fence, and had been looking at my own improvements without knowing them!"

Dobbins, who rarely laughed, did so, nearly pitching over backward. Ed Hanford, though, who laughed easily, eased to his feet with a very sober face.

"You see something, Ed?" asked David.

"Maybe I do, maybe I don't," said the slender man, his narrow features pinched tight with concentration, both hands shielding his eyes as he squinted down the Sound. David scrambled up. A puff of black smoke lay like a thread over the water.

"Ma!" shrieked George McConaha Junior, tumbling through the front door of Ursula's house and stumbling over nine-month-old Austin Bell.

Ursula grabbed her son by the ear. "What do you mean, barging in here like a clumsy ox?" she bawled, yanking him around hard even as Sally Bell scooped up her wailing baby.

Teddy Hanford, chasing after George Junior, hurtled through the door. Too late he saw Eugenia playing with her blocks. The seven-year-old boy veered, swung too wide, ran into the cradle, and the newborn William Richard rolled out, his thin scream piercing the air. Everyone gasped and reached for him while Teddy, trying to avoid landing on the screaming, tumbling baby, threw himself against Mrs. Butler and crashed onto her lap.

"Landsakes!"

"Mama! Mama! Mama!" A half dozen little girls careened inside.

"Mama, guess what?" shouted Becky Horton, finding her mother through the maze of outraged ladies and babies. "The steamer, Mama! The mail boat!"

"The mail boat?" Everyone shrieked at once.

Ursula let George go. He grabbed his ear, pushed past the girls, and ran outdoors.

The girls jumped up and down and clapped their hands. "The mail boat is here! It's here! It's here! The steamer from San Francisco!"

Hats and coats everywhere!

"Oh, where is my bonnet?"

"Sewing bee at Mary Ann Denny's tomorrow!"

"Where is my bonnet?"

"Here it is, Mrs. Blaine."

"Oh, thank you, Mrs. Phillips!"

"Katy!" shouted Louisa, catching sight of her sister's eldest child. "Find your brother, Rollie, he's around here somewhere! Put his coat on! Nora?"

Louisa's six-year-old niece squeezed through the pandemonium. "Yes, Auntie?"

"Nora, help me find Emily Inez's bunting!"

Ten minutes later, sewing bee dispersed, the women walked as fast as they could down Commercial Street, toward the mill, clutching the tugging hands of their older children and holding on to their babies. Mary Ann, Louisa's sister, had her youngest, fifteen-month-old Orion, slung across one hip. Next in line, three-year-old Rollie, charged along ahead of her. Anna, Louisa's sister-in-law, had her new baby (more frightened than hurt) in her arms, with Gertrude, her three-and-a-half-year-old daughter, clasped firmly by the hand. Louisa walked alongside them so swiftly her skirts tangled.

Up ahead she could see Katy and Nora, the eldest of Mary Ann's four children, racing across the Sawdust with their friends. Watch tore after them, barking.

The new steamer had already tied up at Yesler's wharf when they arrived at the mill. Captain Scranton, who'd purchased the steamer and brought it up from San Francisco to service the Sound, and Captain Hunt, the pilot (at least that was who Louisa supposed they were), stood beneath the high tin roof of the mill. Mr. Plummer, Ellender Smith's fiancé and Seattle's postmaster, held the mailbags.

"It *is* the mail!" squealed Anna as the women all pushed into the crowd of men congregated around the platform. "U.S. Mail!" Anna read. "Do you see?"

"I see," said Mary Ann, a plain-looking woman in her early thirties, a sharp contrast to Anna, who was still a young girl with flashing dimples and large green eyes.

Louisa caught sight of David up ahead. "David!"

He angled back through the crowd. "Think maybe we got news from Ma and Pa?" he asked, taking Emily Inez and throwing her over his shoulder like a sack of potatoes.

"Oh, I hope so! It's been so long since we've heard anything! We don't even know if they got their crops in—!" Louisa slapped a hand over her mouth and laughed. Someone had thrown the switch. The shrill saw, whining to a stop, had caught a lot of them shouting in the sudden quiet.

"Wetmore!" called out handsome Mr. Plummer. "Collins! Bell! Nagle! Maynard! Brannan! Smith—William Smith!"

"Shh, shh!" people hissed. "Mr. Plummer's passing out the letters!"

"Denny—Arthur Denny!"

Any number of people could be writing Arthur. Maybe the governor, thought Louisa, enroute home from Washington City and due back any day. Or maybe Delegate Lancaster, still in Washington City. Or Ma and Pa in Oregon. Louisa hoped it was Ma and Pa!

To most people, her family was an odd combination. She, Mary Ann, and Ma had all married Dennys—Ma to Pa Denny; Mary Ann to Arthur; finally, at long last, she to David. Three and a half years ago they'd all lived in Illinois, until Pa took it into his head to move to Oregon. Somewhere along the way Arthur took it into *his* head to build his own city, so when they got to the Willamette Valley of Oregon, he and David, along with Dobbins, came up to Puget Sound. Which meant she and Mary Ann, and Anna, came too. But Ma and Pa with their new baby and the other Denny brothers wanted to stay in the Willamette Valley where they'd originally agreed to live. But oh, how she missed Ma! And baby Loretta!

One by one the names were called off, Mr. Yesler, the sawmill owner, speeding things up considerably by passing out the letters and magazines and newspapers that Mr. Plummer pulled out of the two big leather sacks. A half hour later Louisa, her sister, and sister-in-law boasted several letters between them and were excitedly reading through them in the afternoon's waning light.

"Pa's knee is better!" said Mary Ann.

"Loretta can say her ABCs now!" added Anna.

"Oh, dear, Wiley's thinking of getting married! Married, can you believe it? Wiley?"

"Louisa Denny!"

Startled, Louisa looked up.

"For you, Mrs. Denny!" hollered Mr. Plummer, waving a small brown package over his head. He handed it over to Mr. Yesler and Louisa watched with bated breath as the small parcel was passed hand to hand high over everyone's heads.

"It's from James!" she declared the minute she held the parcel in her hands.

"James? What's he sending you a present for?" demanded Anna, her pretty nose wrinkled with reproach.

Louisa hardly dared look to David. James was Arthur and David's brother. He was hopelessly in love with her, and David, for a long time, had resented him. Terribly.

But David juggled Emily Inez to the other shoulder, and gave Louisa a wink. "Are you going to open it here? Or wait 'til we get home?"

"Open it now!" cried ten-year-old Katy, jumping up onto a log beside Louisa, her red braids bouncing.

"Yes, Auntie!" begged Nora, hugging Louisa.

"What do you think?" she asked David.

"I think you better hurry up and open it before these girls wet their pants."

"Un-cle Da-vid!" the girls bellowed, hitting him until he laughed.

"All right then," said Louisa, "we'll open it!" and she flung herself onto the log. The little girls scrambled down beside her. David stood in front, holding Emily Inez. Mary Ann dragged Arthur over. Dobbins, as usual, was nowhere to be seen.

"What is it?" Katy breathed out.

"I don't know, wait a minute. There!" said Louisa, pulling back the wrapping.

"A book! A real book!" exclaimed Nora in wonder. "Does it have pictures?"

Louisa fanned the pages. "Yes, a few."

"What's the book called?" asked Mary Ann.

A letter slipped out. Louisa passed the book up to David and reached down to rescue the single sheet of paper.

"Read it out loud!" Nora begged, the two girls leaning all over her, trying to read along with her.

"Dear Louisa . . . This book is all the rage in Oregon. Ma thought you and Mary and the children would like the story. Pa says it means eventual war between the States. I don't know. Say hello to Arthur and David. Give the crew a hug from their Uncle James. Presents for them next time—after I talk with Santa Claus. Your loving stepbrother, James."

"Santa Claus!" gasped six-year-old Nora. "He's going to talk to Santa Claus!"

"Don't be a goose," Katy snorted. "There's no such thing as Santa Claus."

"Uncle James—"

"Uncle James doesn't realize we're all grown up!" declared Katy emphatically, ending the matter.

David had the book, and was holding it away from Emily Inez's grasping hands. *"Uncle Tom's Cabin,"* he read. "By Harriet Beecher Stowe."

"That's the book Kate Blaine was talking about!" shouted Louisa, jumping up. "Oh, give it to me, David! Let me see it!"

"I wonder if Harriet Beecher Stowe is related to Henry Ward Beecher, the preacher," said Arthur, taking the book. "Beecher's Bibles and all that."

Beecher's Bibles, Louisa knew, were really rifles, sent by the wagonload to "Bleeding Kansas" to help the Free-Soilers and abolitionists protect themselves from the slave owners.

"She's the reverend's sister," said Mary Ann, waving her letter from Ma in Arthur's face. "Ma says the book came out a year ago, that everyone in the country has read it!"

"Oh, David, let's hurry home!" said Louisa, snatching the book out of Arthur's hands and hugging it to her chest. It was so rare that she had the chance to read something new!

"Don't you want to stay for supper?" asked Mary Ann. "We could read our letters out loud. And try the first chapter in your book, Liza."

"We've got the hens at home," said David apologetically.

Mary Ann pouted. "Pesky raccoons."

"If it's not the raccoons, it's the cougars," David told her. He whistled, a high sharp sound, and in a few minutes Watch appeared. By this time he had Emily Inez strapped to his back and the canoe nosed into the water.

Louisa kissed her sister and sister-in-law good-bye, then her nieces and nephews, and an extra kiss for the new baby. "No falling out of cradles anymore," she told William Richard Boren, kissing him one more time.

"You're not coming back tomorrow?" asked Anna, holding the baby while little Gertrude clutched at her skirt.

"Not unless David has to come. David!" shouted Louisa. "*Did* you get put on Mr. Collins's jury?"

"Yup."

"Then I guess we *will* be back," she said with a sigh, climbing into the canoe and making her way to the bow.

"Not until Friday," said David. "Trials can't start until the attorneys get here. In the meantime"—he pushed off and the canoe glided onto the water—"we best get home and see if we have any chickens left!"

4

Friday, October 28, 1854

This day came Frank Clark who prosecuted on behalf of the Territory and came the defendant in his own proper person, and being arraigned to answer to the indictment herein declares that his true name is David Maurer, and for plea thereto says he is not guilty in manner and form as charged therein and for trial thereof puts himself upon the county and day is given.

—King County Court Journal, 1854
Puget Sound Archives

 o one knew where Mary Ann Conklin came from, or what she'd done before managing Captain Felker's hotel. Few knew her real name; she was Madam Damnable from the start, for obvious reasons (see p. 57).

A small, muscular woman, she wore at all times a grim, determined expression. She also kept a pile of sticks out front, and a pair of vicious Indian dogs tethered out back. Cross her path and you got both sticks and her dogs at your backside. The worst was her tongue. Seattle was a lumber town, accustomed to unholy language, but Madam Damnable's umbrage was enough to make a sailor blush, peel paint off walls, and reduce the toughest of pioneers to a quivering fool. She had but two redeeming qualities: She was a meticulous housekeeper, and she knew how to cook.

Seattle's second term of district court was held in her "Red" room, one of two large parlors on the ground floor of the Felker House. Red flocked wallpaper covered the high walls. Ornate portraits of famous sea captains stared down. On the south wall, beneath an impressive oil of Captain James Cook, a long oak table had been brought in. Friday morning, October 28, Judge Lander from Steilacoom and Doc Maynard, King County court clerk, sat behind this makeshift "bench." Two smaller tables faced them; one for the prosecuting attorneys, the other for the defendants and their counsel. A jury box of twelve empty chairs, three rows of four each, were roped off in a front corner. In the back of the room the grand jury, chaired by Charles Terry, sat in a loosely organized huddle. The petit jurors, twenty-six men in all, sat wherever they could find room, waiting to be called upon.

But first they had to parade past Madam Damnable. She stood in her open doorway, strong skinny arms crossed formidably over her bosom.

"I *licked* my boots clean, just to be safe," whispered big Hillory Butler nervously to David as they sidled past. David snorted through his nose, trying not to laugh. Other men, hearing them, coughed into their fists. Suddenly everything seemed hilariously funny.

There was nothing funny, though, when Tom Russell, Seattle's new sheriff and court crier, thundered, "Hear ye, hear ye, hear ye, the district court of the Territory of Washington is now in session!" David squeezed into a back seat with Arthur and Dobbins, and glanced quickly around the room. A sea of familiar faces sat listening:

Judge Edward Lander. A distinguished-looking man, slightly built, in his late twenties. *From Steilacoom.*

Doc Maynard. Glasses on his forehead. *Seattle.*

Joseph Wright. Bailiff. *Seattle.*

Captain Pease. Captain of the U.S. Revenue Cutter *Jefferson Davis.* Retained to defend Maurer. *San Francisco.*

Frank Clark. Territorial prosecuting attorney. *Olympia.*

Elwood Evans. Attorney for the United States government. *Olympia.*

David Maurer, of course. *Seattle.* Sitting with the captain.

The voice of Judge Lander brought David's focus back to the bench. "We have this morning an indictment of serious import." Judge Lander proceeded to recite the lengthy indictment—a long paper of legal verbiage. He concluded, "How do you plead, Mr. Maurer?"

Maurer glanced over his shoulder at the crowd. His eyes darted frantically from face to face. "Vat ist der question?" he finally blurted out in a trembling voice and with his heavy German accent.

"You are charged with murder," Judge Lander told him gravely. "You are supposed to tell me if you did it or not. Did you string up Masachie Jim? Or are you not guilty?"

Maurer scratched the top of his bald head, which looked like a mushroom, thought David. Maurer stammered, "I guess I bin, Shudge."

"*Not* guilty, you fool!" roared Charles Terry from the back of the room. The chairman of the grand jury popped to his feet and jabbed a finger at Maurer. "*Not* guilty! You're supposed to say *not* guilty, you idiot! By Jove, do you want to get yourself hung?"

"Nicht giltig," said a scared Mr. Maurer quickly.

"Not guilty!" sang out Doc Maynard. "Not . . . guilty," he repeated for good measure, writing it down in the record book. He winked at Maurer.

"Let the record show," said Judge Lander, taking a deep breath, "that Mr. David Maurer pleads not guilty in manner and form as charged herein and for trial thereof puts himself upon the county. Sheriff Russell, call the petit jurors for the case."

Will Brannan, a grand juror, was also a petit juror scheduled to sit on Maurer's jury. For a few moments there was some confusion as Will and eleven others in the audience found their seats in the roped-off jury box. Finally, he, along with Henry Decker, Henry Stevens, Seymore Wetmore, Delos Waterman, Charles Walker, John Hemming, George Bowker, Samuel Bechelheimer, Dexter Horton, William Strickler, and Tim Hinkley raised their right hands to be impaneled according to law. The prosecution began by calling Henry Yesler to the stand.

David listened intently to Seattle's sawmill owner as he relayed what little he chose to remember of that day.

"You saw Mr. Maurer slug David Denny?" repeated Frank Clark.

"Yessiree, that's what I saw."

"But did you see Mr. Maurer," asked Captain Pease in cross-examination, "hang Masachie Jim?"

"Nosiree, I did not see that, sir. No sir."

Five more witnesses were called, all five from the grand jury who, by all rights, should prove good witnesses for the prosecution. They were the men, after all, who felt there was enough evidence to hand down the indictment. But the five witnesses—Henry Pierce, Oliver Eaton, Henry Tobin, Henry Van Asselt, and Franklin Matthias—reported only that they'd seen Maurer punch Dave Denny but no, they did not see Maurer hang the bad Indian. The prosecution began to get testy. The defense started to get cocky.

"Any more witnesses, Mr. Clark?" quipped Captain Pease with a smirk undisguised by his scrubby golden brown beard.

David leaned over and whispered to Dobbins, "Why doesn't Clark call on you? You were sheriff then. I should think your two bits is what he's looking for."

"I wasn't there, remember?" said Dobbins in his customary slow speech. "Liza came and got me."

David sat up straight. How could he forget? It was her race back up the trail to get her brother that had nearly caused her miscarriage!

"The defense calls Dobbins Boren, former sheriff of Seattle!" sang out Captain Pease confidently, the defense's turn to call their witnesses.

Dobbins, dressed in new corduroys—tucked into his boots "Californy" style—clumped on up. David watched his brother-in-law take the stand. After laying his hand on the Bible and swearing to tell the truth, the whole truth, and nothing but the truth so help him God, Dobbins testified, slowly, methodically, that he'd arrived at the scene too late and could only report hearsay. All of which, he told Frank Clark under cross-examination, had been included in his report to the governor.

Eight more men were called. All eight stated exactly the same thing: they had seen Mr. Maurer at the scene of the lynching, but no, none of them had seen him put a rope around Masachie Jim's neck, kick the bucket out from under his feet, or fetch the necessary block and tackle from Captain Pease's ship, moored at that time at Yesler's wharf.

Frank Clark went first with the prosecution's final summation. Captain Pease followed with the defense's. Then Judge Lander solemnly addressed the jury. "You are charged with the responsibility of determining from the evidence brought forth today if Mr. David Maurer is guilty of murdering one Masachie Jim, an Indian. Should you return a verdict of guilt, I remind you I am required to use the full force of the law in passing sentence. If found guilty, I have no choice but to sentence Mr. Maurer to be hung by his neck until he is dead."

David watched the shadowed faces of his friends in the jury box. Slowly he became aware of Maurer. The big German was crying softly at his table, mumbling incoherently.

"You are dismissed," said Judge Lander quietly to the jury. They filed out and locked themselves in the "Blue" room.

"Court will take a short recess while the jury deliberates," announced Joseph Wright, bailiff.

Chairs squeaked, shoes scuffed the floor. "That was pretty pointed instruction," commented Arthur, watching Judge Lander as everyone eased to their feet and stretched. "Wonder how fast it'll take the jury to vote the acquittal."

A historical character of well-known (and infamous) repute in Seattle's earliest days was a woman by the name of Madam Damnable. Some readers may find the name objectionable. This was the name, however, by which she was known. Historical integrity requires that I use historically accurate names. My own sensibilities, however, prevent me from filling my narrative with the expletives that gave birth to such negative appellation. Suffice to say, the name speaks for itself. As my Great-Granny Goodfellow would say, the woman simply could not keep a civil tongue in her head! In way of apology to those who are bothered by the name, listen in on the Reverend Blaine's conversation with Arthur Denny after *his* first introduction to the woman. *"At least she comes by the name honestly, does she not?"*

5

Saturday, November 4, 1854

Mother Damnable reaped a very good profit from this session of court. . . . The bill seemed rather steep to the prosecuting attorney, Mr. Clark. When he went to settle with her, he demanded a receipt. Mother Damnable could neither read nor write; besides, she did not care much for Clark, who, being a young lawyer trying to make a reputation, had worked hard for the conviction of the accused prisoners. She told the young man that she would give him a receipt and stepped back into the kitchen . . .

—Roberta Frye Watt, Katy Denny's daughter
in *Four Wagons West*

There is no such thing as a hasty marriage, thought Louisa as she stole a peek at her husband through the thick smoke of the brush they were burning. *A hasty marriage is no more possible than learning quickly to be a musi-*

cian. Anyone with five fingers can rattle off a scale, but music, real music, takes time. So does a good marriage.

She watched David through the hazy smoke, seeing many reasons why marriage is gradual. Trees growing in the open are symmetrical, their branches grow on all sides. But when trees grow side by side they take the shape of a single tree. This takes time and requires the sacrifice of the branches that stand between them.

We're like two trees transplanted closely together, she decided, heaving an armful of salmonberry vines into the fire. When they'd first married, their old branches had often gotten in the way, keeping them further apart than they'd wanted to be. *Old ways of acting and thinking, old habits wanting to stay green beyond their season of usefulness.*

Like David's automatic acquiescence to his brother; this was a habit deeply ingrained. Arthur, ten years older than David, had been more father than brother to him. Wise and responsible by nature, Arthur had been someone David could look up to. So he still did. Yet David was wise and responsible in his own right; and when he gave up this part of himself to his older brother it interfered with the respect Louisa felt for him.

She too had habits that had been good and necessary prior to marriage. Such as overreacting to danger. Her family tended to "let nature take its course" when someone really needed to "take the bull by the horns." So whenever Ma, Mary Ann, and Dobbins sat back, she stood up. And to do the job right, she used fear and panic and even anger as weapons to drive past their complacency. The more fear, panic, or rage she could drum up, the better; the quicker and easier she got things done. If only to convince them *something* needed to be done. But now that she was married, these exaggerated responses got on David's nerves. She had to learn to put worry and fear in perspective. David was not like her family; he was perfectly capable of seeing trouble and responding appropriately.

59

"Do you think we should start another fire?" she asked him now. While she'd been lost in thought, they'd been dragging and carrying brush deep into the woods, farther than was necessary for their task.

David sized up the clearing. "Should have done it earlier and saved ourselves some trouble," he said with a grin. He began preparing the ground for another fire near the edge of the clearing behind their house. The task wasn't so much *piling* up brush as it was making space *around* the brush already there—to keep the fire from spreading.

They'd been doing this for three days, while Mr. Heebner's jury met and Indian summer held. A week ago, Mr. Maurer's jury had been out only half an hour before coming back with an acquittal. Not so with Mr. Heebner. His trial, which began last Wednesday, November first, had dragged on all day long and the jury—*three days later*—was still in deliberation.

The fact was, too many people had seen Mr. Heebner get the block and tackle from the *Jefferson Davis*. When they'd tried lying about it to Mr. Clark, the prosecutor, Mr. Clark threatened to charge them all with perjury and contempt of court. This had brought most of them around reluctantly. The evidence piled up. So why was the jury still deliberating?

She threw more vines onto the fire, grateful that she and David at least had this chance to get some yard work done. The petit jurors not in deliberation had been dismissed; no new cases could begin until Mr. Heebner's verdict was in. Also, the women had finished Anna's baby quilt so there was no reason for either her or David to go into town. And Will Brannan reported to the sewing circle that Elizabeth wouldn't be coming to Seattle; she'd just had a baby and the canoe ride down White River was too fraught with danger for a frail baby, born two months too early. For Elizabeth as well, still regaining her strength.

"So what's taking them so long anyway?" Louisa asked all of a sudden.

"Who?" grunted David, chopping a branch off an old log with his hatchet.

"The jury."

David picked up the severed branch and carried it over to the fire. Flames licked up around the decayed wood. "I expect they're reluctant to see Heebner hang."

"Do you suppose they're trying to figure a legal way to get him off the hook? Like Doc Maynard did last year with his *mal*feasance versus *mis*feasance when Masachie Jim was hung?"

"I'm sure they are. But if they do, it'll go rough for the rest of us," he told her, whacking at another branch.

She regarded him anxiously.

"If Heebner's jury finds a way to circumvent the facts," he told her, pausing to explain, "people are going to expect the same leniency when it comes to Collins. And that *will* take a stretch of the law."

"Oh, David, what are you going to do?"

"I don't know." His hatchet struck another stubborn branch.

"What happens if Mr. Heebner's jury can't decide?"

"Then it's a hung jury." He laughed.

"It's not funny, David."

"No, I guess not. We'd have to start all over."

She sighed and started back to work. Emily Inez would be waking up soon from her nap and there was still much to do.

"Liza, just leave it to Arthur."

"Leave it to Arthur!"

"Have you ever known Arthur *not* to do what's right?"

She didn't answer. Arthur had an amazing way of taking what he wanted and *making* it right.

But then, what *was* right? she wondered, tackling a clump of tangled deadfall with her rake.

Late that same afternoon Heebner's jury, after deliberating more than thirty hours, finally reached their verdict: Not

Guilty. The prosecution, the jurors explained, hadn't bothered to prove that the name mentioned in the indictment was, in fact, the name of the murdered Indian. The prosecution hadn't bothered to prove it because it hadn't occurred to *anyone* to dispute the name. But the jury wanted to acquit Heebner, and they knew everyone in town wanted them to as well.

"But because the evidence was so plainly against him," Arthur explained to David and Louisa when he came out the next afternoon to bring them the verdict and to notify David that everyone was expected back in court in the morning, "this is the only ground on which we could find to acquit him."

"You weaseled out of it by saying the prosecution had *spelled Masachie Jim's name wrong?*" gasped David.

Louisa, sitting by the fire and reading *Uncle Tom's Cabin*, sensed David's complete dismay.

"The prosecution," intoned Arthur stiffly.

"I had assumed you'd weigh the consequences more carefully," David interrupted.

"The consequences of *not* acquitting him is what I weighed!"

Louisa put down her book, curious, a little scared. Was David going to tell Arthur he was *wrong?*

"If I hadn't gone along with the others," said Arthur, tight-lipped, "I'd have been run right out of town!"

"You weren't run off a year ago when it happened. You stood against the crowd then. In fact, you were hopping mad and ready to string up *Maynard* for wangling Luther Collins—"

"Luther Collins, yes! not Will Heebner! What Maynard did was a disgrace! An obvious twist of the law!"

"And what you just did was *not?*"

Louisa held her breath. Arthur leaned over the table at David. "No-it-was-not! The grand jury charged three men for the murder of Masachie Jim. As far as I'm concerned,

Luther Collins did the killing. Nobody else. If the grand jury indicted Heebner, or even Maurer, on a charge of *accessory* to murder, I'd have been obliged, of course, to render a guilty verdict. But the charge was murder, not accessory, and it was Collins who killed Masachie Jim. Not Heebner."

"Heebner got the block and tackle. Heebner—"

"Don't tell me what Heebner did! I was at the trial!"

"The Indians were at the lynching," said David quietly, his face ashen. "They know the truth. What's going to happen when they retaliate and someone dies, someone completely innocent of any crime? Not even guilty of—*accessory,* is that what you call it?"

Arthur slapped the table so hard his coffee cup bounced. "No one's going to die!"

When David didn't respond, Arthur got up and put on his hat and coat. "No one's going to die, Dave, if you convict Luther Collins."

A full week later David squirmed uncomfortably in the close heat of the crowded courtroom. Sweat dripped down his back and under his arms. *This is it, this is Luther Collins's trial,* he thought. *Any minute I'll be called to the jury box.* He scratched his neck where his beard stopped growing, and kept scratching.

"Hear ye, hear ye, hear ye!" bawled out Tom Russell, "the district court of the Territory of Washington is now in session!"

David was familiar with the procedures by now. For an entire week he and the other petit jurors had been taking turns hearing the lesser cases: five sea captains charged with dumping ballast into the harbor, two scoundrels accused of selling liquor to the Indians. He'd served on one of those juries—Old Jack's, a hermit living on the Duwamish River. It had taken only minutes to acquit the man—though they all knew Old Jack was guiltier than sin. But without evidence . . .

More consultations between the judge and the attorneys. Now a discussion with Luther Collins. David glanced at his watch, caught a movement near the door, and looked up. George Seattle, one of Chief Seattle's sons, strode in. The tall young man was dressed in white man's clothing—except for his moccasins. David felt his heart speed up.

Judge Lander finally started to read the third murder indictment of the session. The verbiage was the same, different only in that Luther Collins was charged with three counts of murder: Masachie Jim and the two Snoqualmie boys indicted the previous spring for killing Mr. McCormick, a stranger passing through town. David scratched his neck again. The town no more wanted Collins convicted than Maurer and Heebner. A pretty dirty trick Arthur had pulled on him, thought David.

He looked again over at George, where he stood by the window. This time their eyes met and, because they were friends, David could read the warning in George's grim expression.

"Mr. Collins, how do you plead?" Judge Lander asked.

David returned his attention to the bench. But before Collins opened his mouth Elwood Evans, attorney for the U.S. government, shushed him and stood up. "The government," said Evans, "withdraws prosecution. Further proceedings in this court are a waste of time and expense. The territory and the U.S. government wish no further involvement in Seattle's determination to obstruct justice."

Silence weighted the room. How would the judge respond? Judge Lander finally reached for his gavel and gave it a weak bang. "Case dismissed," he said, though it didn't sound like he believed himself. Elwood Evans sat down and began gathering up his papers.

"This session of district court," said the judge, clearing his throat and sounding more sure of himself, "is over."

Everyone lingered in their chairs, stunned. Only slowly did they begin, one by one and then in twos and threes and finally in small groups, to get up and go out. Luther Collins beamed. He threw out his chest and slapped his palms against his expanded ribcage. People, passing him, gave him their obligatory congratulations, which he accepted with bluster.

David remained where he was, trying to absorb what had just happened. His initial shock gave way to relief; he'd been spared the distasteful task of casting judgment on another man's life. But almost immediately he felt overwhelming guilt and shame. The government had just condemned Seattle for its mockery of justice. His next thought scared him. *How will the Indians respond to this? What kind of bloodshed will this prompt?* He stumbled hastily to his feet to go find George.

Seattle's son was nowhere to be seen. David took off toward the high bluff of the Point, scrambled down the steep slope to the beach. George, twenty yards away, was pushing his canoe into the water. Before David could call, or chase after him, George was gone, paddling swiftly toward Sqwudux where Chief Seattle was no doubt camped.

Before going home, David decided to stop in at the Felker House. Maybe he could find Judge Lander. Maybe he could talk with him. Maybe there was a way to force a new trial. If he could tell George Seattle that Collins would be tried again—

Mr. Clark, the prosecuting attorney, was the only one in the ornate lobby—mirrors and polished oak gleaming everywhere—when David entered.

"Highway robbery is what it is," Clark barked at him.

"What's that?" said David, coming to a stop.

The prosecutor leaned against the high oak panel of the reservation counter. "She's charging $349 for using this place. Three hundred and forty-nine *dollars!*"

"That is a bit steep," agreed David.

"Listen to this!" Clark held up his left hand, fingers up. With his right index finger he pulled back the first finger of his left hand. "Twenty-five dollars for the use of her best room—" He pulled back on the middle finger. "Two hundred and sixty dollars for the jurors' rooms!" He pulled back on his third finger. "*Four* dollars for using the *furniture! The furniture!* Can you believe it? She charged us for using her rotten furniture!" He pulled back on his pinky. "And last—but not least," he roared, "fifty cents for every meal, a total of sixty dollars! Sum total?" He waggled all four fingers. "Three hundred forty-nine dollars! *Three hundred forty-nine dollars!*"

"Are you going to pay it?" David asked.

"I had to," the attorney grumped, jamming his hands into his pants pockets. "All I know is I don't know what the governor is going to say when he gets back from Washington City. Three hundred and forty-nine dollars and three skunks set loose!"

"Where is she?"

"The lady of the house? Getting me a receipt."

"You asked for a *receipt?*" David glanced quickly around the foyer to see which door Madam Damnable might come flying through at any moment . . . and if there was a door through which he might escape. He hardly had time to back up two steps when she hurtled out the kitchen with an apronful of stovewood.

"You want a receipt, do you!" she screamed like a banshee. "Well, here's your receipt, you dog!" and she threw a chunk of wood at the attorney's head. He ducked. David eased back another step. "I'll lairn ye to ask me for a receipt, you high-flyin' buzzard, you!" she bellowed as she charged after Clark faster than a dog after a chicken. The startled attorney howled in pain and surprise when she struck first his forehead and then his shins. The last thing David saw was Clark racing around behind the counter. The last thing he heard was Madam Damnable caterwauling, "Come out of there, you yellow-bellied coward!"

All the way home David tried to picture Louisa's reaction to the day's events. Should he tell her that George Seattle was there and had seen it all? Should he tell her that George, even now, was probably telling his father how white men meted out justice?

She was not expecting him until tomorrow, at the earliest. So coming up the cliff trail he sang his favorite hymn, "Watchman Tell Me of the Night," to keep from startling her. She met him at the door, startled anyway.

Emily Inez was on the bed, tearing pages out of an old magazine. "Papa!" she squealed, and lunged across the bed to reach him. He caught her just before she would have landed on the floor.

Switching her from one arm to the other, he shrugged out of his coat. Louisa hung it up on a peg by the door. She took off his hat, brushed his hair out of his face, and hung his cap on the back of the door, between her bonnet and Emily Inez's hood.

"What are you doing home?" she finally asked him, going back to the stove to stir the stew.

He told her everything. She went to the table and sat down weakly. "I wonder who will die now," was all she said. He was grateful she did not burst into tears.

That night, on the west side of the Duwamish River, shadows fell ominously over a lone log cabin. Inside, Old Jack was drinking his Blue Ruin, playing chess with himself. He heard what he first thought was an owl.

PART 2

Treaty Making

The return of Governor Stevens from Washington City in December of '54 with authority
to make treaties with the Indians outshadowed
all other events.

—ROBERTA FRYE WATT, KATY DENNY'S DAUGHTER
IN *FOUR WAGONS WEST*

6

December 1854

Governor Stevens was welcomed back to the territory by the citizens of this place on Friday of last week, after an absence of some 9 months on official bastions at Washington, whither he had repaired in conformity with the desire of the last legislative assembly to report to Congress the result of his Pacific Railroad survey, and further the interest, by his personal presence, of that great national work, in the direction of the route pursued by him from the east to the north to the shores of Puget Sound.

—*Pioneer & Democrat*, December 9, 1854

*G*overnor Stevens returned in time from his duties in Washington City to address the opening session of Washington Territory's second Legislative Assembly.

"I wholeheartedly congratulate you, my fellow citizens," he began on a bitterly cold Monday morning, the fourth of December, "on our first year of existence. Our population is rapidly increasing. A legislature has twice assembled. Laws have been made by representatives of the peoples' own selection. Courts have been held and general justice has been meted out to all—"

Arthur Denny, representative from King County, sat with his fellow politicians in a meeting room of Edmond Sylvester's Olympia House at the head of the Sound. He did not like Isaac Stevens. The short, energetic governor was, in Arthur's opinion, ambitious but woefully shortsighted. He'd rescued the northern railroad survey from oblivion, true, but the territory needed someone who understood the native population—particularly now that Elwood Evans, U.S. prosecutor, had refused last month to try Luther Collins.

For a moment Arthur's mind left the meeting room and the governor's congratulatory speech. He was back stumbling through the dark again, always through the dark . . . looking for Old Jack's cabin. Pat Kanim, chief of the Snoqualmies, had been the one to bring the news, barging into the house late that night, scaring Mary Ann and the children half to death. Arthur too, when he heard what the chief had to say.

Just past one in the morning they'd found Old Jack dead in his hut. Bloodied chess pieces lay scattered across the earthen floor, many of them broken. Old Jack had put up quite a fight; Doc Maynard reported fifty-seven different knife wounds at the inquest. Since then Arthur could not rid himself of the sight of the old hermit, mangled almost beyond recognition, kicked into a heap in the corner and left to die in his own growing pool of blood. Arthur could see him now, even with his eyes shut, and he shuddered with moral indignity. Not just over the retaliatory murder, but because a few stupid fools dared suggest Jack's death was due to Heebner's acquittal! Yet Old Jack—and how anyone could mix this up was beyond Arthur—had been hacked to death following the motion of Elwood Evans to drop all charges against Collins! If blame was to be assigned, blame rested squarely on the desk of the U.S. prosecutor. No one else.

"I earnestly call your attention to the importance of organizing an effective militia for the defense of the territory," sang out the governor. His words broke through Arthur's thoughts. "Without dwelling upon our Indian relations, which have at several times the past season been critical, we need roads through the mountains to facilitate military movement between our settlements. Time is of the essence," he stated. "To that end, I will be leaving shortly to begin treaty negotiations with the Indians and see to it that they are removed to reservations, separated from the whites. I believe that the time has now come for their final settlement."

The Indian relations were, indeed, critical. But Arthur knew this was not the motivating factor behind the governor's proposal. Snoqualmie Pass, east of Seattle, had proven the best spot for the railroad to cross through the mountains and while they all wanted the railroad—it was *imperative* to their economic future that they get the railroad!—the land still belonged to the Indians, and they were in no hurry to sell. Skill and time were necessary to negotiate satisfactory settlements. A marathon of ten treaties in six months' time, as proposed by Stevens, would only alarm the Indians. And if he persisted in rescuing the railroad by rushing the Indians, everyone would pay.

"In view of these important duties which have been assigned me," the governor finally concluded, "I throw myself unreservedly upon the people of the territory, not doubting they will extend to me a hearty and generous support in my efforts to arrange, on a permanent basis, the future of the Indians of this territory!"

A thunderous applause resounded, and though Arthur joined his colleagues, he did not do so with much enthusiasm. The governor, he fretted, was not a man inclined to listen to anyone but himself. Such men were dangerous.

Two weeks later Arthur sat miserably in the middle of Yoke-Yakeman's canoe, wedged between his sleeping roll, a box of books for Mary Ann, several bolts of calico, gifts for the children's Christmas—from himself as well as James, who, true to his word, had sent packages from Oregon—and other sundry sacks and boxes full of trade goods for his new store. He sat cross-legged for as long as he could stand it, then shifted his legs straight out for as long as he could stand it, then crossed them again.

By canoe, this was a two-day trip from Olympia to Seattle. Plenty of time to shift, and think, and wish *two* steamers, instead of only the one, plied the Sound. The governor had taken the liberty of appropriating the *Major Tompkins.*

Soon after his arrival, the governor had enthusiastically decided with whom and where to hold his peace treaties, and hired the new steamship as escort for himself and staff. Christmas or no Christmas, he was even now at the Nisqually Plains, determined to conduct his first treaty with the Indians of upper Puget Sound. His unexpected acquisition of the new boat had left Arthur and the other legislators—if they wished to go home for Christmas recess—to their own resources. Thank goodness, thought Arthur, he'd run into Yoke-Yakeman and Lucky, two Snoqualmie boys he knew well. Otherwise he'd be celebrating Christ's birth away from his family. Well, maybe he wasn't all that fortunate, he thought, shivering in the rain as it drizzled steadily down the back of his neck.

To offset the annoyance, he reflected on the progress they'd made so far in the legislature. A joint resolution had been passed requesting Congress to recognize the citizenship of George Washington Bush, a freeborn colored man from Missouri. Bush had been in the first party of settlers to arrive on the Sound but, as laws currently stood, only white men were entitled to a claim under the Donation Act. By passage of this one resolution alone Washington Territory had emphatically declared itself "free soil" under the obnoxious Kansas-Nebraska Act.

He'd also reintroduced women's suffrage, but like last year his motion had failed to carry. Same with his second bid for temperance. Too many people like Doc Maynard in the territory. But his motion requesting federal authorization for two volunteer companies had carried. As had his motion for a man-of-war to patrol the Sound. Now the decision to send a warship was up to Washington City.

Quite suddenly Arthur found himself looking forward to reconvening after New Year's. He had in mind a whole new bill. Every new territory within the Union was allowed one township for a university, with a hefty $30,000 congressional appropriation. What if the university were in Seattle? Just think what kind of trade that would generate! *To say nothing of being an added draw for the railroad!*

He stayed that night with Ezra Meeker, an amiable man who'd settled on a small island within shouting distance of the fort at Steilacoom, a convenient layover point between Olympia and Seattle. The two men quickly discovered they shared many of the same dreams and they stayed up late, rain drumming the roof, speaking of the future. Both believed in progress, both believed in encouraging immigration. Both believed the country's first transcontinental route was destined to terminate on the Sound, though they argued over whether the railroad would terminate in Seattle, or Steilacoom.

When Arthur awoke in the morning his congenial host asked, "Sleep well, Mr. Denny?"

Arthur carefully regarded the floorboards that had bruised his bones all night. "You have a very good foundation under your floor, Meeker."

"How's that?"

"Didn't find any spring to the bed."

7

Saturday, January 20, 1855

For days hundreds of canoes came from all directions and nosed their way in along the beach. Along the trails and from out of the forest came other natives. Twenty-five hundred of them in all assembled awaiting the arrival of the governor.

—Roberta Frye Watt, Katy Denny's daughter
in *Four Wagons West*

The lower Sound Indians arrived at the designated treaty ground by sea, nosing their dugouts into the sand: the Lummi, the Tulalips, several bands of the Duwamish. Hundreds of others emerged out of the woods: the Snohomish, the Skagits and Snoqualmies, the Muckleshoots. Louisa, nursing Emily Inez inside Doc Maynard's large bedticking tent, listened to the tumult of the ever growing crowd as Indians from all over northern Puget Sound gathered for the governor's second treaty.

His first treaty had gone well, the Nisquallies, Puyallups, Steilacooms, and six other tribes surrendering two and a half million acres in exchange for $32,000, three small reservations encompassing just 3,480 acres, and other amenities like schools, doctors, a blacksmith shop, and fishing rights. There was rumor of dissatisfaction. Leschi, a Nisqually elder, was unhappy. Yet the majority seemed content, sixty-two chiefs and subchiefs signing an X to their printed names on the agreement. Louisa hoped things would go at least half as well at this treaty.

She and David had been here two days already, camping in the damp cold at Mulkiteo somewhere north of Salmon Bay. David, Doc Maynard, and Henry Smith, who knew the Suquamish and Duwamish languages fluently, were needed to help clear out the underbrush, erect the big council tent, and explain to the Indians all that was happening in preparation for the governor's arrival tomorrow. Catherine Maynard had come along, too, to do the cooking, and Louisa was grateful for her company.

Too bad Arthur isn't here, she found herself thinking. Strange. She didn't normally appreciate his presence. But the men could use Arthur's help, particularly with a few of the Snoqualmies who were still short-tempered, despite the vengeance they'd taken out on Old Jack last fall. But Arthur had returned to Olympia. The Legislative Assembly had reconvened on January third and probably wouldn't dismiss until sometime in February. There was much yet to do.

For a moment her thoughts were diverted. Arthur blamed the U.S. prosecutor for Jack's murder. He said it was because the prosecutor had dropped the charges against Mr. Collins that the Indians had sought their revenge. But peel the onion back a layer. *Why* had the prosecutor dropped the charges? To her way of thinking, Arthur and every other man on Mr. Heebner's jury held the blame. The rest of Seattle was just fortunate nothing more had happened.

Emily Inez fell asleep; Louisa felt the sudden increase in her daughter's weight the instant she dozed off. *How could a whole year have gone by since your birth?* Louisa ran a finger softly along her daughter's cheek. Emily Inez was a whole year old now—one year and a month, and growing so fast her baby clothes had to be put away. Not only that, in a couple of days, Louisa realized, she and David would be married two years! *Two years!*

The tent flap lifted. A shaft of light sliced across the gloomy interior, and Catherine Maynard's cheery round face brightened the doorway. "Louisa," she whispered, "Chief Seattle's coming in. You really ought to come see this!"

Louisa hastily tucked Emily Inez under a low eave of the tent, covered her up, gave her a soft kiss, then crawled out. The bright sunlight glittered on the water with sharp sparkles like thousands of diamonds. Louisa blinked painfully. "The sun, it's come out," she said with a smile.

"Just in time. Look . . ." Catherine Maynard pointed west, across the water.

Using her hands for a shield, Louisa caught sight of a large flotilla of Indian dugouts, the Suquamish tribe advancing from Port Madison. An imposing sight, their frail boats manned with an order and precision that would credit any military movement. They slipped quickly across the smooth water in regular platoons and in the most perfect dress and order. They wheeled into line to front the treaty ground in admirable style.

"Wow," said Catherine Maynard beside Louisa. "I doubt I'll ever see anything so grand if I should live to be a hundred."

"Nor I," whispered Louisa, awed by the display of greatness. She'd never before considered the Sound Indians particularly militaristic or regimental.

The first to disembark was Chief Seattle, an old man by Indian standards. Few lived to be Seattle's sixty-five. He was followed by his two regal sons, Jim and George. David was anxious to see George, Louisa knew. They hadn't seen him since his disconcerting departure last fall. Seattle's eight slaves came next, scampering ashore to secure the large war canoe. The forty warriors who'd manned the canoe barked orders. Men, women, and children from the other canoes splashed out. Louisa saw David and Dr. Henry Smith disappear into the commotion. Doc Maynard was there, making jokes. She could hear the Indians laugh, and then Doc's own infectious laughter float over the top of the tight crowd.

With the arrival of Chief Seattle, head chieftain to six of the collected tribes, the crowd swelled to twenty-five hundred men, women, and children. Louisa gazed around at the huge throng. The women were busy, some laying out blankets and fixing fires, others propping together small lean-tos made from downed cedar boughs, or draping grass mats and animal skins across the keels of their overturned canoes. Children and dogs ran wild. Suddenly Louisa felt very small and vulnerable amidst this strange busyness.

Catherine sensed her quickened insecurity. "What do you say we find Princess Angeline?" she asked, referring to Seattle's forty-five-year-old daughter.

"I can't leave Emily Inez."

"I'll find the princess then, and invite her to tea. You know how she loves sugar cubes."

"Yes, of course," said Louisa, cheering up.

"We can tell her all about Ellender Smith's wedding to Mr. Plummer!"

"I'll get the fire started and put on some water!" called out Louisa. But dry wood was hard to find. *This is like the Oregon Trail! Only without the handy buffalo chips!*

The treaty ground at Mulkiteo was a large acreage of grassy flatland easily defined on its western edge by the Sound. To the north lay the gurgling Snohomish River. To the east and south stood the woods. The sea, river, and forests framed the parklike setting and, by late afternoon, and despite a return of the rain, the clearing fairly simmered with festivity and movement.

Along the beach a company of blue-uniformed soldiers, brought up from Fort Steilacoom to impress the Indians, wandered amongst a short row of their army tents. Woodsmoke from their fires sharpened the tantalizing smell of hot coffee. Closer to the woods and all along the river, half-naked Indian children, oblivious to the rain, ran in and around the campfires—which looked warm and cozy in the wet January dusk. Dogs tore back and forth. Grown-ups walked in groups, talking, their heads protected from the steady rain by drawn-up blankets or identical conical straw hats. Sometimes the buzz of harmonicas could be heard. Sometimes two or three overlaid each other in discordant duets and trios.

The hats and harmonicas, as well as small jugs of blackstrap molasses, had been presents to put the Indians in good humor to greet the governor come morning. After supper, David and Louisa went out for a walk, holding Emily Inez's mittened hands so she could toddle clumsily between them. She wore a pair of beautiful new moccasins, a gift this afternoon from Princess Angeline. They walked away from the short row of army tents to visit the Indians and to get a feel for their mood. They found that the gifts had, indeed, put most of the Indians in rare humor.

Older women sang while burying camas roots in the ground where the nutritious root would bake all night beneath a well-tended fire. Old men sat around the fires, smoking, watching young braves gamble with polished bone fragments. Pretty girls giggled and whispered and laughed out loud whenever a brave had to hand off his shirt and sit shivering in the cold. The braves, however, didn't seem to notice either the cold or the girls.

David pointed to a trio of adolescent boys sitting under a large fir tree. They all wore hats, and were breathing in and out on their harmonicas and eating blackstrap all at the same time.

"They sound like a bunch of bumblebees," said Louisa.

She jumped suddenly. "Jim! George!" she yelped, gasping with relief when she saw who it was. Seattle's two sons had snuck up behind her, and whispered "boo" in her ear.

"Scare her good, mm?" said George to David. David nodded, delighting in Louisa's shining face. He too was happy to see Jim and George.

"Don't do that again!" Louisa chided the two young men, younger half brothers of Princess Angeline. "You scared the tar right out of me!"

"*Tar?*"

"Yes, tar," said Louisa, playfully pushing Jim Seattle's chest with the flat of her hand. He pretended to stagger backward.

"Tar?" he asked again.

David tried to explain the word in Suquamish, then Duwamish. But the closest he could come was tree sap and the color black.

Jim looked at Louisa, incredulous.

"It's an *expression*, Jim. I don't really have tar—"

"Es—" He tried the word but his tongue slithered over the tricky combination of *x, p,* and *r.* "Esression . . . ?" he repeated.

"Never mind," she told him, shaking her head.

George stooped down to pinch Emily Inez's nose, then scooped her up in his arms. "May I?" he asked Louisa, indicating he wanted to put her up on his shoulders.

She nodded.

Jim and George wore brown corduroy pants and hickory shirts and the new conical hats. Each had a woolen Hudson's Bay blanket draped over his shoulders. George let his fall so he could swing Emily Inez up onto his neck. She teetered a little, then lunged forward and seized him around the head, covering his eyes and knocking off his hat.

"Ach!" he grunted, clawing at her mittened hands to make her let go.

Like their father, Jim and George hadn't had to paddle their own canoes as children. Consequently, they stood tall and straight, without the deformed, bowed legs of their slaves or the majority of their tribe. They towered now above Louisa, who was five feet two. Emily Inez, allowing George to place her hands beneath his chin, beamed proudly down at her mother and father.

"Seattle would like to speak with you," said George suddenly to David. "Can you come?"

"Me too?" asked Louisa, picking up George's muddied blanket, and fallen hat. By way of an answer Jim affectionately threw an arm around her.

Down at the beach, Louisa gazed across the darkening sea. In the deepening twilight, light seemed to radiate from every object, as if the logs and trees and all the stones along the shore had stored their own light during the day to draw upon when dusk came. This flatter light, this strange darkness without any shadow, was vibrantly alive with the smells and sounds of the world, and she breathed deeply of the rich salty air, smelled the pitchy incense of the fir trees, and listened with content to the rich timbre in the men's low voices.

The rain had softened into a slight mist, and they sat comfortably enough on damp logs around a roaring beach fire, she and David between Jim and George, Chief Seattle opposite them, Doc Maynard, Henry Smith, Pat Kanim of the Snoqualmies, and Chief Nelson of the Muckleshoots filling in the rough circle. Emily Inez sat happily in the wet sand, flinging bits of seaweed and gravel at the fire, her whole face lighting up when the fire sputtered under the assault. Chief Nelson, a square, squatty man with an obvious love for children, tut-tutted at her but kept giving her bits of twigs and bark to throw.

Seattle did most of the talking. All the talk was in Duwamish, though Pat Kanim was Snoqualmie and Nelson

Muckleshoot. Perhaps it was the language common to them all, thought Louisa. She herself understood only a few words. Yet by watching Seattle's facial expressions and his energetic hand movements, she could guess at their discussion. *Old Jack.* Despite George's quick warning, both Seattle and Pat Kanim had been helpless to prevent his murder. Perhaps they hadn't wanted to. They both refused to name the men responsible, which was unlike either of them.

The allied chief, easily the most influential on the Sound, and the Snoqualmie chief, another influential man, were cousins of sorts, though Seattle was twice Pat Kanim's age. He was also much larger, and more powerfully built, with huge broad shoulders and a square head that sat atop his body on a short, thick neck. Some said he was homely, but Louisa found the opposite to be true. She saw his sharply creased face as quite grand, and she loved to watch him. She could almost see the keen workings of his mind behind those dark eyes, shining now in the firelight like glimmering marbles. Behind his eyes was something you could trust, as you trusted the earth.

David suddenly eased forward, elbows on his knees. He stared into the fire, then offered some kind of comment to the discussion. Doc Maynard objected. Nelson seemed to agree. Seattle acted surprised. The Muckleshoot chief grew angry, and he and Chief Seattle argued. Louisa glanced anxiously to David.

"Nelson just found out the Muckleshoots are to be put on the same reservation as the Duwamish," he explained.

"But the two tribes hate each other! Do they *have* to be put together?" she whispered, unable to imagine such a thing. It would be like having to live in Arthur's house all over again, like she did before she was married. *"Do they have to?"* she repeated.

"That's the way the governor mapped it."

"Didn't he bother to ask anyone how it should be arranged? Anyone who knows anything about them could have told him!"

"He's like Arthur," said David, surprising her. "He doesn't ask, he tells."

She was still trying to absorb this further evidence of change in David's attitude toward his brother when Doc Maynard took off his wet boots, peeled off his wet socks and stuck his wet feet near the fire. "Ahh," he said with a shiver, wiggling his cold wet toes over the heat of the flames.

Nelson reached over, picked up a boot. He saw the huge hole and clucked his tongue.

"Remind me to steal your moccasins next time it rains, Nelson," said Doc Maynard in English, and they all laughed. Then Seattle stood up. The evening was over.

The Indians dispersed. Louisa, Doc Maynard, Henry Smith, and David, holding Emily Inez, headed down the beach toward the trail that would take them up to the grass and their communal tent.

"So what was the powwow all about?" Louisa asked, more than just a little curious.

"Seattle was trying to get a consensus for the governor tomorrow," grunted Doc Maynard, trying to get used to his wet feet inside his wet boots again.

Henry tucked his chin in under the collar of his India-rubber parka. "If you pinch a baby it'll yell and kick all over the place," he said. "But a perceptive man takes the knife out of his heart without fanfare."

"That supposed to mean something?" snorted Maynard.

"Seattle sees things as they are. Not the way he wants them. He knows we all have to go on, that living in the past will only result in more bloodshed between us. He's willing to withdraw to a reservation . . . painful though it may be. But Nelson's still thinking in terms of all or nothing."

"I can't say as I blame him," said Louisa thoughtfully. "David, where is Suwalth? Why isn't he here?" she asked, referring to the subchief of the Duwamish band that stuck to the settlers—like glue, was the way Doc Maynard put it. His was the encampment in town.

"He doesn't want to sign the treaty. The Duwamish don't want to live with the Muckleshoots anymore than the Muckleshoots want to live with the Duwamish."

"But if Chief Seattle signs, it's as good as done. He *is* chief of the Duwamish."

"What about the Duwamish out by the coal mine?" put in Henry. "Near as I can tell, they get along fine with the Muckleshoots."

"Tecumseh's bunch, the Lake Indians?" asked David, naming another of the Duwamish subchiefs living between the coal mine and the south end of Lake Washington. "They keep their distance, Henry. The two tribes have hated each other for generations."

Louisa watched the young doctor clamber up the short, steep cliff to the grassland above. She took a deep breath and made her own run up the slope. "Why doesn't the governor give them separate reservations?" she panted, wheezing at the top beside Henry and wiping her gritty hands on the folds of her skirt.

David shifted Emily Inez in his arms and lunged on up the path.

"Seems simple enough to me," she said.

Doc Maynard was the last up. He sighed wearily. "That's the rub, Mrs. Denny. Our governor is of the opinion that the fewer the reservations, the better. He did this to the upper Sound Indians as well. He lumped the Nisquallies in with the Puyallups. Much to Leschi's disgust."

Catherine was sitting by the fire when they approached the tent. "Coffee's on!" she called out. "And hot rice pudding."

"Does it have raisins?" asked Doc. "Ah, good woman!" He hauled her to her feet and gave her a noisy kiss, then reached round and pinched her bottom.

"OHH!" she gasped, jumping back and slapping at his hands. "You stay away from me or I'll sleep outside in the rain!"

"You'll sleep with me," he said matter-of-factly. "I need a hairy animal to keep me warm."

"You can get yourself a bear!"

Doc Maynard took a gulp of coffee, his light blue eyes twinkling in the firelight. "I just might do that."

Louisa whispered to David, "I know he's only joking, but don't *you* ever do or say that to me."

David followed her into the tent. "I prefer soft skin."

"I don't know who's worse, you or Doc Maynard."

They stood with Emily Inez between them.

"You know," she said, "if you could arrange for a moon on these occasions, I just might be able to see who's kissing me."

8

*Sunday,
January 21, 1855*

The second treaty arranged by Governor Stevens—the Treaty of Point Elliott—was attended with great pomp and ceremony. It was made in January 21–23, 1855, at Mulkiteo with Chief Seattle's Duwamish and Suquamish Indians and with the Snohomish, Snoqualmie, Skagits, and other tribes from northern Puget Sound.

> —Roberta Frye Watt, Katy Denny's daughter
> in *Four Wagons West*

*I*n the morning, a Sunday, the gray hulk of the *Major Tompkins* could be seen lying offshore, veiled by rain. Governor Stevens had chartered the steamer for seven hundred dollars a month: The duties of Captain Scranton, owner of the vessel, and Captain Hunt, pilot, were to supply the governor's table as well as carry and distribute food to the Indians for the duration of each council. The Indians would not have time to hunt and fish. When Louisa poked her nose out of the tent, the crew were rowing back and forth in the pouring rain with the supplies and doing their best to hand out bags of flour and large slabs of bacon to the excited Indians.

"Good morning," said Catherine from under the dripping wet tent awning, where she stood frying flapjacks in an iron skillet over the protected fire.

"Where are the men?"

"Seeing how Governor Stevens wants everyone to be seated tomorrow."

"They're waiting another day?" Louisa asked, surprised. "I thought the governor was in an all-fired hurry."

"Seattle says it's the Sabbath."

"But the governor was adamant."

"So is Chief Seattle!" said Catherine with an amused laugh.

"It's nice to know someone in this wilderness keeps the Sabbath," said Louisa, wishing again she and David could go to church in town. But Reverend Blaine disdained the Indians. . . . And David didn't want anything to do with such a man.

She dressed quickly, her icy cold fingers fumbling with the buttons, then got a very sleepy Emily Inez into dry diapers and warm, clean clothes. Emily Inez resented the ordeal and thoroughly woke herself up by screaming the whole while.

"I have porridge ready for her," Catherine announced when Louisa finally emerged with a squalling Emily Inez. "I didn't know whether you wanted me to put sugar on it."

"No, we don't give her sugar," said Louisa, thanking Catherine for her thoughtfulness and accepting the tin cup full of warm cereal.

"Here comes Princess Angeline," said Catherine. "Three guesses as to what she wants, and the first two don't count."

After flapjacks and berry jam, the three friends drank tea around the fire, sitting cross-legged on rubber mats. Louisa described to Princess Angeline the brand-new house Mr.

Plummer was building for Ellender Smith. Catherine told her about the green blinds Ellender had ordered, for every window, on *both* floors.

Angeline was not impressed. She told them about her brother who was thinking about buying a wife today, from the Sklallam tribe.

"Jim or George?" asked Louisa curiously.

"*See-an-ump-kun,*" said Angeline. *Jim.*

"Isn't he the one who wanted to marry you, Louisa?" teased Catherine.

"They *both* wanted to marry me."

"You naughty woman, you," said Catherine.

Angeline, who looked more like sixty than forty-three, stuck her two sugar cubes between what was left of her front teeth and sucked her tea right through the sugar. "Mm, good! More?"

Catherine and Louisa gave her two more sugar cubes.

Angeline happily slurped up the tea. "God d—"

"*Bless* you, Angeline," interrupted Louisa quickly, smiling at Catherine. "It's God *bless* you. You *have* to learn to get it straight."

"God *bless* you!" said Angeline, and her smile was one that pierced the heart.

Council began at nine o'clock sharp the next day, a cold but bright Monday morning. The Indians strode into the conference in single file. In dignified silence they took their seats upon the ground in a semicircle before the governor and his staff. The four head chiefs—Seattle of the Duwamish and Suquamish and their allies, Pat Kanim of the Snoqualmie, Goliah of the Skagits, and Chow-it-hoot of the Lummi Indians in northern Puget Sound—sat in front as befitted their high rank. The subchiefs, like Chief Nelson of the Muckleshoots, occupied the second row. The various tribes then took their places behind their chiefs.

What a spectacle of savage pageantry, thought Louisa, gazing across the stupendous gathering from where she sat on a teetery green camp stool with the few whites not directly involved with the signing. Such dignity! this great semicircle of warriors in their gay barbaric dress! gathered before a handful of white men to listen in respectful silence! Behind stood the evergreen forest and the high Cascade Mountains; in front, the wide blue Sound; and beyond, the glittering, snow-capped Olympics.

Mike Simmons, the "Daniel Boone" of the territory and the governor's chief Indian agent, got things started by leading the crowd in a rousing three cheers for Governor Stevens.

"Aye Iah!"

"Aye Iah!"

"Aye Iah!"

The governor then rose somberly from behind a large table, cleared his throat, and began to speak in a distinct, resolute voice.

"My children! You are not my children because you are the fruit of my loins but because you are children for whom I have the same feeling as if you were the fruit of my loins!" He glanced over to Colonel Shaw. Shaw, dressed in blue uniform and silver buttons, began the Chinook translation. Designed as a trade jargon by the Hudson's Bay Company, Chinook was nothing more than a three-hundred-word mishmash of French, English, and various Indian dialects. It worked well enough to barter beaver pelts but was a poor tool, Louisa knew, for something as complex as treaty making.

Listening absently to the inadequate translation, she realized how extremely short the governor was. At five feet three inches, he hardly came to the shoulders of the military men who flanked him. In size, he seemed a frail, half-grown boy, with a head much too large for his body. But Louisa knew that Isaac Stevens was not frail. He was as strong as big Mr. Butler, if not stronger. Today he wore his usual red flannel shirt, his dark frock coat. His corduroy trousers were tucked into the tops of his high black boots "Californy style." Under a wide black felt hat, his face was swarthy. His eyes were blue. His dark blond beard was slight but thick. Looking into his face she could almost see the devils of determination that drove him beyond natural limits and which made him, as David once said, a giant of a man to be reckoned with.

"What will a man do for his children?" the governor asked, the Chinook translation of his opening comment completed. "He will see that his children are cared for, that they have clothes to protect them against the cold and rain, and that they have food to guard against hunger." He went on to explain, pausing for translation, how he'd traveled many moons back to Washington City where the Great Father lived, to see the Great Father on their behalf.

"Thought he went because Jeff Davis was trying to stop his railroad!" snorted someone Louisa didn't know.

"He stopped him, didn't he?" grumped Doc Maynard beside Louisa, irritated by the interruption.

"My children—" Quickly Louisa turned her attention back to the governor. "I have told you the heart of the Great Father. But the lands are yours and we mean to pay you for them. The Great Father has many white children—who are his children the same as you! They have come, some to build mills, some to till the land, some to fish, and some to sail ships. The Great Father wants you to learn how to farm and for your children to go to a good school. He wants me to make a bargain with you. You will sell your lands, and in return we will provide all these things! You will have certain lands set apart for your homes, and receive yearly payments of blankets, axes, and medicines. All this is written down on this paper which will be read to you!" He held up the treaty.

"I believe I have your hearts," he concluded. "You have my heart. Together we will put our hearts on this paper and then we will sign our names. I will send that paper to the Great Father and if he says it is good, it will stand forever."

To Louisa's surprise a mass was then sung, after the Catholic form, led by Bishop Demers under whom Chief Seattle had been converted two decades before. *"Glory . . . God on high, and on earth peace to men of goodwill . . . we adore thee, we bless . . . O only begotten Son—who taketh away the sins of the world, have mercy upon . . . who sittest at the right hand . . . most high in the glory. . . . God the Father, God the Son, God the Holy Ghost . . ."*

She'd never seen or heard anything quite like this and she was entranced: the black-robed priest, the white vestments, the glimmering gold cross, the sprinkling of incense and water, the reverent Indians now intoning a Gregorian chant that none could understand but which held some kind of ritualistic meaning she could not comprehend.

"Ah-ah-mennn," the priest finally sang.

"A-men," the Indians answered in near perfect echo, everyone among them making the sign of the cross.

The last shuffle subsided. Everything grew quiet. The governor again resumed control, and Louisa took Emily Inez over to play with a circle of Indian children. "Did I miss anything?" she asked breathlessly upon rejoining the small group of whites.

"No," said David. "He's just started to read the treaty. Emily Inez all right?"

"She's fine. Happy to run wild for a bit."

A babel of noises arose suddenly from a dozen different quarters.

"What is it? What's happening?" Louisa asked in alarm. She grabbed David's arm and leaned forward, straining to hear, to see.

"They want the treaty read in their own language, not Chinook."

"Is he going to allow it?"

"Nope," grumbled Doc Maynard, leaning back on his camp stool.

"There's no need for any fuss," Catherine chided him gently. "The Indians know Chinook, it's no loss."

"Ridiculous. The very idea of taking a language with nearly half a million words and mashing it down to three hundred—and expecting anyone to understand what's meant . . ."

"Now, dear," said Catherine, patting his hand, "Colonel Shaw is doing his best."

"Wake nika cumtux, six!"

The governor looked up impatiently.

"The Skykomish missed the last line," explained Colonel Shaw.

Governor Stevens's swarthy face darkened with anger or impatience, perhaps both, but he repeated the sentence.

"You know what this is?" asked Maynard, whirling on his wife. "This putting English into Chinook?"

"No, what is it, dear?" she said kindly, for he was fast getting into one of his moods.

"It's like pushing a bouquet through a knothole! It's one dang hard pull and all you know in the end is that someone thought to send you flowers!"

"And you have no idea," quipped David from the other side of Louisa, "if they were roses or skunk cabbages."

Doc Maynard's laugh came out his nose.

"The paper is now read!" shouted the governor. "Is it good? If it is good, we will sign it; but if you dislike any point, say so now!"

Pat Kanim went first, pronouncing the treaty good. Then Chow-it-hoot, then Goliah. Nelson stood up next, but Seattle, in terse quick words, gave the Muckleshoot chief reason to think twice and he sat back down, quickly.

"David?" whispered Louisa anxiously.

David grinned, then reached for her hand and tucked it into his jacket pocket with his own. "Seattle," he whispered in her ear, "just told Nelson it was high time he learned to get along with his *red*skinned brothers."

Chief Seattle prepared to speak. As an allied chief, he was not about to demean himself by speaking Chinook. A handful of nouns and even less adjectives ill-suited his allegorical mind. Thoughts came to him in pictures. He would speak Duwamish, a precise, versatile language.

When he began, everyone within a half mile heard him easily, for his voice was a well-trained instrument. As a boy he practiced with stones in his mouth, his father standing farther and farther away to force volume and clarity. Today Seattle's voice rumbled up from his stomach and rolled in thunderous waves across the crowd.

"ʔəslabəd čələp ti dukʷibət ʔut əči(l) dxʷʔal ti swatixʷtəd."

Henry Smith, sitting on the stool in front of Louisa, whipped out a note pad. Seattle's clear enunciation and oratorical rhythm, spelled by Shaw's feeble Chinook translation, gave Henry ample time, scribbling quickly, to record the address. Louisa leaned forward to read over his shoulder the words of the mighty chief.

"Yonder sky has wept tears of compassion upon my people for centuries untold, but that which appears changeless and eternal may change. Today is fair. Tomorrow may be overcast with clouds. My words, however, are like the stars that never change. Whatever Seattle says, the great chief at Washington can rely upon with as much certainty as he can upon the return of the sun or the seasons.

"The White Chief says that Big Chief at Washington sends us greetings of friendship and goodwill. This is kind of him, for we know he has little need of our friendship in return. His people are many; they are like the grass that covers vast prairies. My people are few; they resemble the scattering trees of a storm-swept plain. The great—and I presume good—White Chief sends us word that he wishes to buy our lands and is willing to allow us to live comfortably. This indeed appears just, even generous, and the offer

94

may be wise also, as we are no longer in need of an extensive country.

"There was a time when our people covered this land as the waves of the wind-ruffled sea covers its shell-paved floor, but that time long since passed away with the greatness of tribes that are now but a mournful memory. I will not dwell on, or mourn over, our untimely decay, nor reproach my pale-faced brothers with hastening it as we too may have been somewhat to blame.

"... Our good father at Washington ... sends us word that if we do as he desires he will protect us. His brave warriors will be to us a bristling wall of strength. His ships of war will fill our harbors so that our ancient enemies far to the northward—the Haidas and Tsimpsians, will cease to frighten our women, children, and old men. Then in reality he will be our father and we his children. But can that ever be?"

A full minute passed before Seattle resumed. Doc Maynard leaned around back of Louisa. "David!" he hissed. "I guess we're listening to just about the greatest orator ever! Judge Chenowith's father in Olympia swears the old man is the best! Pretty high praise coming from a fellow who's heard Henry Clay and Daniel Webster and John C. Calhoun ..."

Seattle began again, angrily. David and Maynard both sat up straight. Louisa peeked over Henry's shoulder.

"Your God is not our God! Your God loves your people and hates mine! He folds his strong protecting arms lovingly about the paleface and leads him by the hand as a father leads his infant son—but he has forsaken his red children—if they are really his! Our God, the Great Spirit, seems also to have forsaken us! Your God makes your people grow strong every day! Soon they will fill the land while our people ebb like a receding tide that will never return! The white man's God cannot love our people or he would protect them! They are orphans who can look nowhere for help!

"How then can we be brothers? How can your God become our God and renew our prosperity and awake in us dreams of returning greatness? If we have a common heavenly father he must be partial—for he came to his pale-faced children. We never saw him. He gave you laws but had no word for his red children whose multitudes once filled this vast continent as stars fill the sky. No! We are two distinct races with separate beginnings and separate destinies. There is little in common between us!

"To us the ashes of our ancestors are sacred. Their resting place is hallowed ground. You wander far from the graves of your ancestors, seemingly without regret. Your religion was written upon tables of stone by the iron finger of God so that you could not forget. The red man could never comprehend nor remember it. Our religion is the traditions of our ancestors—the dreams of our old men, given them in solemn hours of night by the Great Spirit, the visions of our shamans, and written in the hearts of our people.

"Your dead cease to love you as soon as they pass the portals of the tomb and wander way beyond the stars. They are soon forgotten and never return. But our dead never forget the beautiful world that gave them being. They still love its verdant valleys, it murmuring rivers, its magnificent mountains, sequestered vales, and verdant-lined lakes and bays, and they ever yearn in tender affection over the lonely hearted living. Often they return from the Happy Hunting Ground to visit, guide, console, and comfort them."

Abruptly he changed his tone and turned to the governor. "However, your proposition seems fair. . . . I think my people will accept it and retire to the reservations you offer them. Then we will dwell apart in peace, for the words of the Great White Chief seem to be the words of nature speaking to me out of dense darkness."

He turned to face the crowd once more. "It matters little where we conclude our days. The Indians' night promises to be dark. Not a single star of hope hovers above his horizon. Sad-voiced winds moan in the distance. Grim fate seems to be on the red man's trail, and wherever he goes he will hear the approaching footsteps of his destroyer and prepare stolidly to meet his doom, as does the wounded doe that hears the approaching footsteps of the hunter.

"A few more moons. A few more winters—and not one of the descendants of the mighty hosts that once moved over this broad land or lived in happy homes, protected by the Great Spirit, will remain to mourn over the graves of our people—once more powerful and hopeful than yours. But why should I mourn at the untimely fate of my people?

"Tribe follows tribe, nation follows nation, like the waves of the sea. It is the order of nature. Regret is useless. Your time of decay may be distant, but it will surely come, for even the white man whose God walked and talked with him as friend with friend cannot be exempt from the common destiny. We may be brothers, after all.

"Yes, we have pondered your proposition, and we will accept it, but I here and now make this condition! We will not be denied the privilege of visiting at any time the tombs of our ancestors, our friends, and our children!"

He scooped up a handful of muddy grass, held it out so all could see.

"Every part of this soil is sacred in the heart of my people! Every hillside! Every valley! Every plain and grove has been hallowed by some sad or happy event in days long vanished! Even the rocks, which seem to be dumb and dead as they swelter in the sun along the silent shore, thrill with memories of stirring events connected with the lives of my people! And the very dust upon which you stand responds more lovingly to our footsteps than to yours, because it is rich with the blood of our ancestors and our bare feet are conscious of the sympathetic touch!

"Our departed braves, our fond mothers, our glad, happy-hearted maidens, and even the little children who lived here and rejoiced here for a brief season, will love these somber solitudes and at eventide they will greet shadowy returning spirits. And when the last red man shall have perished, and the memory of my tribe shall have become a myth among you, these shores will swarm with the invisible dead of my tribe, and your children's children think themselves alone in the field, the store, the shop, upon the highway, or in the silence of the pathless woods, but they will not be alone. For at night when the streets in your cities and villages are silent and you think them deserted, they will throng with the returning hosts that once filled them and who still love this beautiful land. No, the white man will never be alone . . ."

He paused, drew himself up to a great height, squared his massive shoulders and concluded: "Let the white man deal kindly with my people, for the dead are not powerless. Dead, did I say? There is no death! There is only a change of worlds!"

Governor Stevens thought Seattle's speech too long. Time and time again he consulted his watch. He arranged, then rearranged his pens and ink bottle on the table. When Seattle at last finished, Louisa watched the governor breathe a sigh of relief. She smiled, amused. David smiled too. He'd been watching the impatient governor as well.

"Now what?" she whispered. They were close, like children whispering in school.

"I guess they start signing now."

"I'll go see what's become of Emily Inez."

She found her daughter toddling around on a sandbar where a half dozen old women dug clams. A score or more children kept her away from the water's edge by tearing after her and playfully scaring her another direction. Her cheeks were rosy red when Louisa finally caught up with her. Her nose was runny, her eyes bright.

"NO! NO!" she yelled, and kept yelling until Louisa set her down again.

"You don't mind playing with her?" Louisa asked the children in Chinook.

"*Wake, wake!* no, no!" they chorused. Just then one of them spotted Emily Inez sneaking away. The alarm went up.

The whole horde ran after her, laughing, calling out, *"Chako! Hyak chako, hyas klootchman! Copet!"* Emily Inez turned around to watch them tear like the wind after her. She wobbled and went down on her bottom with a plop. A very skinny little Indian girl, laughing so hard she could hardly pull Emily Inez up, brushed off her bottom and somehow got her steady on her feet again. The game was on and Louisa, satisfied that her daughter was safe and happy, returned to the treaty ground.

She arrived just in time to see Seattle, the last to sign, present the governor with a white flag. "My heart is very good toward Dr. Maynard," said the chief. "I want always to get medicine from him. And by this," he added, handing the flag to the governor, "we make friends. We will never change our minds."

The governor thanked him, and said, "We too have gifts." He nodded toward Mike Simmons. Simmons, taking cue, climbed onto a chair and held out his arms to quiet the crowd.

"Tomorrow we will have gifts for you and next summer we will give you some more! After that," he shouted, "you must wait until the paper comes back from the Great Father! The gifts we give you now are not in payment for your lands! They are merely a friendly present! Tomorrow we will do this! Tomorrow will be our *potlatch* to you!"

BOOM! B-B-B-B-B-*BOOOM!*

David and Louisa jumped. So did everyone else as more gunfire roared off the water. But it was only the *Major Tompkins,* firing a thirty-one-gun salute!

The Indians recovered, and began laughing at themselves. Good joke! they chortled. One by one and then in tribes they made their answer until the air vibrated with the echo of their high, bloodcurdling war cries.

The hair on the back of Louisa's neck stood up straight, though she was used to such cries. Many a night she'd lain awake in bed, listening to the natives go through their barbaric racket. *But so many? All together?* Her heart stopped.

Just then she caught sight of the children hauling a terrified Emily Inez up the beach. Louisa's heart began beating again, chaotically now.

David reached Emily Inez first. "She's trembling all over, Liza," he said weakly when Louisa caught up.

"Will she be all right? Shh, shh," she crooned to Emily Inez. "Just the Indians yelling again, and the boat making bad noises."

"Bad noise!" bawled Emily Inez, twisting around in David's arms to point.

"It's not the Indians that scared her," said Louisa, amazed. "It was that stupid boat and their stupid guns!"

"Let's just be glad Emily Inez has no fear of the Indians," said David calmly.

"I don't know if that's good or bad."

"It's good, trust me." David started back up the beach. "Because the minute we start being afraid of the Indians we might as well pack up and go home."

Louisa quietly slipped her arm through his. "David, let's pack up and go home!"

"What?" He stared down at her.

"Not Illinois!" she remonstrated. "*Home!* Our claim!"

He leaned over to kiss her forehead. "You are a pickle, a sweet pickle. Very well, Mrs. Denny, let's get *right* home."

9

*Monday Evening,
January 22, 1855*

IMPORTANT FROM EUROPE. Sebastopol Not Yet Taken! Great Battle between the Russians and Allies! Sebastopol is represented to be in a horrible condition, fever having attacked the garrison in consequence of the exhalations from the thousands of unburied bodies in the city killed in the great battle of the 5th of November . . .

—*Pioneer & Democrat,* January 19, 1855

*D*avid and Louisa paddled without speaking. The incoming tide slackened and stood still, brimming the beach. Heavy boughs of cedar and hemlock swept down over the quiet flood. Beneath the branches the shoreline lay in shadows of darkness while away from the shadows the water resembled a dim polished mirror, reflecting stars.

Louisa paddled wearily. The beach came to an end. They rounded a point. Ahead lay a great dark emptiness.

"Elliott Bay," said David from the stern. "We're nearly home."

Within minutes they passed Smith Cove, a lonely looking pocket of darkness but for the single light in a cabin window. "I didn't know Henry left early too," said Louisa. "Oh, of course, his mother is home."

"Do you want to stop and say hi?"

"I could use a warm cup of tea. And Mrs. Smith is probably lonely now that Ellender is married and living in town."

"But if we keep on, we'll be home before you know it."

"Let's go *right* home!" said Louisa with a quick laugh.

He laughed back at her. "Maybe the mail is in? Oh, Liza, I'm just having fun," he said when he saw that she'd taken him seriously.

"But maybe Mr. Mercer went into town," she argued, paddling with new energy. "Maybe he picked up our mail and brought it out!"

Tom Mercer, their "Lake Union" neighbor, was looking after their chickens and dog while they were gone. But he'd hardly go into town on a fool's mission, thought David. Seattle hadn't had mail in eight weeks and wasn't likely to get any either; not until the governor finished with the *Major Tompkins.* He said as much.

"But Mr. Mercer and the girls probably went in yesterday, for church."

"Tom wouldn't have picked up mail on a Sunday."

"He's not all that strict about the Sabbath. Besides, Mary Jane"—Mary Jane was Mr. Mercer's eldest daughter, fifteen years old—"has been waiting since before Christmas for her catalog order. Maybe the *Major Tompkins—*"

"Liza, there is no mail." David wished he hadn't brought it up. "Until Governor Stevens finishes his treaty making on the Sound, we're back to square one—no boat to carry the mail."

"But maybe the *Major Tompkins* dropped it off on the way up to Mulkiteo yesterday!"

David laughed. "You *are* persistent! And maybe that new side-wheeler Captain Webster keeps promising the coal company is here too!"

"Oh, David, don't be a spoilsport," she pouted.

A high, cold wind came off the land. The canoe began to bob, the water no longer mirror smooth. Emily Inez, asleep in a pile of fur skins on the bottom of the dugout, stirred. In minutes the stars dimmed.

"A northeaster!" shouted David. "Quick! If we hurry, we can make it home before the storm breaks!"

By the time they got the canoe beached David's clothes were wet through, his feet were soaked, and much to his disgust he couldn't keep the sleeting rain out of his face or off his neck. Louisa hurried a sobbing and shivering Emily Inez up to the cabin, leaving David to haul up their plunder and secure the dugout. If he kept his chin up, the icy stuff beat into his jacket collar at his throat. If he tucked his chin in, the rain ran off the rim of his soaking wet hat and found the back of his neck. "Ah, phooey," he muttered, letting the sleet have its way, and heaved the canoe upside down. Quickly, with cold, painful fingers, he got the painter tied to the usual stump growing out of the bank. He figured it would take five trips up the trail before everything was off the beach. It took seven.

Inside, Louisa had the fire started, two lamps lit, and was just starting to strip off Emily Inez's wet clothes when David dropped the last bag onto the floor just inside the door. "Can you put the kettle on?" Louisa asked without bothering to look up, drawing Emily Inez's arm out of her bunting.

Mechanically he set to. "Should we give her a bath? She's pretty dirty," he said, eyeing first Emily Inez and then the tub on the wall. "Or wait until tomorrow, when she's not so fussy?"

"She's got sand in her ears, David. She even has it in her bottom!"

"That a yes?"

Louisa looked up this time, her eyes inviting in the cozy light. "Yes."

An hour later, everyone bathed, fed, and Emily Inez asleep in her trundle bed, David and Louisa flopped with exhaustion into their chairs at the table and regarded each other wearily, but happily. At last, time to be alone, just the two of them.

Outside, the sleet had turned to a wet snow. The darkened window at the end of the table had begun to ice. No need to mention how glad they were *not* to be in a tent tonight. Or to speak of their close call on the water. Another ten minutes and it would have gone hard. "You're right," Louisa finally said. "No mail."

He suppressed a smile. "Check the stove shelf."

She leaped up, squealing, "Why didn't you tell me?"

"Between the soap tin and sugar box," he told her.

Quickly she pulled down a stack of newspapers and one precious letter. Without bothering to look at who it might be from, preferring to save the surprise, she laid the back issues of the *Pioneer & Democrat* on the table, the most recent on top, the oldest on bottom. She waved the letter in his face.

"No mail?" she chided.

A slip of blue paper, torn from the inside of a sugar barrel, fell to the tablecloth. She picked it up. "A note from Tom. *David, Louisa,*" she quickly read, skimming the short note, skipping every other word. "'*Steamer put in on way to Mulkiteo. Sunday, did not get mail. Two loggers no scruples. Fetched mine, yours, the good reverend's.'*

"HA!" she declared triumphantly, waving the letter again in his face. "The *Major Tompkins* did stop in with the mail!"

"Ha! but Tom—being Sunday—did *not* get the mail," David shot back, and snatched the letter.

"So we're both right. '*Amazed to find no mail from outside world,'*" she read on. Her grin gave way to puzzlement. "'*Problem not preemptive use of steamer. Instead, mail not getting up the Cowlitz Trail in winter weather. Men now demanding sea route direct from San Francisco. No more overland "puddle jumping." Will check Wednesday, see if cabin fine. P.S. Dog good. Chickens, not good. No eggs.'* So who's our letter from?" she demanded suspiciously, "if there's no mail from the outside?"

"Has to be someone in Olympia." He turned the envelope over.

"The Lows?" she guessed, referring to one of Seattle's founding families who'd since sold out and moved to a farm somewhere near the territorial capital.

"Nope, but good guess. Too bad. I'd like to hear from John and Lydia, hear how things are going for them."

"David, we don't know anyone else in Olympia."

"We know Arthur."

"Arthur! Well, of all the disappointments!" she declared. "I thought—oh never mind."

"Come on," he cajoled, handing over the envelope. "Sit down and read me his letter while I take a gander at these newspapers. He's probably sent an update on the legislature." His eyes happened on a headline. Quickly he snatched up the January 19 newspaper, gave it a snap, and leaned forward to gain what little light he could from the table lamp. "Europe's still at it, Liza, and it sounds awful. It says here that the Allies have Sebastopol under siege, but that the Russians are putting up a fight."

Her disappointment over the mail gave way to a strange despondency. Slowly she eased into her chair. "Do you suppose there will ever be a time," she asked him, "when people aren't fighting somewhere on this earth?"

He leaned closer to the flickering flame.

"'The Allies have effected a breach,'" he read, "'and it is stated that the Turks were to lead the van in the assault. The Russians are making great preparations to receive them, having planted cannon to sweep the streets, and fortified the houses in satisfaction of the Allies gaining an entrance into the city. Both sides fight desperately, and the destruction of life frightful.

"'Deserters from Sebastopol report the town to be in a horrible state. The inhabitants were in want of water. The

105

Russians, being unable to bury their dead, were throwing the bodies into the bay; but the sea rejects them, and the beach is strewn with corpses. The great hospital has been destroyed by fire, and two thousand sick and wounded soldiers had been burned—'"

"Don't read anymore. It *is* too awful."

He agreed, and set the paper aside, inviting her eyes to meet his. "This world is full of trouble, isn't it? All of Europe at war. The U.S. . . . fighting in Kansas. And the Rogue River Indians in southern Oregon are raising another rumpus. Aren't you glad we live here, Liza? Where people at least are trying to get along?"

"Do you think Chief Nelson will be able to live with the Duwamish? That everything will be fine?"

"If Chief Seattle has anything to say about it."

"Does he?"

"Are you going to read me Arthur's letter?"

"No, I can't see that he'd write anything interesting."

She was right, thought David, the letter was pretty dry. King County's boundaries had been redrawn, everyone north of the Puyallup River had gone over to Pierce. "Say, here's something," he said. "Arthur's somehow pulled his prohibition bill out of the sink. It's to go to a referendum at next summer's election. Looks like the people will get to vote on whether Washington Territory goes dry or not."

"The *people?*" she asked adroitly.

"All right, the men."

She got up and blew out the lamp. "What *man* is going to vote for prohibition? Besides you, Arthur, and Dobbins."

"What about Maynard?" he drawled. "Don't you think we can count on him to sway a few folks our way? Hey, what are you doing?"

"Going to bed. Last one in is a rotten egg."

"Hope you like rotten eggs," he said in the dark with a contented smile.

10

February 1855

All of the stores on Commercial street were doing a thriving business, a fourth having been opened by a Jewish firm by the name of Bettman.

—Roberta Frye Watt, Katy Denny's daughter
in *Four Wagons West*

The fourth and final Puget Sound Indian treaty took place the last day of January on the Olympic Peninsula. The Quinalt, Neah Bay, and Port Madison Indians signed away the entire northern peninsula in exchange for a few small reservations and the usual promise of a school, doctor, and blacksmith shop. Ten days later, on February tenth, the *Major Tompkins* steamed into Esquimult Harbor of Vancouver Island and struck rock. Crew and passengers made it to shore, despite the gale, but the brand-new steamer, in service less than four months, sank.

Captains Scranton and Hunt returned to San Francisco. Governor Stevens chartered the Hudson's Bay Company's *Beaver* back to Olympia.

Immediately he began preparations for another flurry of treaties with the plains Indians of eastern Washington, and while he waited impatiently for the snow in the mountain passes to melt, the pioneers, pleased with his quick and easy settlement on the western side of the mountains, rushed with burgeoning confidence into spring.

In Seattle, the busy tap of hammers competed with the shrill whine of the never-ceasing sawmill as new settlers arrived and old settlers expanded their horizons and hopes. Stores, houses, and new industries popped up everywhere.

Bettman & Brothers, an Olympia-based Jewish firm, joined the rank and file on Seattle's Commercial Street.

Judge Lander moved up from Steilacoom.

Captain Hewitt, another attorney, hung out his shingle—CHANCELLOR IN PROCTOR AND ADMIRALTY. He also went into business making oxbows.

Arthur Denny's commissary did so well he took on two partners: Dexter Horton to do the books and David Phillips to mind the store.

A block down the road and kitty-corner to David Maurer's Eatery & Guest House, Plummer & Chase expanded their general mercantile and post office to include, in the basement, the bowling saloon they'd been talking about.

Mr. Plummer, apart from Mr. Chase, bought a lot at the foot of Main Street from Doc Maynard and built a wharf. Captain Webster's new *Water Lily* had arrived and Charles Terry, last to leave Alki, Seattle's original site, gave up his land interests to pilot the forty-nine-foot side-wheeler up and down the Duwamish River. His job was to haul Webster's coal from the mine at Mox La Push and put into Seattle at Plummer's new pier so the coal could be onloaded into ships destined for all parts of the world. Between runs, "Captain" Terry took over the mail contract of the demised *Major Tompkins*, fetching whatever mail came overland to Olympia. In very short order Plummer & Chase and Plummer's Pier became the center of Commercial Street activity. Busier than even the mill at mail time.

Away from the Point, across the Sawdust and up, up the precipitously steep hill of Mr. Yesler's "skid road"—down which he skidded logs from the back of his claim to his mill—the ring of hammers competed not only with the high whine of the saw below, but with the incessant rat-a-tat-tat of forest woodpeckers. Misters Woodin and Wetmore were building a water mill, up by the gurgling stream that crossed "skid road," for their new tannery and shoe shop.

Hammers north of the mill added further happy notes. Guthrie Latimer, Louisa's uncle, was needed back east to close out his brother's affairs. He closed out his own affairs by simply handing over his boardinghouse to Reverend Blaine—who'd been using the downstairs for church services. Within a week Reverend Blaine sold the Latimer House to a sea captain for two thousand dollars. He and his faithful church members started at once to build their own church building.

Yet more hammers rang out. A half block up the hill, around the corner from the church and tucked inside the woods, Widow Holgate watched her own new house take shape. She'd come west the spring before with her three sons, her two daughters, her daughter's husband, and their three children. But she hadn't enjoyed living on the joint claims of her eldest son and son-in-law. Lem Holgate and Ed Hanford had filed south of the Point, and as much as Widow Holgate liked living with her daughter's family, she preferred living in town with her own. Preferably near the church, she said. She was Baptist, but if the Methodist-Episcopalians were putting up a building, they would, she said, do in a pinch.

On the Sound itself, further evidence of progress could easily be seen. Four different freight lines, each with its own fleet of ships, regularly plied the water in search of Puget

Sound lumber, cedar shakes, and cord wood. The Sound's twenty-four sawmills could hardly keep up with the increasing demand—not just in San Francisco, but around the world. Which meant the settlers and mill owners obliged as quickly as they could, and in whatever way they saw a profit.

David Denny and Tom Mercer worked together, clearing a grove of alders from a fertile valley they shared southwest of Lake Union. They intended someday to farm the land; settlers would be spreading north as Seattle grew. They'd need potatoes and beans and whatever else could be grown here. As for now, the alder commanded a high price in cord wood and was easy enough to clear. The thud of David's and Tom's axes biting into the brittle trees echoed back and forth from morning to night, even as meadowlarks trilled in the wavering branches overhead.

David had great plans for this valley. He loved the meadow and, as the trees came down, the commanding view of Mount Rainier to the south. On clear days this singularly high, snow-crowned mountain stood up against the sheer blue sky like the monarch it was. "You know," he said one day to Tom when they stopped to mop their brows and have a look at the mountain, "I can't talk Louisa into moving out here. She says I'm plumb crazy—"

"Maybe you're going about it the wrong way," interrupted Tom, a strong-looking man with broad shoulders, kind eyes, and prematurely gray hair. His wife's death on the Oregon Trail had worn him out in a way that all the hard work of trying to keep four growing girls fed and clothed could never do.

"No getting around her," said David. "She's got her heart set on the Sound. She loves the water. Particularly now with so many ships passing up and down. Way back here, she says, she'd feel too isolated."

"Isolated?" Tom cast his eye north, to his own fine house somewhere through the trees, overlooking Lake Union. "She'd be a might closer to me and the girls. Unless, of course, she doesn't consider us company."

"That's not the problem."

"Guess she'd miss Mrs. Bell, and her girls. And their boy, Austin," said Tom, speaking of the Bell family who held the claim between the Denny brothers.

David said, "Louisa worries about Sally. She visits frequently, does what she can to help out. I asked Henry about it once, he says Sally won't last a year. He thinks William ought to take her to a dryer climate, California maybe."

"Easier said than done, I suppose." Tom thought about his own wife. She'd taken cold at The Dalles, had sickened and died before he'd hardly known she was ill. "What's William say to California?"

"He knows as well as any she's failing. If they go to California she may live another year. She may die on the way."

"I heard once that this was a great country for curing consumption."

"Great for curing fever and ague, Tom. Consumption only gets worse in these parts. Too damp."

"We can always pray otherwise, son."

"Sure." David never argued the power of prayer, especially coming from a man like Tom Mercer.

"But in the meantime, about that wife of yours," said Tom, leaning on his axe handle, "if you're going to move her around, you got to look at things from her point of view. *Why* does she like living on the water? I mean besides the ships and pretty view."

"She likes knowing she can get into Seattle if need be." David eyed another tree, guessed it would take about five swings to knock the spindly thing over.

"Out here, you have the road."

David started over to the tree and began tromping down the brush with his boots so he could find his stance and get a clear swing. "She's scared of the cougars, Tom. Says she'd rather get into town by water than court a chance of running into one on the road. Can't say as I blame her, not after that big one jumped her last winter."

111

Tom eased his axe around his head a few times to loosen his shoulders a bit. "If Louisa was the timid type I'd say you had a point, but your wife doesn't scare worth a nickel. She can stare down an Indian and still have sense left over to spend some. No, I'd say if you're serious about wanting to move her around, I guess you're going to have to put a carrot in front of her nose. Find something she *really* likes. Then I expect she'll move along 'bout as happy as a hungry horse coming into the barn."

"You going to lend a hand, or jaw all afternoon?" David took his first swing into the gray bark of the slender tree. His muscles tightened obediently, driving the axe blade deeply into the wood . . . exactly where he'd figured. He gave the axe handle a quick back-yank. The blade squeaked out and he let fly again. On his fifth stroke the tree creaked. Tom arrived in time to give it a push and the tree fell over with a graceful "swoosh."

David looked up. The mountain stood serenely untouched.

"Hey, where're you going?" hollered Tom.

"Just found my carrot!"

Tom swung around. Yup, he thought, scratching some bug under his beard. Louisa had a fondness for mountains. The Sound was special, but her preference lay in the mountains beyond. Give her a gawk at old Rainier—*Tahoma the Indians called it, The Mount That Was God*—on a day like this? Why, in no time at all, Tom thought to himself, he'd be swapping a brick of butter for half a dozen eggs. Maybe even one of his calves for her next brood of chicks.

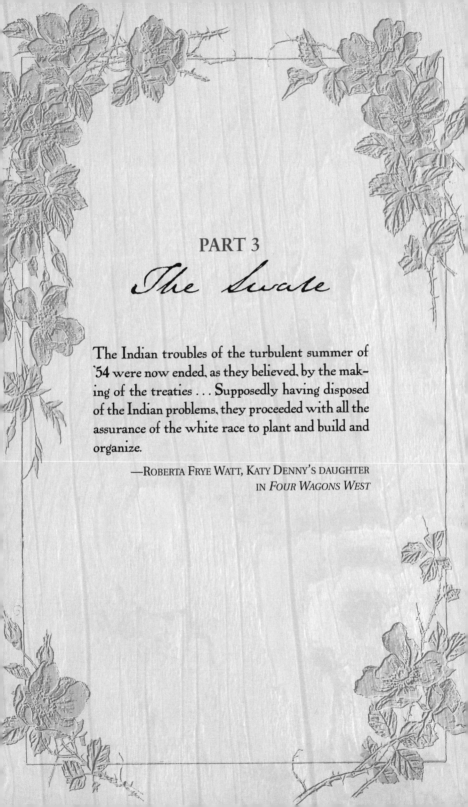

PART 3

The Swale

The Indian troubles of the turbulent summer of
'54 were now ended, as they believed, by the making of the treaties . . . Supposedly having disposed
of the Indian problems, they proceeded with all the
assurance of the white race to plant and build and
organize.

—ROBERTA FRYE WATT, KATY DENNY'S DAUGHTER
IN *FOUR WAGONS WEST*

11

Friday, March 22, 1855

In the spring he built another cabin further east on the donation claim, east of what is now Box Street, between Mercer and Republican.

—Emily Inez Denny, David and Louisa's daughter
in *Blazing the Way*

Six weeks later Louisa awoke earlier than usual. Another cloudy morning, she decided. Nothing different than all the other cloudy mornings during March. Yet today felt different; something in the air buoyed her spirit.

"The Chinook!"

She sprang from bed and ran to the window. A rabbit darted across the clearing. Chipmunks raced around and around and up and down the trees. Yes, the soft gentle Chinook wind had come, warming the earth, readying it for spring. "The Chinook! The clouds will be gone within two shakes of a dead lamb's leg," she told David excitedly.

"Spring's here, that's good." He swung his legs off the bed and sat blinking in the gray dawn. "We can get more done now."

They felt no lack of anything as they hurried along the trail to their "swale." They hurried as if to make up for the inertia of five thousand years of untouched wilderness and their own delay in recognizing the sequestered paradise David had found.

When they came to the trail's end and entered a high, grassy meadow, the clean, peeled logs of their new, unfinished cabin stood before them, bathed in morning's first glow of light. The clouds, indeed, had blown away and the logs shone as if made of gold, not fir. The great trees standing two hundred yards beyond the cabin, hazy with more of the golden rays, made for an enchanted distant forest. It was a beautiful lonely place.

But there was nothing frightful about the loneliness; to the south, the swale opened onto a brilliant dome of snow floating in the sky. Mount Rainier had been, and would always be, there forever, and David and Louisa's new affinity to the eternal landmark rooted them to this place they already called home.

Louisa could hardly believe she'd been so stubborn about staying in their little cabin on the water. "Oh, David," she said now, "you must cut a big window, a *huge* window, in the south wall! So we can see the mountain each morning when the sun comes up!"

She set Emily Inez down in the high, dewy grass and took David's hand, and, hands swinging slowly between them, they stood admiring their last few weeks of work. It was the most beautiful house on the Sound, Louisa thought with pride. Sixteen by twenty feet along the front with an attached room, twelve by fifteen, out the back. A cat-and-clay chimney. A front porch. Plans for five windows was an extravagance, she knew, but such a fine house deserved extravagance. In her mind's eye, she could see her sweetbriar growing along the porch railing. And her vegetable garden? Where would she put that?

Emily Inez tottered off. Watch, quick to tag after her, set the wet grass into motion with his tail. Emily Inez laughed at the tickling blades and rubbed at her nose. A butterfly fluttered up. She stared, wide-eyed, in wonder.

"I know just how she feels," whispered David, tightening his fingers through Louisa's. "Everything looks so pretty and new." The world was softly bathed in golden sunlight. Birds sang ecstatically. Leaves and shoots not there yesterday today held a soft green. Impulsively David brought Louisa's hand up to his lips and kissed the dry, tight skin on the back of her hand. She pushed her hand again to his lips. "You like this, do you?" he said.

She laughed and pulled away, picked up her skirts and ran through the wavering grass to the house. "Oh, David! It's so beautiful! When can we move in?"

"We haven't even got a roof yet!" he hollered after her, amazed to think there was a time she didn't want to move. But one look at Mount Rainier and her resistance had vanished.

He watched with pleasure this morning as she raced to the little shed he'd built six weeks ago. She pulled the bolt. The plank-slab door swung open. She began pulling out the saws and other tools. "Can I help make the shingles?" she asked, pausing for breath.

"You can make them all, if you can find the froe," he told her, striding forward and wondering if any Indians would show up today. A few folk in town insisted the natives were indolent and unreliable. But they could be counted on, David figured, same as the weather. Though *how* they accounted for themselves could sometimes, like the weather, be a surprise. You had to learn to read the signs.

They were always more than willing to *watch* a man work, for they were incurably curious. But given the right mood—

or a half dozen brass buttons in trade—they could sometimes even be cajoled into overcoming centuries of thought
that decreed building and planting woman's work. Today
maybe he could talk them into grubbing stumps. This was
a task unfamiliar to them. Maybe, the men wouldn't think it
beneath them.

"Do we have one?"

"Have one what?" he asked.

"A froe!"

"Oh," he said, coming back to reality. "Yes . . . maybe even
two. Tom, I think, left his the other day. Have you seen my
saw?"

She handed it over.

"My axe?"

She pointed, and he called for Emily Inez to follow him
over to the big windfall cedar log he'd been saving for the
shingles. She scampered after him, talking away to herself
in baby talk, interspersing a few English words, occasionally
a bit of Chinook. He set her up on a stump and gave her a
flower to play with. Watch sniffed at the underbrush, circled
around on himself three times and lay down.

David's cedar tree was five feet thick, perfect for sawing
into shingle-length drums. He set his saw into the deep cut
he'd made the night before. He'd sawn most of the way
through before giving up and going home.

This morning he went at it again with fresh energy and
counted twenty-three strokes, one for each year of his life.
On his twenty-fifth stroke the drum trembled. On twenty-
seven it broke loose and sank further into the ground. He
paused to rub his wet forehead with his shirtsleeve, then laid
aside his saw and pushed his shoulder against the bark. Giving a determined heave, he laughed to feel the lightness of
the detached drum as it rolled easily away from the rest of
the massive log. Two more feet and he upended it with a thud
among the ferns.

"Boom," said Emily Inez from her perch.

"Boom," he agreed, looking down into the heart of the drum.

The center had been hollowed out by dry rot, which explained the lightness. But the rest of the dull, red wood was perfectly seasoned. Four or five swift blows of his axe, and the drum split open like a melon. A dozen or more blows, each time his axe releasing the fragrance of a thousand summers, and he had as many bolts.

The froe Louisa handed him was an L-shaped tool necessary for making the shake shingles. "How do we do this?" she wanted to know.

"The wooden handle," he explained, pointing, "is the vertical. The steel blade, with this wedge-shaped section, is the horizontal. See here? The blade's thick back is dented. Shows you how it's been used."

She nodded and sat down on a rock. He handed back the froe and she took it awkwardly between her small, work-worn hands.

"Hold it with your left," he instructed. "You have to hold your maul with your right, remember, to make the blow." She juggled things around a little, then watched carefully while he showed her how to set the froe's blade near the edge of one of the upright cedar bolts she'd tucked between her knees. "Across the grain, that's it. Now strike with your maul."

She did. The wood split partway. By prying and wiggling a little on the froe handle she detached something resembling a shake. But it was irregular and bulged in the middle. "Not very good, is it?" she said, kicking at it.

"Try again. You'll get the hang of things."

But her second try wasn't good either.

Her third was spoiled by a dead knot, which made a hole right through it.

"We'll save that for over your side of the bed," he teased. She pretended to hit him with her maul. He lurched backward, out of her way. "Give up?" he asked.

"No. I can do this as well as any man."

But her fourth attempt was the worst of all.

"People usually get *better* at things, Liza."

"Shush." She bit her lip and tried again. This time she set the blade across the grain half an inch from the edge of the bolt and struck firmly with the back of her maul. Pop!

"Well, look at that! Just flew off like it didn't belong!" she declared proudly, bending over to look more closely at the board she'd just whacked loose. "Would you look at that," she repeated, amazed. "Flat as a breadboard—except for these little crinkles."

"Need those for the rain to run off!" he said with his own rush of pride at her accomplishment.

She tried again. Another perfect shake. "Wow, this is fun!" She popped off a third perfect shake. A fourth, a fifth. She kept it up until the entire bolt vanished into the pungent smell of cedar and trampled ferns.

They worked together in rhythm, David sawing more drums off the log and splitting them into a dozen or more bolts, Louisa whacking loose her shingles in steady pops. An hour flew by.

"Think we have enough?" she asked.

"Enough to get started." He had to laugh at her bewildered expression. "Come on, we'll stack them up next to the house so I can take them up to the roof poles."

Emily Inez staggered back and forth behind them, trying to haul some of the shingles herself. She dropped each one slowly and torturously, but triumphantly, by her parents' neat pile.

"Look," said Louisa, measuring a shingle against Emily Inez's shoulder while David set a ladder against the back wall. "They're almost as high as she is!"

Watch suddenly started to bark.

"Hey, breakfast time!" shouted David.

Louisa dashed to look. Mr. Mercer and his daughters were traipsing up the meadow, swinging their baskets and bundles through the well-worn grassy trail that led from their house a half mile away to the new clearing. Louisa gave them a wave, and the two youngest broke loose and came running, knees banging into the baskets as they came on.

"Fresh bread and cold venison!" shouted six-year-old Alice with a giggle.

"Fresh bread?" David hollered, already a good way down the trail. "Did you get up extra early to do that, Mary Jane?"

Fifteen-year-old Mary Jane blushed.

"Wait'll you taste it!" shouted Tom from the rear of the line. "She wrapped it hot, and I brought butter!"

Louisa greeted each of the girls—Mary Jane, fifteen; Eliza Ann, thirteen; Susannah, eleven; little Alice, six—then helped them lay out their picnic cloth on a big flat stump and unpack the baskets. Every morning for the last six weeks they'd had breakfast like this. Mr. Mercer and his girls supplied the food. And then every day, after the younger girls had gone on to school at the Blaines' house in Seattle and Mary Jane had taken Emily Inez back up to Tom's house, he stayed on to help in whatever way he could.

Six weeks sweeping by, thought Louisa. Like a holiday! Soon the fun would end. Very soon, if all went well. *But then it'll be even more fun, when we get moved out here!* Quick! So much to do! Hastily she spooned the rest of the applesauce into Emily Inez's mouth and wiped her face clean with a damp cloth Mary Jane always thoughtfully provided.

"Thank you," she told the young girl.

"You're very welcome, Mrs. Denny."

Tom stood up, brushed the crumbs out of his beard. He squinted critically at the T-shaped house. "Did you get the shingles done?"

"A good lot of them. Louisa did," boasted David.

Up popped Tom's eyebrows. "You'll ruin this country, ma'am, with so much fine female energy!"

Louisa's turn to blush.

"Roof today?" he asked. "Tomorrow your floor? You are having a real floor this time, aren't you, Mrs. Denny?"

"Only if we can hurry up! But I'm so anxious to move in, I can hardly stand to wait!"

"Well, hold on. Dexter Horton's coming up with the floorboards this afternoon. He'll bring them in the wagon when he brings the girls home."

"Mr. Horton is bringing us home today? We don't have to walk?" shrieked Eliza Ann, Susannah, and Alice all at once. They began jumping up and down, Emily Inez, too, in imitation. Alice shimmied up her father's back. "Can Becky come for a visit?" she demanded, throwing her arms around his neck, nearly choking him.

Susannah, eleven years old but small for her age, stood in front of her father. She threw her small, skinny arms around his waist. Chin on his belly, she looked up at his face adoringly. "Can she, Father?"

"If her ma says yes, I expect we can put up with her. But you girls better get to school now, you don't want to be late."

Eliza Ann, Susannah, and Alice grabbed their lunches. Watch trotted on ahead. He knew the scent of cougar and could be counted on to intercept any danger.

Louisa helped Mary Jane gather the leftover scraps.

"Is that Salmon Bay Curley and Madeline, Mrs. Denny?" said Mary Jane.

Louisa glanced up. An Indian couple were coming along the trail from the Mercers'. Salmon Bay Curley—named for his unusual hair and for the long, narrow inlet on which he lived just north of Dr. Smith's claim—waved and leaped the creek that crossed the trail. Madeline, his *klootchman,* her customary three paces behind Curley and balancing a huge basket on her head, hesitated.

"What's he got her carrying?" cried Louisa. "David, you must give her a hand! She's liable to get herself soaking wet trying to jump the creek with all that!"

David and Tom jogged off, chuckling, and passed Curley, who stared after them curiously.

Tom took Madeline's basket. Nearly dropping it, he saved himself from a bad fall by staggering back a pace or two. David laughed, Madeline too. But then Madeline screamed. David had her off her feet and was splashing playfully through the creek water with her in his arms.

"*Wake! Wake!*" she screeched in Chinook. "*Copet!*" No, no, stop!

Curley stomped up to Louisa. "*Whiteskins!* Fool to make such fuss over woman!"

Louisa gave the indignant man a quick peck on his leathery cheek. She knew it would make him mad. "You're the old fool," she scolded, "treating your wife like that. As if she's some ugly old horse."

Curley slapped at his cheek. "She *is* ugly old horse."

Curley had brought them what he thought was a funny story. The newest settler to stake a claim near Salmon Bay had poisoned an Indian.

"He *memaloosed* Limpy!" Curley chortled, holding his stomach and grimacing, and falling to the ground in a dead heap to show the others what he meant. He sat up laughing uproariously.

"You think that's funny?" gasped Louisa, aghast, looking hard at David and Tom, both of whom were frowning. Mary Jane stared with equal consternation.

"Ha, ha!" wheezed Curley, scampering to his feet, though he nearly fell over, he was laughing so hard.

Madeline chimed in, "Eat bad food, *memaloose!*" She too grabbed her stomach and clumsily keeled over.

Curley rattled off the whole story in Duwamish. David translated. Mr. Utter had put out a few slabs of poisoned beef to kill off the cougars bothering his livestock. Old Limpy, named because of a gunshot wound he'd received years before from an upper Sound Indian, happened to be passing through and spotted the meat. He helped himself to what he figured was a right handy supper, sitting there on the ground like that, just waiting to be roasted over a fire.

"But that's awful! Madeline! Why are you laughing?" Louisa stared in complete amazement. Madeline had collapsed onto her bundle, her mirth so uncontrollable she had to wipe the tears from her eyes with both hands. "In Happy Hunting Ground, Limpy say, 'Good joke!'"

"They have the sorriest sense of humor sometimes," said Mary Jane in disgust. "Like that time Yoke-Yakeman stepped in a cow pattie and then pretended to lick his foot clean!"

This set Curley and Madeline off all over again.

"Look at them," said Mary Jane.

"At least they're laughing," said her father. "Which is a sight better than having them get all steamed up and in a royal hullabaloo."

Louisa suddenly looked around for Emily Inez. She'd not seen her daughter for a few minutes, and panicked. "Oh my . . ." she gasped, frozen to the spot. Her daugher had climbed the ladder around back of the house and was trying to haul herself onto the top log of the back wall. Louisa must have managed to squeak some kind of sound despite her constricted throat. Curley whirled, following her frightened gaze.

As lithe as a cougar, he raced across the yard to the cabin. Louisa found her feet and started around back. David, quick on Curley's heels, passed through the front door just in time to see his daughter slip, then fall, her soft baby hair poofing up like dandelion fluff.

Curley caught her and lurched backward. David caught Curley. The three of them landed in a heap on the ground, looking straight up at Louisa who, breathless and white-faced, had all but hurled herself over the top of the wall trying to grab Emily Inez.

"Is she all right?"

"Mama!" cried Emily Inez happily, catching sight of her mother. She pulled out of Curley's arms and stood up, clapping. "Again! My do again!"

"No you don't," breathed out David, staggering after her and catching her up in his arms. "This is as high as you go, Half-pint," he told her, and swung her up on his shoulder. "Thanks, Curley." He held out a hand.

"Bad little girl!" said Curley.

12

Friday, March 22, 1855

A bulwark during these years was Dexter Horton... When the mill and farm hands and the trappers and loggers from the surrounding country were paid, they would ask Mr. Horton to keep their money for them. They gave it to him tied in little bags with their names attached. He tucked these money-bags away behind boxes, or more often in the coffee barrel. Weeks after, perhaps, when someone came back for his money, Mr. Horton would dig around in the coffee barrel until he finally found a little cloth bag, smelling of coffee...

In this store continued a business that led to the biggest banking system in the Northwest.

—Roberta Frye Watt, Katy Denny's daughter
in *Four Wagons West*

A few more Indians arrived and agreed to help David and Tom with the shingling. The women joined Louisa in her garden. She and Madeline had already staked out a forty-by-forty square southwest of the house. David told her she should dig and burn out all the alder stumps, and then plow. But she didn't have time for this. She'd just have to work around the stumps.

She worked feverishly, dropping her hoe into ground that had never known cultivation. Every root torn loose seemed to her a triumph over the wilderness, a root that would never grow again, and she made certain of this by shaking the earth carefully from each and every one and dropping what was left onto a nearby pile. When she had enough for an armful, she carried them over to Madeline's brush fire.

She was determined to weed out every root and explained to the women who'd come to help how to cultivate deeply. "When you can find no more roots with your hoe," she told them, "put your hand in the dirt and feel for any strands you might have overlooked." Each root they found, they grubbed loose, and when the women left they each possessed half a yard of red calico for their trouble, and Louisa had the keen satisfaction of a well-dug garden. Delighted, she buried her hands deep into the earth to feel the loose soil through her fingers as she broke and crumbled the last damp clods.

"Soon camas will bloom," Madeline said when she and Curley prepared to leave. For all her husband's "old horse" description, Madeline was, in fact, a regal, dignified woman. She wore a red bandanna around her head to keep her hair off her face, and adorned her fingers and forearms with numerous rings and bracelets. She loved silver and her jewelry was made of flattened silver coins, ornately carved. "When the salmon run, camas ready to pick," she said, pointing toward the marsh between the cabin and Lake Union, silver bracelets banging together in a pleasant clinking sound.

The marsh was a sheet of beautiful blue—blue like flax— shining among the green freshness of spring. *So this is the camas blossom,* thought Louisa with satisfaction.

"She dig camas roots good," said Curley. He started to laugh suddenly and poked his fat, dignified wife in the ribs. "She dig good! She digs with toes, not hoes!"

"Pretty proud of himself, isn't he?" said Louisa to David, watching them go.

An hour later a conestoga, drawn by two magnificent horses fighting their bits, emerged out of the trees to the east and came jouncing across the meadow. Long, dark shadows trailed, for the day had begun to fade. High on the wagon seat sat a small man with a brown goatee, his black hair back-combed beneath a big straw hat. "Whoa!" he hollered, pulling hard on the lines. Even as the wagon rolled up to the house, the little girl sitting beside him hopped off.

From the back of the still-moving wagon from off a high load of fir planks six more girls dropped to the ground. They twisted their ankles a little as the wagon rattled on and the ground stood still, but they recovered and joined Becky Horton in her race up to the new cabin.

"Auntie! Me and Nora and Gerty are here! We came with Becky and the Mercers!"

Louisa, inside the cabin marking the logs where she wanted her windows cut, was surprised to hear her nieces' voices. She tucked her pencil into her apron pocket and ran out to meet the oncoming wagon.

"Whoa! Whoa!" shouted Mr. Horton. Tib and Charley reluctantly came to a final stop alongside the house. They pawed the ground and rattled their lines. The wagon bounced and finally creaked still. "Guess they smell their own barn and don't want to stop!" greeted Mr. Horton as he set the brake and dropped off the wagon seat to shake Louisa's hand. "Hey there, Mrs. Denny!"

"Mr. Horton," she greeted.

Tib and Charley, a docile black mare and a spirited white Arabian gelding, belonged to Tom, though they were kept in town at the livery. Dexter and Tom operated Seattle's only transport company. Tom owned the team and wagon. Dexter, who lived in town, did the hauling . . . when he wasn't working at the mill or adding up figures at Arthur's store. "Smart horses," he told Louisa. "They knew right away this wasn't their turnoff. Hey there, Uncle Tommy!" he greeted, holding out his hand again, this time to greet the older man stepping carefully off the ladder. "Hey, what happened there? Beaver come along and chew out the bottom rung?"

"Nope," said Tom, accepting Dexter's offered hand with a big smile. The two men had come across the prairie together and were close friends as well as partners. "Had a bit of an accident a while back," Tom started to explain, then disappeared around the other side of his horses where he began running his hands up and down their legs and talking to them, making sure they were all right. "Emily Inez climbed up onto the roof so we took out the bottom rung to keep her from trying it again."

"Emily Inez climbed up the ladder? All the way to the top, Auntie?" marveled six-year-old Nora. "Did she fall?"

"She fell on top of Curley," said David, coming up behind and lifting Nora onto his shoulders. Her pink gingham skirt hung down over his face and he pretended to trip and lurch all over the place. "Stop, stop!" she screamed hysterically.

"My turn! NO FAIR, *MY TURN!*" shouted four-year-old Gertrude, Louisa's brother's daughter. She raced after them, grabbed her uncle's knees, and tried to make him stand still.

"Your turn in a minute, Corkscrew! Then you next, Missy Alice!" David hollered over to Alice Mercer who stood waiting hopefully with her thumb in her mouth.

Becky Horton handed lollipops all around. Katy explained to Louisa that Mr. Horton had invited them to come along for the ride, to see the new house. "It's so big!" she exclaimed, circling around and finally stepping through the front door to look inside. Like her mother, she stood with her hands on her hips to give it a proper examination. "Blazes, but this is big!"

"Don't say blazes, it's slang," Louisa reminded her.

"Where's everything going to go?"

Louisa began pointing with pride. "My stove here, in the corner. And a long cupboard over here. Above the cupboard—see where I've made pencil marks?"

Katy nodded, squinting and standing up on tippy-toe. With the sun going down and the roof almost finished it was getting hard to see inside.

"Uncle David's putting a big window here, so I can look out to Mount Rainier while I work."

"You can see Mount Rainier from *here?*"

"On a clear day."

"Blazes, but I wish we could—sorry, I keep forgetting." Katy turned around, and her mouth dropped. She'd spotted the huge fireplace. Quickly she rushed over and stepped onto the hearth to measure herself. "Wow! I can almost stand up inside!" She peered carefully up the chimney. "Looks like Santa Claus can get down this one without trouble. Guess who has to have Christmas at their house this year, Auntie," she said with a very grown-up grin.

Louisa smiled.

Katy swung out the iron wand that was secured in the stone wall of the firebox. "What's this?"

"My crane. I can hang a soup kettle over the fire or swing it out over the hearth to cool off."

"It'll be nice for making soap. You won't have to stoop so much."

"Maybe I won't burn myself either."

"Papa should have thought of this for Mother," said Katy. "It's a very good idea." She stepped out of the fireplace and wandered over to the door in the middle of the back wall. She poked her freckled nose through. "If this is your bedroom, you have space for more than just a bed."

Amused, Louisa showed her niece where she planned on putting a clothes cupboard someday, as soon as they had the money. "I want a proper commode too, with a marble top."

"Here's a good place for a rocking chair." Katy spread out her arms. "Perfectly harmonious," she announced.

"Then I must add a new rocking chair to my list," said Louisa grandly.

"You should see Widow Holgate's new rocking chairs. She has two, and they *are* the loveliest! Milton made them out of two halves of one of Doc Maynard's old salmon barrels. He cut five staves out of the sides, stuck them upside down on some legs and rockers, and Widow Holgate made perfectly sumptuous cushions out of calico. You've just got to see them, they're the prettiest chairs I've ever seen."

"Prettier than your chair?" Louisa asked, thinking of the little chair they'd carried across the prairie.

"That's a silly little chair for babies," scorned Katy. "When you come into town next, I'll take you up to Widow Holgate's new house and show you."

Louisa realized with a jolt that her eldest niece was growing up. Soon she'd be a young lady like Mary Jane Mercer and Eliza Ann.

"Where's Emily Inez?" Katy asked all of a sudden, going back out to the main room. "Did she really climb up the ladder and fall down on Curley? What was Curley doing here anyway?"

Louisa didn't know which question to answer first. "Emily Inez is up at the Mercers'. Yes, she really did climb up the ladder, sixteen months old! Right up and over the top." Louisa positioned Katy in the path of light coming from the open front door and turned her around to face the south end of the back wall. "Right there," she said, pointing.

"That's awful high up."

Louisa felt weak all over again, just thinking about it. "It's extra high because Uncle David is putting a loft over the kitchen. He's been waiting for those floorboards."

"That'll be nice."

Louisa could hear the men outside, unloading the lumber. Soon they'd be finished and find themselves hungry. "Do you want to go with me to the Mercers'? Mary Jane is making everyone supper."

"Can we leave all the other girls here?"

"If you want. But they'll follow shortly."

"I know. But if we hurry, we can have a nice walk, just us two."

Louisa smiled, "All right. Let me get my bonnet."

After a hearty supper of boiled potatoes and roast duck, David and Louisa rode with Dexter as far as the cutoff to their old cabin. They sat with him on the wagon seat, a tight, comfortable squeeze. In the back, Becky, Katy, Nora, Gertrude, and Emily Inez curled up in a half dozen old blankets. The older girls whispered and giggled softly. Once in a while someone fussed at Watch who kept wanting to lick their faces. Soon they'd be asleep; let them fuss, thought Louisa. They'd played hard all evening.

"Got your window measurements right here in my pocket," said Dexter. "You're sure you want five, Mrs. Denny?"

"Yes," she murmured, snuggling in close to David. She was so tired she wondered if *she'd* fall asleep. Her hands throbbed with pain. Probably from splitting all those shingles. And all that hoeing!

The moon stood off to the left, nearly full and casting a pretty blanket of light across the stumpy road. Shadows and night sounds lurked everywhere. Far away a cougar screamed and Louisa shivered and pushed even closer against David.

"Just think of it," said Dexter. "This is the most famous road in America."

"How so?" David readjusted Louisa's head on his shoulder. "Only you and Tom use it. And me once in a while. Maybe more, when we get moved out."

"No, sir, you fail to see the significance of this pretty cut through the trees. Keep going, past Seattle I mean, and where do you end up?"

David thought about it for a moment.

Louisa said, "You end up at the Beach Road."

"Then where?" said Dexter.

"Why, I guess the Military Road," said Louisa. "That intersects out by Mr. Collins's and Mr. Van Asselt's farms."

David was beginning to get the drift of Dexter's thinking.

"Sure enough," said Dexter. "And we all know where the Military Road goes."

"Fort Steilacoom?"

"Fort Steilacoom, then Olympia, then right on down Ford's Prairie, the Cowlitz, across the Columbia, right into Portland."

David chuckled. "You're saying this is the Oregon Trail?"

"In a few years we'll cut it the other way, to the north, right on through to Bellingham, maybe even British territory!"

David smiled. "You're starting to sound like my brother."

"Must come from working with him, I reckon." Dexter jiggled the lines and clucked his tongue. Tib and Charley speeded up a little and Louisa felt the comfortable lurch of the wagon.

"How *is* the store doing?"

"Selling everything from plows to thimbles to women's tonics. One of us is going to have to go to San Francisco, I reckon, for more stock. So much cash in Seattle these days, people are spending like there's no tomorrow. Matter of fact, payday comes along and people ask me to keep it for them!"

"Really?" asked Louisa, lifting her head. "People in town are getting scared to keep their own money?"

"Don't think it's being scared of other people taking their money, Mrs. Denny, as much as trying to save it from themselves. If I have it, they don't, you see what I mean?"

"Where do you keep it all?" asked David.

Dexter laughed, a good sound in the chilly night. "In little sacks. I bury them in the coffee barrels behind the counter. Some I hide behind boxes or bags."

"Sounds like you better bring a safe back with you when you go to San Francisco," said David. "And it's not the Oregon Trail," he added, part of his brain still working on the previous subject. "At least not until we get a shortcut through the mountains. People traveling the Oregon Trail come down the Columbia and stay. They don't head up this way."

"We got the Naches Pass, east of Olympia. That puts us on the direct line."

"But how many people made it through that eye of a needle some call a pass? Last year only one wagon train. This year, two. Small ones at that. All we got out of this year's immigration—six thousand people—were a half dozen families and they settled way out by White River. If this part of the road is ever to be called the Oregon Trail, it has to start farther back on the Columbia—The Dalles, or Walla Walla. Where immigrants can save a couple hundred miles by coming direct through Snoqualmie Pass."

"If I didn't know better," drawled Dexter, laughing a little, "I'd say it was *you* sounding like Arthur! Hey, this your turnoff?"

A shaft of moonlight pointed out a straight path amongst the intricate maze of trees, its soft pretty light falling onto the round, shiny leaves of a salal bush. Struck by the pearly moon shaft, the coarse salal looked more like a shrub of silver growing in the night, and David was almost tempted to pick a few coins and hand them over to Dexter for safekeeping. "Looks like it," he said. "Thanks for the ride."

Two minutes later he and Louisa stood alone, Emily Inez waking up long enough to look around and see where they were before laying her head back down on her father's shoulder and falling asleep again. Louisa followed David as he pressed toward their cold little cabin on the Sound, the moon finding loopholes through the trees and slanting its paths ahead of them. The ferns and deadfall and rhododendrons with their long, polished leaves and clusters of growing buds almost seemed to glow in the iridescent light. The night held a cool refreshing fragrance. *A sort of green-and-brown smell,* thought Louisa. *A smell of salt and fir and damp leaves.*

"This'll be one of our last nights here," David grunted when he at last pushed in their door.

Louisa was about to say she was almost sad, for she was attached to this cabin. But then she bumped into the table, hurting her hip. "I can hardly wait," she whispered in the dark, then she nearly screamed. "Who's there?" she squeaked out instead, instantaneously reaching for the matches on the table.

13

Late Friday, March 22, 1854

Dr. Choush, an Indian medicine man, came along one day in a state of ill-suppressed fury. He had just returned from a Government "potlatch" at the Tulalip agency.

—Emily Inez Denny, David and Louisa's daughter
in *Blazing the Way*

*T*heir visitor was startled almost as badly as David and Louisa, for they'd woken him up from a sound sleep. "Dr. Choush!" Louisa gasped. She was so surprised, and relieved, to see the Indian medicine man that she dropped the lit match onto the floor. Quickly she struck another and once she got the table lamp lit, the darkness retreated to the corners.

"David, he looks upset. Ask if he wants barley soup. He likes barley soup."

While she scurried around the crowded dim cabin, she grew more worried. Dr. Choush was working himself into a temper, sleepy and disoriented though he'd been at first. Why was he so angry? What had happened?

She got Emily Inez into bed, then went to make the soup, measuring a cupful of barley into a pot of water David had put to boil on the stove. She cut up some carrots and potatoes, an onion, tossed in a bit of salt and pepper, and then added a dash of sage.

"He says they were given crummy presents at the government potlatch," said David wearily, his voice full of discouragement.

"What potlatch? What presents?"

"At the treaty signing, do you remember when Governor Stevens promised to send more presents? To show good faith on the part of the Great White Father?"

"It's only the end of March. He said this summer," Louisa said.

"He says a lot of things!" cried David in sudden exasperation. "The presents must have come early! He must have told his agents to hand them out!"

"What agents?"

The cabin was freezing. David decided he'd better light a fire. He rumpled up some newspapers and jammed them down between two cold logs in the fireplace. "Governor Stevens," he explained, "appointed Indian subagents for each of the proposed reservations. I have no idea who they are, though I'd sure like to meet the fool in charge of the Tulalips." Gently he blew on the first flickering flames. "He gave them blankets torn into strips, six to eight inches wide. What are they supposed to do with those?" An edge of bitterness crept into his voice. "Dr. Choush says the women tried sewing several together. All that did was leave most of them with nothing."

Torn up blankets as a gesture of goodwill? Louisa stared at Dr. Choush's dark, square face, the ill-suppressed fury behind his eyes. He was a well-respected Tulalip medicine man, and wore a long hickory shirt and a dogs' wool blanket. He trembled, but not from cold. From rage.

She motioned him to sit by the sputtering fire, then pantomimed that she had soup if he wanted. He didn't answer, but squatted on the hearth and held his hands to the flickering flames and started muttering again. Slower this time, so David could translate.

"Little Man In A Big Hurry promised a big *potlatch*. Rich Indian men fight to give best gifts at *potlatches*. They give their greatest wealth. Their canoes, their slaves, their dogs. When one man gives much, another gives more. They give and give until the rich man has nothing. The rich man even gives his blanket that he wears. The rich man becomes poor, but he becomes the richest in honor."

Dr. Choush stood up suddenly and started for the door. "You say the Great White Father is a rich man? He did not make himself poor! He is poor in honor! We have been tricked!"

"Don't go!" Louisa pointed to her soup and to his stomach. He said something to David, and shook a fist in his face. "Wait!" She grabbed the new Hudson's Bay blanket they'd bought for Emily Inez's trundle bed and raced after him out of the cabin. "Wait, Dr. Choush! Wait!"

He paused at the corner. Moonlight reflected off his greasy black hair. Shadows made his menacing face look brutal. "I'm sorry," she told him. "I'm sorry. Please, take. Yours. My *potlatch* to you. My best blanket."

He took it, and said something she didn't understand. When he was gone, she nearly bumped into David going back to the house, for he'd followed her out.

"What did he say to you when he left the house just now?" she asked. She could still see Dr. Choush's angry gestures, David's responding dismay.

There was little point, David knew, in keeping anything back. "He said white people are few, that our doors are thin.

That if they want, the Indians can easily break the doors and kill all the Bostons inside." Hand on her back, he guided her inside the cabin and shut the door behind them. Louisa just stood there, wringing her hands in despair. He reached out and gently folded his hands over hers.

"Was he serious? Well, of course he was serious," she answered herself fretfully.

"I'll ask Arthur to find out what went wrong, see what he can do in Olympia. Maybe more blankets can be issued—"

"Maybe! Maybe? That's the problem, David! We have an idiot for a governor! You said so yourself, he doesn't listen to anyone but himself! How's *Arthur* supposed to influence him?"

"You're jumping to conclusions again, Liza," he said gently. "And you're forgetting that Dr. Choush is a friend. When he left, he said you were heap good woman."

"He did not," she argued, though she smiled a little. "Nobody talks like that unless they're from Missouri or born in a barn."

He shrugged. "So I took a little liberty with my translation. But that's what he meant. More or less," he added.

"What did he really say?"

"He said your *potlatch* was a fine gift. That you possess rich honor. He said thank you."

"But it was such a feeble gesture, it hardly rights the wrong."

"Maybe in the end that's all we can do."

"What?" she asked.

"Try to right the wrong."

14

Monday, April 1, 1855

Papa offered to buy Uncle Dobbins' claim for $700. Uncle Dobbins' wife refused it. She was a mighty mean, cantankerous woman, so she sold it to Terry for $500.

—Katy Denny, Arthur and Mary Ann's daughter
Denny file, Museum of History and Industry, Seattle

*D*avid and Louisa moved to the Swale the last weekend in March. April first she entertained her first dinner guests, for she was proud of her new home and anxious to show it off. Not everything was perfect of course, at least not yet. Her wall borders still had to be made. The old chairs needed new calico cushions. And the Indian mats no longer looked as cheery on the new wooden floor as they had on the old dirt floor. She wanted a rag rug now, with bright colors. But one thing at a time. For now, it was enough to know that everything was new and bright.

"So who was waiting for you in the dark like that?" Mary Ann asked David.

"David, don't," warned Louisa. "If the girls hear, you may frighten them." She was mashing potatoes at her new kitchen counter. "It was only Dr. Choush," she told Mary.

"What did he want?" Mary Ann insisted, leaning over the stove to pick at the tender flakes of pheasant meat David was carving. He made a playful slash at her fingers. She withdrew. "Why was he in your cabin? Sitting in the dark like he owned the place?"

"If he owned the place," said David with the special smile he reserved for her, "he would have *made* himself at home and lit a fire."

"Ah, but lighting a fire is women's work!" said Mary Ann, laughing.

"We'll tell you all about it later," Louisa said firmly, giving one last punch at the potatoes. "Little pitchers have big ears . . ."

"That serious?" Mary Ann's eyes turned dark with worry.

"No," said David. "Liza, Mary and I can finish here if you'd like to get everyone seated at the table."

Louisa nearly forgot to untie her apron before calling breathlessly over to Mr. Mercer by the fire. He glanced up, looking a little disoriented. Twenty minutes ago he'd found *Uncle Tom's Cabin* on the shelf and had been engrossed ever since.

"If you'll kindly come to the table, we're about to eat."

"Oh, I'm sorry." He held up the book. "A very stirring story, may I borrow it?"

"It's a sad story, Mr. Mercer," said Mary Ann, helping David set out the food. "I don't know what's to become of our country over this ugly slavery business."

"Of course you may borrow the book," said Louisa. "I should *give* it to you, after all the work you've done around here. Except it's a gift from David and Arthur's brother. Yes, over there, please, just watch your knees, we've got lopsided boxes holding the table under there." She pointed to the spot she had set for him. "Yes, by all means, borrow the book. The girls will enjoy the story too. Don't you think, Katy?"

Katy slid onto a bench beside Nora. "Yes, but you'll cry when Eva dies."

"Why did you tell him?" hissed Nora.

"Arthur, I'll put you over here," said Louisa. Emily Inez whined to be picked up. Louisa obliged, then pulled out a chair and pointed Arthur to it.

One by one she got her other guests, the Mercer family and her sister's family, seated around the large makeshift table David had put together, boards propped atop a few boxes and crates, covered over by a long, white linen tablecloth. She was anxious for all to go well, though things had not started off as planned. Dobbins and Anna had not come.

Her table, such as it was, sat in the center of the large open room that made up the front of the house. On one end was her kitchen, the other her parlor. The kitchen, on the south, boasted two counters either side of the stove, with cupboards beneath with real board doors that locked shut; a new sink; a pump—no water, David hadn't dug the well yet—her big, regulation ship's stove; more cupboards attached high on the walls.

On the parlor side, on the north wall, was her large fireplace with a beautifully sanded oak mantel—wide enough to set pictures and knickknacks. Bookshelves made of half rounds had been fitted into the log walls, to frame David's stonework.

Through the open door of the back wall she could see her high bed with its old, worn-out comforter falling down over the lockers David had built beneath the mattress. After the floor, his lockers were her greatest pride, filled now with clothing, diapers, linens, and a new bolt of *blue* calico, calico she wasn't about to trade with the Indians for *anything.*

She glanced around again, seeing in her mind's eye how her house might look when she got the finishing touches done: the calico border along the top of the walls, pictures on the walls, the new cushions—

"Are you going to sit down?" Arthur asked.

Embarrassed, she sat quickly. "Oo!" she squealed, popping back up. "And what's this, pray tell?" she chided playfully, picking a pinecone off her chair and laying it on the table.

"APRIL FOOLS'!" the little children shouted, wiggling in their chairs with glee at their joke.

"It was ME! ME!" shouted Alice. "ME! ME! I did it!"

"I helped!" Nora put up her hand as she'd been taught in school.

"Me too," said little Rollie.

"A fine joke," said Louisa. "Is it safe to sit down now? You didn't put a spider there, too, did you?"

"A *spider!*" giggled Nora.

"Are you girls ready to say grace?" David asked, glancing down the table, Tom and his girls on the one side, Arthur and Mary Ann's family on the other. Emily Inez sat on her mother's lap at the far end. She caught his eye and gave him a sweet wet smile, then folded her hands and bowed her head.

"She's so cute!" exclaimed Katy.

"Shush," hushed Arthur. "You mustn't make her vain."

"Sorry, Papa."

David began his prayer as always, "Heavenly Mother and Father . . ." Louisa knew this irritated Arthur, and she sensed him getting testy. But this was David's way of acknowledging the other Hebrew names for God, the way the Quakers did. When he was done, Arthur said, "Amen."

Everyone had brought something to share. In addition to Louisa's roast pheasant there was a saddle of venison from Mr. Mercer, with venison liver and bacon, and heated stones in the basket to keep it warm. There were loaves of bread and bricks of butter, three kinds of pies from Mary Ann and jugs of milk and cream. Louisa passed around the hot coffee and tea. Mary Ann put the kettles back on the stove.

"When the girls came out with Dexter last week," said Arthur, helping himself to the potatoes, "they said Curley and Madeline were here."

"Madeline was of the opinion," said Louisa, "that we will starve so far from the water. She brought me a whole pantry of her very best stores. Some camas, kalaise, dried clams, smoked salmon, dried berries—"

"Did she take all your sugar in exchange?"

"She was very kind, Arthur. She left me two cubes in the bottom of my tin."

Arthur roared with laughter. "Ha! She's as bad as Mandy, Yoke-Yakeman's *klootchman!* Sometimes I actually kind of enjoy their sense of humor!"

"Wait'll you hear what they thought was so funny at Salmon Bay," said Mary Jane with a roll of her eyes.

"Do we have to talk about that?" asked Louisa. "It was such a sorry accident."

Arthur insisted. "What happened?"

"A week ago," Eliza Ann told him, "Ira Utter poisoned Old Limpy. By accident," she qualified. "And Madeline and Curley actually thought it was funny."

Arthur set his elbows on the table. "I suppose he was trying to kill off the cougars?"

"Set out raw meat laced with strychnine," said Tom.

"Maybe somebody better pay him a visit. Remind him we have Indians living around here, in case he hasn't noticed."

"David," said Mary Ann, changing the subject. "How in the world did you get Louisa's stove moved? It weighs a ton."

"No one helped him, he did it all by himself, like a fool," said Tom, his mouth full of food but too anxious to tell the story to wait. "I found him coming across the swale like a turtle, staggering along with the stove on his back—"

"On his back!" Mary Ann looked over in dismay to Louisa.

Louisa pointed to her forehead. "He had one of those Hudson's Bay *voyageur* straps, you know, to help distribute the weight over his neck and shoulders."

"You let him do it?" her sister asked in dismay.

"What could I do?"

Arthur jabbed his fork at David. "That's a regulation ship's stove, cast iron, must weigh four hundred pounds if it weighs one. You're lucky you didn't bust a gut."

"That's what I told him," said Tom, chuckling. "He said it wasn't the stove that wore him out, it was the two-hundred-pound sack of flour he had in the oven!"

Mary Ann clapped both hands over her mouth.

Tom burst out laughing. "Pulled *my* leg, too, Mrs. Denny. I jumped right quick. Should have known better!"

Over tea and pie, and sitting around the fire—the little girls playing upstairs in the loft and Mary Jane and Eliza Ann washing dishes on the far side of the room—the adults discussed Dr. Choush's visit.

Mr. Mercer and Mary Ann sat in the best chairs, Mr. Mercer leaning forward, elbows on his knees, looking softly into the fire. Arthur sat on the floor, next to David. Louisa took the footstool.

Arthur had his boots off and was sitting with his shoulders back, his arms thrust behind him and locked at the elbows to hold himself up. With his long, strong legs stretched out in front of him, his heels resting on the low hearth to catch the heat, he looked like a Titan launched feetfirst through space, contemplating the universe, thought Louisa.

"It could be worse," he said, "but we've got two things going for us. One, Pat Kanim is the Tulalip's strongest ally and he has always been a friend of the white man."

"Not always," David reminded him.

"Long enough. Two, Doc Maynard was appointed subagent for Seattle's Indians, and rather than snub anyone he made up his shortage by purchasing enough blankets to go around, one apiece, to everyone in all six of Seattle's tribes."

"Who paid for them?" asked David, surprised.

"He did."

"Out of his own pocket?"

"Where did he get that kind of cash?" asked Tom. "That many blankets must have cost him upwards of five, six, maybe seven hundred dollars."

"He sold off some lots," said Arthur. "Ten or eleven, I think."

"Will he get reimbursed?" asked Louisa. "Can the next Assembly—"

"If I'm elected again I'll see what can be done," Arthur told her. "I probably won't get anywhere though. Maynard did this on his own, without proper authorization."

"Maynard can take care of himself," said Tom. "I'm worried about the Indians who got the short shrift. Can't something be done about them?"

Arthur reached up and scratched his head. "It's not that simple—"

"I know, but something must be done," Tom broke in. "We can't have the Indians getting riled up—not when we're coming to terms."

"Our primary problem," said Arthur, still in his laid-back posture, "is that we were preceded by the Hudson's Bay Company. They had the power to act on their promises, unlike us. McLoughlin was King, he made his rules. He saw to it they were followed. The Indians learned to hold him and all the English, accountable. And the English, the King Georges, proved themselves trustworthy. Democracy, unfortunately, works differently."

"Are you coming to a point with this, dear?" said Mary Ann.

"In democracy a governor can make all the promises he wants," said Arthur, with only the mildest of glances toward his wife. "But it's up to Congress to keep the promises. And as much as I'd like to point the finger at Stevens for making the Tulalips mad on this one, there's not a whole lot he can do if Congress chooses to get stingy and reneges on the agreements. Which is what Congress, of course, has done from the beginning. They always have enough money to fight the Indians. Never enough to honor their bargains. For instance," he asked, "how much was Governor Stevens given to treat with the Indians? $100,000? $150,000? Yet the Senate just passed a bill authorizing the President to send us a man-of-war to patrol the Sound, and to enroll three thousand volunteers for service against the Indians. Two and a half million dollars has been appropriated to that end."

"*You* wrote the motion," Mary Ann reminded him.

"I did, but I requested *two thousand* men, and I said *nothing* about millions of dollars."

"Well we mustn't leap too far ahead," suggested Mary Ann sweetly. "David, you'll be interested to know that Dobbins just sold the front half of his claim to Judge Landers and Charles Terry. We're looking forward to seeing more of Charles now that he'll be in Seattle—"

Louisa and David both sat up, surprised, Dr. Choush forgotten.

"Dobbins sold, why?" said David.

"Are they—" started Louisa, but she couldn't bring herself to ask if they were separating.

"No, they're not . . ." Mary Ann obviously couldn't say the word either. "But things aren't good. Dobbins takes to the woods for days at a time. Remember when we were growing up how he used to get when he wasn't happy? How he'd just go away and we'd never know where he was?"

Arthur said, "He sold the west half, what he figures is Anna's part of the claim. He's giving *her* the money."

"Are they . . . divorcing?" Tom asked, the only one amongst them who could actually voice the concern.

Louisa jumped up to get fresh coffee, upset. Anna had always been difficult. Last spring, when she was expecting William, she'd even told Louisa she *hated* Dobbins. *Why,* wondered Louisa, *can't they be happy?* But then Dobbins and Anna had never been happy. From the very beginning they'd brought out the worst in each other. Louisa remembered her analogy of marriage . . . two trees transplanted closely together. Some couples learned to sacrifice the branches that stood between them, and were better for it. Others, like Dobbins and Anna, couldn't find ways to accommodate and so they suffered. Terribly.

Maybe it would be better if they did d— No, she would not say the word. Let Mr. Mercer say it if he wanted. She wouldn't even think it.

"You've done a fine job," she told the Mercer girls in an attempt to change the subject. "Everything looks so lovely. You've even been able to figure out where I put things!" She smiled upon opening a cupboard or two.

When she returned to the fire, coffee in hand, David asked Arthur how much Dobbins got for the land.

"SHE'S NOTHING BUT A MEAN, CANTANKEROUS WOMAN!"

Louisa swung around and gawked up at the loft behind her. Katy, leaning over the rail, her red braids swinging down past her furious face, was shouting angrily: *"Papa offered Uncle Dobbins $700, but she said she wouldn't sell to Papa! So she sold it instead to Mr. Terry for $500! SHE'S A MEAN, WICKED WOMAN!"*

Arthur leaped to his feet. He had Katy down from the loft and out the front door so fast it made the rest of them breathless. Louisa poured her coffee in uncomfortable silence.

"He's not going to belt her, is he?" said Tom.

"No, I don't think so," said Mary Ann. "He can hardly do that. She's only echoing what he said himself, this morning. When he found out he'd been hoodwinked out of the best land deal Seattle will ever see."

"Cream, Mr. Mercer?" asked Louisa. "Sugar?"

Arthur brought Katy back in and made her apologize for her outburst. Feeling sorry for her, Louisa offered to brush her hair.

"Sit on the floor in front of me. You can tell me if Uncle David and Mr. Mercer left any splinters."

Katy sniffed a little, but came and sat down.

The conversation lagged, but then picked up with discussion of the new church. Doc Maynard had contributed a new pulpit. Sam Maple was waiting on the paint to come in from San Francisco.

"What color?" asked Katy.

"White," said her mother. "And when it's done, God's house will look ever as smart as the Felker House!"

Mary Jane joined the group. "Are you going to come to the dedication?" she asked Louisa.

"When is it?"

"Next month. Mr. Matthias says he'll be done about mid-May."

"Is Reverend Blaine preaching?" asked David.

"No," said Tom. "Brother Roberts from Olympia is coming up."

"Oh, David, let's go!" said Louisa.

He smiled at her and her alone.

"What I want to know," she told him later, when everyone had gone and they were lying in bed and staring at the ceiling, "is where Arthur was going to get that $700 to give Dobbins? His store can't be doing *that* well."

This was only their third night in the new house, and though the new noises were beginning to sound a little familiar, the large airy room still felt strange. Louisa wondered if she'd ever get used to having a bedroom separate from her kitchen and parlor.

"My guess," said David with a thoughtful sigh, cupping his hands behind his neck, "is that he made that much on those blankets he sold Doc Maynard."

She eased up onto her elbow and looked down at David's gentle face in the strange moonlight. "You don't think he'd try to make money off this Indian mess, do you?"

149

He met her eyes. "That's not the way Arthur would look at it. He'd only see it as making money off Maynard."

She flopped back down on the mattress and pulled the covers up to her chin. "What a skinflint! I guess I don't blame Anna for not selling to him!"

David freed his hands suddenly and pulled her in close. "Anna knows how to nurse a grudge, and when to play her cards. But let's not talk about the family. Let them worry about their own troubles, we have enough of our own."

"We do?"

"One, I'm freezing, I need someone to warm me up."

"Two?"

He kissed her eyes shut. "I don't know, I can't remember."

"David?"

"Mm?"

"Let's have another baby."

He lifted his head a little, to see her face. "All right. When?"

She counted on her fingers. "March?"

PART 4

James

The world spun out of focus, only James held it in place. Then slowly, slowly, the whirling unraveled and Louisa crumpled into his arms. His hand came up and cupped the back of her head; everything was stable, secure. He was her friend, her brother, and she kissed his cheek the way she always did.

Neither of them saw David on the crest of the hill. He stood looking down on them, his jaw drawn tight ...

—*SWEETBRIAR*

15

Sunday, May 12, 1855

We had our dedication last Sunday. All went off pleasantly notwithstanding the day was very rainy and unfavorable. I tell you it seemed real good to go to meeting in a comfortable house after we have been without so long. Brother Roberts was very much pleased with the church, says he has seldom seen so small a house that combined so many excellencies and so few defects.

—Kate Blaine, minister's wife
Letter dated May 19, 1855

ouisa woke wet with sweat, heart pounding and screaming *"James!"*

David's head came off the pillow. In the narrow path of moonlight slipping through the bedroom window he could vaguely see Louisa's shoulders, her straight back. She was

153

absolutely still and for a brief moment he had the absurd notion she was dead. But that couldn't be.

Nervously he glanced over to Emily Inez's trundle bed. Thank goodness she was still asleep. *Babies sleep through anything . . . amazing,* he thought to himself. He eased up beside Louisa. "What is it?"

Her voice was hollow, not her own, more like a returning echo. "I had a dream, an awful dream. James is dying."

"My brother?"

"Mm-m."

He reached over to hold her hands, startled anew to find them trembling. "Come here." He gently pulled her into his arms and eased back onto the mattress. He tucked her head against his shoulder, astonished to find her forehead damp with a cold sweat.

"Do you remember Ma's dream?" she whispered. He took her hand and held it over his heart, a signal they'd established somewhere along the line to indicate cherished conversation. *"When my father died?"*

He nodded, remembering the story. One night Ma dreamed she saw a horse sidesaddled and bridled at the gate, with a messenger telling her she must mount at once, and ride to go see her husband who was deathly sick. In her dream Ma obeyed, riding over a strange road, crossing a swollen stream at some point.

At daylight, when she awoke, the same horse was sidesaddled outside, the same messenger called to tell her she must go at once to her husband, he was dangerously ill at a distant house. As in her dream, she was conducted over the same road, forded the same swollen stream, and arrived at a house where her young husband lay dying.

"My dream was like that," whispered Louisa fearfully. "Not the same details, of course. For it was James, not Father. Oh, David, James is dying, I know he is. We must go to him, in Oregon, before it's too late."

He was about to say they couldn't afford such a trip. Yet if it was true, of course they would go. He had a whole season's timber piled up, waiting to be hauled down to the mill. He could use the money from that. "Tell me what you dreamed," he said.

"Pa came. Charles brought him on the *Water Lily* from Olympia. His hair was all white, like snow."

"Anything else?"

"Yes, we took the overland route. Pa said it would be faster. The road was terrible, and never seemed to end."

"Tell me what Ford's Prairie looks like." When she didn't answer, he explained, "Ford's Prairie is a layover point on the Cowlitz Trail, where travelers can stay the night."

"Is it a log cabin with an outside stair to the loft? A huge stone chimney? Surrounded by a field of high blue grass?"

How did Louisa know about the outside stair to Sid's loft? She'd never been to Ford's Prairie! And the blue prairie grass? The chimney of which Sid was so proud?

"Shall I sing you back to sleep?" he asked.

When she nodded against his shoulder, he interlaced his fingers with hers, their hands laying atop his heart where he could feel the disturbing, too-rapid beat of his fear. Nothing must happen to James, dear God no, he prayed. He'd spent too many years resenting James, bitterly so, before he'd ever been able to forgive him. But forgiveness was the wrong word. James had done nothing wrong. The sin lay within himself, in his own heart, for hating a brother whose only crime was an abiding love for Louisa.

When had his resentment begun? David asked himself now. Long before leaving Illinois. This much he knew. Probably ever since Ma married Pa and had brought Louisa to live with them in the big farmhouse outside Cherry Grove. How well he remembered the spark between Louisa and James; they'd been captivated by each other from the very beginning. James, seven years older than himself, Louisa an unbelievable five years older . . . leaving him, a kid of sixteen, to watch from the sidelines. It was this difference in their ages, his and Louisa's, that had caused his terrible insecurity. And he'd carefully hidden within that insecurity, never noticing that Louisa loved him, not James. It had taken her near capture by the Indians on the Oregon Trail to see it, her falling into his arms, their eyes close, their hearts beating wildly together, only then had he finally seen. Seen what a fool he'd been.

"David?"

He realized he'd not yet begun to sing. He chose one of Ma's favorites, a song she'd often sung back home, in the cool of the evening. And around the scorching campfire when coming across the hot, lonesome prairie.

> "Come my heart and let us strive
> For a little season,
> Every burden to lay by
> Come and let us reason."

"If Pa comes?" she asked, "may we go?"

"Oh, Liza," he murmured, drawing her close and kissing the top of her head. "Do you need ask? Now, shush, go to sleep. It'll be morning soon and we're going to church. Remember? for the dedication?"

> "Feeble, faint, and fearful
> How can I be cheerful?
> Think on what your Savior bore
> In the gloomy garden.
>
> "Sweat and blood through every pore
> Crying, 'O My Father!
> 'O behold my hands and side.
> 'To redeem the nations I was crucified.'"

They sang the same hymn the next morning in church. Louisa reached for David's hand; the hymn was not a common one. He sensed her quickening fear and glanced down at her uplifted face, looked up again and resumed singing, the resonant tenor of his voice joining the others. He felt a little fearful himself.

Most of Seattle had turned out for the dedication. *Everyone must be curious about the new church,* thought Louisa, because so few attended on a regular basis. Or perhaps they felt the same way as she and David? Hungry to hear someone other than Reverend Blaine preach?

Seattle had but the one minister, Mr. Blaine, who regarded the natives with abject contempt. He even taught that their mortal souls were without redemption. Such judgment was so anti-Christian David often wondered why anyone would attend his church. But the Reverend Blaine did have his faithful few: Arthur and Mary Ann, the Mercers, the Phillipses, Dexter Horton and his family, John Nagle from Lake Washington. And now that Widow Holgate had moved into town, she and her family: John, Milton, and Olivia. It was their hard work and dedication that had made this lovely church building possible.

Louisa couldn't help but admire the simple beauty of the building. In the hall at the back, two winding staircases descended to a small basement. Ahead was a small, neat pulpit, with two chairs situated close behind it. Further back, three climbing, wide steps for the singers. Louisa counted fifteen pews off either side of the three-foot center aisle. Maybe as many as a hundred and fifty people, she calculated, could be accommodated, although this morning only a third that number were present. Seattle was not yet a big town.

Louisa suddenly realized that her brother and Anna were not here. Surreptitiously she scanned the crowd again. *Was Dobbins gone again? Where was Anna?*

Mrs. Butler got up to sing a solo. Louisa set Emily Inez onto the pew beside her and listened to Mrs. Butler's pretty voice.

In Illinois Louisa too had sung solos, and had been in the church choir. Oh how she missed those days!

Slowly she forgot all her worries: the unhappiness in her brother's home, even her dream of last night and her sick worry over James. And when Brother Roberts got up to speak, she became fascinated by his account of the history of the Methodist church.

"Maybe you better make Emily Inez sit down," whispered David all of a sudden.

"But if I put her in my lap she'll get fussy."

"She keeps walking back and forth on the pew, leaning over and grinning at the Hortons."

Louisa eased around. "Is she bothering you?" she whispered to the woman behind her, a pleasant, plump young woman with bright blue eyes, sitting with Mr. Horton and their daughter Becky.

"Not in the least," breathed the kindly woman, leaning in to lay a hand on Louisa's shoulder. "She's a sweet little thing, reminds me in a strange way of my other little girl that I lost."

"Oh, I'm sorry . . . I didn't know . . ."

"Yes, before we left home, but that's quite all right, and don't you worry about Emily Inez. She's a good little baby."

Louisa turned back around, wondering about all the sad secrets in people's lives. Suddenly she was thinking of James again and, with an icy cold shudder that swept through her heart and left it thudding, she *knew* he was dying. She knew this as certainly as she knew that a hard rain had begun and was harshly drumming on the roof overhead.

An anxious half hour later, coming out of church, the rain beating down so hard it bounced off the wooden steps before her, Louisa reached for the banister even as her gaze sought the Sound—down the steep stumpy hill, past the mill near the beach, across the Sawdust. Her heart sped up painfully. Through the rain and mist she could see a boat putting into Mr. Plummer's pier! David, speaking briefly to

158

the two reverends, stopped abruptly. Someone shouted, "It's the *Water Lily!* The mail is here!"

Everyone plunged down the steps, snapping open their umbrellas and jostling past Louisa in their haste to get to the Point.

"Do you see what I mean?" she heard Reverend Blaine talking to Reverend Roberts. "No one in Seattle has any respect for the Sabbath!"

"Better than having no respect for your fellow man," said David harshly. He grabbed Louisa's elbow. "I shouldn't have said that, I lost my temper," he told her as they plunged down the stairs. "Liza, you don't suppose Pa is aboard ship, do you?"

"Oh, David, I *know* he is!" she cried, grabbing at her shawl in the wind. They cut down the hill, the wind blowing her shawl loose again.

"Liza! David! Aren't you coming for dinner?"

Louisa turned around. Her sister was hailing from the church steps fifty yards back. "Yes!" shouted Louisa.

"So where are you going?"

"We want to get our mail first!" she blurted out, not wanting to broadcast her fears. Too late she realized Arthur had taken offense.

He stood beside Mary Ann, holding Rollie and Orion, one boy in each arm. "We can wait for our mail until tomorrow!" he hollered.

Pa was not on the boat. Relieved, Louisa sank weakly onto a pier piling, her knees completely giving out. But then David dashed her relief by saying, "Maybe there's something in the mail."

He and Emily Inez were gone a long time. Mr. Plummer had had to run back to his big new mansion on the far side of the Point, to get his keys, then open up his post office in Plummer & Chase. And the mail, as usual, had not come for six weeks or more, so there was oodles to sort through. Alone on the pier in the pouring rain, Louisa shivered and fretted, sick to her stomach.

When they'd left Illinois, James was twenty-seven, two years older than she. He was a powerfully built man with muscles hard from farm work. The Nordic traits that cropped up now and then in the Denny line had certainly gone to him; his skin was almost russet in color. His hair and beard and mustache were red too, but more like the color of burnt fields in autumn, she'd once decided. Everything about him was red, except his eyes, which were robin-egg blue. He was a handsome man, full of strength and warmth, temper, vitality. He was her favorite stepbrother, and if she didn't love David so much she would have married James. It made sense. James was in love with her, and Ma and Pa had thought he was the better man for her. Their objection to David had been that David was five years younger than she. And while she could understand how it made sense to everyone else that she marry James, love never made sense. And she loved David. *Oh but poor, poor James!*

In that moment she was back in Cherry Grove, Illinois, the morning they'd left forever. She'd had to say good-bye to Pamelia, her dearest friend on earth. Tears in her eyes, she was cutting through the meadow to where the wagons stood ready to go West.

"Louisa? You all right?"

"Oh, James . . ."

In one stride he had her in his arms, and she pushed her face into his shoulder.

"Liza, it's all right," he whispered. "It's bad, I know, but it'll pass, I promise."

"I miss her already!" she cried into the blue flannel that was his shirt. "And what about Ma, the babies . . . What if something happens?" She looked up at him. "I'm afraid, James."

He said nothing and she searched his face for assurance—he always had it for her. "It's going to be all right," he promised, and she felt his arms tighten around her back.

160

"How old was your Ma when she died?" she demanded suddenly.

He took a surprised step back.

"I want to know how old your Ma was when she died."

He whistled and yanked his cap from his head, and ran a hand through his thick red hair. "You know all this. Happened maybe ten years ago now."

"How long was she ill?"

"I don't know . . . as long as I remember. What's this got to do with anything?"

"I'm just wondering about my own Ma is all."

"Ah!" He laughed—suddenly, spontaneously, as was the habit of all the Denny men. "What'd you and Pamelia talk about?" he teased. "Rattlesnakes and Indians?"

He grinned and leaned forward, hands on his hips. "We have to get you laughing again, Louisa Boren." He spoke to her as he did to Kate and Nora. "This is a good day and we can't have you spoiling it. What's Ma's verse? 'This is the day that the Lord has made. Let us rejoice in it and be glad'?" He made an exaggerated pout to make her smile. "Can't have Ma seeing that long face of yours. Tell you what. We're going to race over to that oak tree." He laughed low in his throat and gray darts of light came to his eyes. "It's where I kissed my first girl!"

James could always make her laugh. It was the way he took charge, the way he smiled and gave in so easily to his own laughter, as if he owned it all and was willing to share. "Go on, I'll give you a head start. On your mark!" he hollered. "Get set, GO!"

She ran swiftly, lifting her skirts high as she leaped over the mud puddles, soft and messy with the warming sun. The breeze lifted her hair from off her neck and whipped into her cheeks. She could hear him lumbering up behind, closer, closer. His arms swung out and caught her. She hugged tight, head down, as he twirled her around and around in mad circles.

161

The sound of someone's boots striking the pier brought Louisa back to Seattle. She tore her gaze away from choppy gray water, dimpled by the driving rain and ruffled white by the wind, and away from the *Water Lily* tied to the pier, to see who approached. "Read it," said David with a big smile. He handed her a letter. "Ma and Pa are full of news about the farm, that's all."

She could hardly believe it and sprang to her feet, tearing open the letter at the same time. David steered her along the narrow pier so she could read as they walked. They were passing the mill when she finished the chatty, newsy letter. "You're right! James is fine! He must be, or they'd have said something!"

David tossed Emily Inez into the air and pouring rain, and laughed.

"What's so funny?"

"There's a letter for Arthur from the acting governor. Governor Stevens must have gone over the mountains to complete his treaties. Do you think we should let that cat out of the bag over dinner? Should we tell Arthur he has a letter from the man left in charge?"

Louisa laughed too, finding herself almost giddy with relief that James was all right. She understood now why David had laughed. "Oh, David, do! He'll wish he hadn't acted so high and mighty! He'll just die from curiosity!"

Like mischievous children they scrambled up the hill, skirting the stumps as they passed through Suwalth's Indian camp. Since the treaty signing, more and more Indians had come into town. Nearly a dozen new cedar-slab cabins clustered the bluff. Louisa waved to a circle of children squatted around a sorry-looking fire, doing their best to shield their sizzling fish from the rain. "I'll bet you tomorrow's dishes," she puffed, reaching out to catch David's coattail, "that if you say anything about the letter, Arthur will overcome his scruples in short order and go fetch it."

David nodded to an Indian coming off the beach, then stared after him when he ducked into one of the shanties. *A Kljkitat?* The Klikitats were of the Yakima Nation, a vicious breed.

"*Before* four o'clock," said Louisa.

He stopped, and whistled.

"Is it a bet?" she asked him.

"I don't know . . . *Tomorrow's dishes?*"

"My dishes against your pile of wood that needs chopping. I win, you do my dishes. You win, I do the wood."

He shifted Emily Inez and stuck out his hand. For a moment she stared stupidly at him. "It's a bet," he said.

She moved to shake on it.

"No wait, we have to spit first."

She thought it strange, but spit without questioning it.

He chuckled, and shook his head at her, amused. "Not the ground, you goose. You spit into your palm."

Her eyes went all big and round. "*I do?*"

"You spit, I spit, we shake. That way neither of us can back off our word."

"My hand? Are you *sure?*"

"It's raining to beat the band out here. Have we got a bet or not?"

"Oh, ugh," she fussed. But she screwed up her nose and spit anyway.

He spit, and they shook.

"You have a very silly father," she told Emily Inez.

16

Sunday Afternoon, May 12, 1855

A fine basket of crabs traded from an Indian were put in a tin pan and set under the table; several were cooked, the rest left alive. As one of the children was proceeding with the dismemberment necessary to extract the delicate meat, as if it seek its fellows, the crab slipped from her grasp and slid beneath the table. Stooping down she hastily seized her crab, as she supposed, but to her utter astonishment it seemed to have come to life. It was alive, kicking and snapping. In a moment the table was in an uproar of crab catching and wild laughter.

—Emily Inez Denny, David and Louisa's daughter
in *Blazing the Way*

Louisa was surprised to find Gertrude setting Mary Ann's table with no evidence of Dobbins, Anna, or the baby in sight. The four-year-old sensed her confusion. "Father went to the mountains to hunt with Klap-ki-latchi," she explained. Carefully she placed her forks to the left of each plate, her tangle of black ringlets shimmering with each movement of her small shoulders. "Mother has the worst case of dys-en-tery since George Washington—"

"Gerty, that will do," cautioned Mary Ann. "We don't speak of our infirmities. It's not polite."

"Mother said I may come to Sunday dinner though," Gertrude went on. "Aunt Mary Ann is having crab."

Yes, Louisa could see that. Rollie and Nora were under the table, poking sticks at the live crabs Mary Ann had put in a bucket and pushed out of the way.

"Should I go see how Anna's doing?" Louisa asked her sister. "See if I can't get her to come over?"

"You can try. Lord knows I have. But she's still not speaking to Arthur and she *is* poorly. Katy, if you could, please come mash the potatoes."

"I'll go see what I can do." Louisa rebuttoned her coat and whispered to David on her way out that they shouldn't wait for her. Anna's stomach was probably in a knot because she herself was in a stew, and Louisa was resolved to meet the unhappiness that lay ahead.

A well-tramped trail lay between Arthur and Mary Ann's log cabin on the north end of town and the little cabin belonging to Dobbins and Anna two and a half blocks closer in. The forest between the two homes had given way entirely to the axe. Charles Terry and Judge Lander, Louisa realized, had wasted little time in clearing out this section of their new land purchase. She could easily see the church through the rain curtain, a whole block to the east, and the Blaines' pretty little parsonage next to it. The church, with its unfinished square belfry, beckoned. Impulsively Louisa cut through the deadfall and stumps.

"I wish people could be made to feel a little pride in our church, darling," she overheard as she climbed the stairway. "You know I told you how hard I worked to clean the floor, but look, they've tromped in all this mud, they set their umbrellas all running with water right in the seats. And mothers actually let their children climb and crawl all over the pews!"

Louisa started back down the stairs. Quickly.

"No one even stayed to help clean," Kate, the preacher's wife, whined. "I shall have to clean it all by myself!"

"Let everyone see you, my dear," said Reverend Blaine in his annoying, high-pitched voice. "Maybe someone will take the hint."

Louisa hurried to Anna's house along the trail called Second Street. *Why are they upset about a little mud and water? This is Seattle after all . . . and it is raining.* To beat the band, as David had said. *And the ridiculous martyrdom?* she wondered, irritated, as she passed the fancy parsonage behind Reverend Blaine's tidy picket fence. Why didn't Kate just *ask* for help? Mary Ann or Mrs. Phillips would be more than happy to scrub the floor each week!

The baby was alone, crying fretfully when Louisa knocked and let herself into her brother's cabin. "There, there," she crooned. Quickly she shrugged out of her wet coat and shawl, and was shocked, when she went to pick up her nephew, at how small and pale William was for eight months old. *He is not thriving,* she thought sadly, looking into his dark, tearless eyes. And he was soaking wet. As she changed him out of his deplorable state, for even his bed sheets were soaked with urine, she gazed around at the surrounding mess. Dirty dishes on the table. Bed unmade. The fire nearly gone out. She could not help but compare the stuffy dark room with her own new airy, sunlit house.

The door swung open. "Liza! You caught me in the outhouse. I've had the worst—never mind. I suppose you're here to try and talk me into going to Mary's for dinner? Well, it won't work," said Anna breathlessly, emphatically, and she draped her coat and bonnet over the back of a chair and flopped petulantly onto the disheveled bed. "I won't ever go visit there again. I despise that man!"

"May I?" Louisa indicated that she'd like to rock her nephew by the fire.

166

Anna nodded, then got up with a disgruntled sigh to stir the embers with a broken poker. She added two more logs, took the footstool opposite Louisa. Automatically she reached for her knitting.

Louisa settled William over her shoulder. He stunk, but she could hardly give him a bath without insulting Anna. "So who do you dislike the most just now?" she said brightly, for she might as well jump in with both feet. "Arthur or Dobbins?"

Anna slipped her needle into a stitch, and set her hands. "Is this any of your business?"

"No . . ." Louisa acknowledged. "But you told me once you hated my brother—" *What am I doing?* she wondered in a moment of panic. But the fact of the matter was she felt a little sorry for Anna. She wished Anna could find some kind of happiness in life. Everyone deserved to be happy. And even though she knew Anna was terribly disappointed in her husband, Louisa also knew her brother was not a brute. Surely he and Anna could learn to live together, in some kind of truce.

"For some reason," Louisa pushed on as best she could, "you and Dobbins rub each other the wrong way, though why, I'm not sure. Except you *are* so opposite in temperament. Also, when I look back, I can see he should never have brought you out West. You were the belle of Knox County, raised for garden parties and ballroom dancing and playing croquet on manicured lawns. Not for grubbing stumps, and making your own soap, certainly not for living in—" She looked around the rustic cabin. "So I understand a little your unhappiness. I can't help but wonder if this isn't why you keep getting those dreadful stomach pains—"

"You understand nothing!" snapped Anna all of a sudden, and she glared so furiously at Louisa with cutting green eyes that Louisa shrank back a little. "What would you know of my miserable life? You're married to a saint! What would you know about living with a man who couldn't care less if you lived or died—except when he wanted something out of you! He never talks to me, your brother. He doesn't even *look* at me!

"Once I hid under the bed for three whole hours," she continued, knitting quickly and all but spitting the bitter words out of her mouth, "and your brother didn't even so much as get up and look out the window after me! The baby cried and cried. Did he take notice? No. He just kept reading by the fire. I swear, the whole house could have burned down around his ears for all he cared! He'd have to be in flames himself before noticing anything amiss!"

"Dobbins doesn't mean to be aloof," Louisa defended helplessly. "That's just the way he is."

"OOOH! *That's just the way he is...*" mimicked Anna cruelly. "I am so tired of hearing that excuse! What about me? Don't I count? Am I not entitled to a little civility? A little friendly companionship? Or do I exist only to cook your brother's meals, have his children, wash his clothes? Am I supposed to spend the rest of my life in subservience to him, like a slave—without a tender word, not even a simple thank-you? Why, a *squaw* gets more courtesy and reward than I! Oh, I see how you and David," she went on, "exchange secret little smiles, how even Arthur and Mary Ann have their ways of loving each other! But have you ever seen Dobbins do the same for me, have you ever *once* seen it?"

"But you knew this about my brother before you married him," answered Louisa lamely, realizing for the first time how truly desperate Anna was. How truly lonely she was. "You knew he's never been one for talking, or showing affection. He doesn't mean to be rude or inconsiderate, he's just quiet. He lives inside his own head."

"You can say that again. And there's no room for anyone in there but himself!"

"And why are you feuding with Arthur?" Louisa plunged in even deeper. "Don't you have enough misery without adding to it? Heaven knows I can get pretty put out with him myself. *But bite off your nose to spite your face?* Anna, he offered you $700 for your claim, yet you sold it to Charles and the Judge for five hundred!"

"I have my pride," said Anna stiffly.

"Meaning?"

"At least *you* realize Dobbins is no prize. But Arthur? No! He so much as told me it's a woman's job to overlook the sins of her husband."

"Why should Arthur have cause to say something?"

"Because," huffed Anna, "Dobbins offered to sell him my half of the claim, and Arthur asked why in the world he wanted to sell when property will go sky-high once the railroad is built. Dobbins told him *I* wanted the money—"

"Did you?"

"Of course I did! But Mr. High-and-Mighty came straight over here all full of holy smoke. You should have heard the things he said! He said I was henpecking Dobbins to death, that I was making him look the fool to everyone in Seattle! All because I wanted a little money!"

Louisa laughed awkwardly. "Oh, Anna, can't you at least be glad you're not married to Arthur? Things could be worse, seems to me." She added, "If Mary Ann can put up with Arthur and his absurd notions, you should at least be able to put up with Dobbins—who has no notions. Except to *try* and make you happy. Because he does try, you know."

"He hasn't done a single thing to try and make me happy!"

"He let you sell half the claim! And why, whatever for?"

Anna narrowed her eyes.

"What are you up to, Anna Boren?"

Anna exploded. "ME! What am I up to, you ask! *I'm* doing something? Do you see me running off? Do I run away whenever I can't stand it anymore? It's always the woman to blame, isn't it? You're just like Arthur! Get out of my house, Louisa Denny! You don't understand a thing! None of you understand! NONE OF YOU!" Anna whirled off her stool and threw open the door. "GET OUT!"

Louisa eased to her feet. Woodenly, she handed over the baby. He'd started to cry in the ruckus, and now Anna snatched him none too gently.

"Anna, I didn't mean anything," she stammered. "I just want to help." She put her hand on Anna's arm.

Anna flung her off. "Get out!"

Happy shrieks of laughter, an alien sound, reached out to greet Louisa as she approached her sister's cabin moments later. Mary Ann's dog bounded out. Louisa bent down to pat Moreover's head with both hands. Inside, the children and Arthur were under the table in a rowdy, noisy tangle.

"I have him!"

"No, no, I do!"

"Oh blast, he got away!"

David rocked back away from the table, laughing hard. He looked up, saw Louisa. "Katy dropped her crab while trying to get the meat out, but when she bent down to pick it up, it came alive and bit her!"

Louisa tugged off her soaking-wet shawl, shivering. "Did one of the live ones get out of the tin?" she asked, forcing herself to forget Anna and her unhappiness. At least for now.

"Looks like it." David suddenly threw out a foot, to ward off an eight-inch crab clattering sideways, suddenly, out from under the table. Arthur reached around with a long arm and snared the crab with a tight, but careful, grip.

"Nora! Rollie! Gerty! Quick! Pull out that bucket! Before he eats my thumb for Sunday supper!"

The children, still under the table, pushed and shoved against the heavy bucket. "Careful," cautioned David. He reached down and gave a long, easy pull. "We don't want anymore of these ladybugs escaping."

"Ladybugs!" giggled Nora, her brown curls bouncing softly around her face.

"Pa, Pa, did you really get him?"

Louisa slowly looked around. Mary Ann had Katy by the fire and was bandaging her fingers.

"Did you, Pa?" asked Katy again.

"Sure did, Woodpecker!"

"Don't call me Woodpecker!"

"Oh, Katy, did you get bit hard?" asked Louisa, Anna slowly leaving her mind.

"Her skin was broken," said Mary Ann. "And she'll bruise. But no broken bones."

"Shall I get some skunk cabbage?"

"Yes, but wait until after we finish eating."

"No!" shouted Katy. Vehemently she yanked her hand away from her mother. "Don't you dare put any of that smelly old skunk cabbage on me!"

"Hush now," scolded Mary Ann. "It'll keep down the bruising and take out the pain. Arthur, please, will you pour off some of that water in the bucket so this won't happen again? I can't, for the life of me," she told Louisa, motioning for her to come sit down to the table, "imagine how one crawled out. *And don't you dare put that salt water on my garden!*" she hollered after Arthur.

David sang out, "Your crab must have heard he had a letter waiting for him at the post office!"

Arthur turned around on the threshold, bucket in hand.

"From Acting Governor Mister Mason, no less!" said David with a wink to Louisa.

Arthur came in, snared his oil slicker off the back door hook. "Maybe I should get some skunk cabbage while I'm out."

"Maybe you should," said David, laughing at him.

Louisa went over to her husband. "I don't know why you're laughing," she told him, kissing his saintly cheek. "I won the bet."

He clapped a hand around the back of her neck and brought her face down close to his own. "It was worth losing," he whispered up at her with laughing brown eyes.

She whispered back. "Tell me that tomorrow night, when you're up to your elbows in soap suds."

"*I will.*"

17

May 1855

WALLA WALLA SATISFACTORY TO ALL: By the arrival at this place, last week, of Mr. W. H. Pierson, from the Walla Walla valley, we are informed of the ratification of treaties with four of the principal tribes in the vicinity of the Walla Walla valley, consisting of Nez Perce, Walla Walla, Cayuse, and Umatillas, by Governor Stevens . . .

Entire success has thus far attended—all are sanguine as to the future—and no exertion will be spared by Governor Stevens to terminate all things amicably, and return this section of the territory in good season.

—*Pioneer & Democrat,* June 29, 1855

*D*uring the remaining weeks of May and into June, on the far side of the world, the Allied forces prepared to meet in Vienna, in an effort to stabilize peace in Europe. But the Conference was destined to disband as soon as it met, leaving the contending powers to arbitrate the war's destiny by sword alone.

Simultaneously, on the continent of North America, halfway between Washington City and Washington Territory, a different kind of war began. Hundreds of Missourians poured over their border to stuff Kansas ballot boxes in that territory's first election. By the end of May, the presidentially appointed governor of Kansas figured that in the city of Lawrence alone, in an election with only 369 legitimate voters, 781 proslavery ballots and 253 free-soil votes had been cast. In the territory at large, of 6,207 votes, more than 5,000 were determined spurious, an excess of 80 percent. Nevertheless, Governor Reeder, fearing the Southern-controlled President Pierce and his Southern-directed Secretary of War, Jefferson Davis, upheld the election. The results stood: One Free-Soiler in an otherwise all proslavery legislature. Before the year would conclude "Bleeding Kansas" would form two opposing governments and Kansas armies would face off, their cannon peering over separate fortifications. They'd fire the first shot of a battle that would eventually spread to include the entire nation in a civil war that would last until 1865. On December 6, Thomas Barber, a Free-Soiler, would be the first of 600,000 men to die.

In Washington Territory, Governor Stevens crossed the Cascades and opened his Walla Walla Treaty Council, six thousand Indians in attendance. May was not a good time to talk treaties. Washington's southeastern Indians had just learned of Oregon's plan to force the Willamette Indians eastward, across Oregon's Cascades. In their own territory, the eastern Indians saw for themselves the encroaching number of whites. Too, they saw the growing numbers of federal troops and the building of new forts. Their animosities ran hot; distrust ran deep. Chief Kamiakin of the Yakima Nation made it clear. "We welcome the King Georges," he said in reference to the English employees of the Hudson's Bay

Company. "But we do not want the Bostons with their guns, wagons, and plows!"

Father Ricard, in charge of the missions among the Yakimas, Cayuses, and Walla Wallas, wrote Governor Stevens to warn him that if Kamiakin attended the Walla Walla Council "it would be with a hostile purpose," and that the governor, if he insisted on going, would do so at a great "hazard of his life."

Yet Governor Stevens determined to proceed and, as the month wore on, the many eastern tribes finally began to trickle in: first the Nez Perce under Chiefs Lawyer and Looking Glass; next the Cayuses and Walla Wallas; the Umatillas; finally Chief Kamiakin and the sundry Yakima tribes.

Peppered speeches heated tempers, the natives almost unanimous in their sentiment against the governor's terms of sale. Once again, Governor Stevens insisted on consolidation, this time going so far as to consign all the eastern tribes into one communal reserve.

Kamiakin, head chief of the Yakima and their allied tribes, bitterly opposed him. As did Old Joseph and Looking Glass of the Nez Perce. The Cayuses too. Even Peo-Peo-Mox-Mox, an old friend of the whites. All refused to be party to such an offer. Only Lawyer, head chief of the Nez Perce, was willing to comply.

Hot days, more speeches. May turned into June. The animosity ignited, and Chief Lawyer of the Nez Perce discovered a plot to massacre the governor and his men. The massacre, Chief Lawyer warned Stevens, was but the start—a signal for the capture of the military post at The Dalles and a war of extermination of all whites in Washington Territory.

Lawyer declared that he would protect "Little Man In A Big Hurry" and all through the night he had the Nez Perce pitch their tents in a circle surrounding Stevens's camp. In the morning Little Man In A Big Hurry reconvened the Council. Stubbornly he defended his proposal. One large reservation, he explained to the hostile crowd, would allow the

Great Father to give them better protection from the encroachment of the whites than if they were scattered far and wide. He focused on the benefits to the chiefs especially: houses, annual salaries, the power to select the goods to fill tribal allotments. Some chiefs pretended capitulation. Chief Tomayhas of the Cayuse openly held out. "I will never leave the land of my mother!" Knowing Tomayhas to be the man who murdered missionary Dr. Marcus Whitman eight years before, Stevens hastily adjourned for the day, to let tempers cool.

In the morning, messengers arrived with the disturbing news that extensive gold had been discovered in the Colville area. Four French Canadians, former employees of the Hudson's Bay Company, had found three pounds of dust valued at $16.75 an ounce. Others were reported to be making ten to thirty dollars a day with simple mining equipment. The need to conclude the Indian treaties was imperative. Miners of all description would soon be pouring into eastern Washington; the land *had* to be cleared for settlement. Stevens relented, without telling the Indians why.

He offered the tribes three separate reserves. One for the Walla Walla, Cayuse, and Umatilla. Another for the Nez Perce. A third for the Yakima. The chiefs conferred. "This is only a pretense," Kamiakin and Peo-Peo-Mox-Mox warned their people, "a snare laid to trap us. This is a promise these commissioners do not intend to keep. Would the Great Father, of whom they talk so much, keep this treaty more sacredly than the treaties made for him with the Willamette tribes?"

In the end Kamiakin made his mark to the paper. So did Skloom, his lieutenant, Owhi, his brother, and eleven other Yakima subchiefs. They would meet insincerity with equal insincerity. And when the time came? The Yakima Nation would show they had not been deceived.

Five days later Governor Stevens departed for northeastern Washington. At Hell Gate in the Bitter Root Valley he made a treaty with the Flatheads, Kootenay, and Upper Pend d'Oreilles. From there he pushed east to make a treaty with the warlike Blackfoot across the Rockies. What he didn't know, what he preferred *not* to know, was that Kamiakin had left Walla Walla with thunder rumbling in his heart and mind. If Stevens had stopped to reflect, he would have seen the hatred smoldering in his wake.

Oddly, in western Washington, while the newspapers were quick to headline European and Kansas hostilities, they were equally quick to dismiss all rumor of hostility in their own backyard. The *Pioneer & Democrat* reported the Walla Walla Treaty signed to the satisfaction of all, the Indians willing, even eager, to exchange their sixty thousand square miles for less than a tenth that much. The majority of pioneers accepted this acquiescence without question. Few stopped to listen to what the Indians themselves reported concerning the event.

Arthur and David, Doc Maynard, Henry Yesler, and Henry Smith were among the few. All month long and into the next Pat Kanim and others came to them with varied warnings: naming the reluctance and distrust across the mountains; telling of Kamiakin's doubts; of seeing strangers in their own camps at night; of hearing plans to purchase and stockpile ammunition. Then came word that Leschi had gone to Willamette Valley in Oregon to speak to the disaffected Indians there.

Yet what could any of them do?

Their governor was gone, blithely making new treaties. They could only wait and see, and go on best they could. And try to ignore these persistent undercurrents which stubbornly remained without name or focus.

David and Louisa often wondered where things might lead, and David remembered the Klikitat he'd seen in Suwalth's camp. But he and Louisa weren't unduly alarmed. The two races had collided and quarreled for three years, yet life had somehow carried on. They found they had little energy to distract themselves with the same level of concern they'd once had. Their own Indians remained friendly, and if the Duwamish or Snoqualmie sympathized with their brethren beyond the realm of Puget Sound this was understandable. As for the murders that had happened—and which they knew could always happen again—wasn't it better to live here, in veiled uncertainty and threat, than to live in Chicago where some three hundred murders occurred each year? Or in San Francisco where, in the last seven years, over forty-two hundred people had met their deaths by violent means? An unheard of six hundred a year? Or Kansas? or Europe?

With this as their perspective, David and Louisa kept busy in the Swale. Soon they no longer even discussed the whispers of unrest; they could ward off trouble no easier than they could stay the hand of winter. Life had its seasons and this was summer, full and pleasant.

David dug his well, built a better henhouse, started grubbing stumps to prepare the first acreage for his farm. Louisa planted a flower garden. She transplanted her sweetbriar from the front of her old cabin up to the front of her new one, and brought up her dahlias, her pink Mission roses—that Dobbins had gotten for her at Fort Steilacoom—and her Sweet Williams. She continued with her vegetable garden as well, expanding all the time, and by the end of May, she and David were employing more and more Indians to help. They had potatoes to plant, corn to put in, stumps to root out. Split-rail fences had to be made as well, to keep back the deer.

Tom Mercer, a half mile away, worked equally hard, and because he and David paid a white man's wage, a small community of Indians from the various local tribes were soon camped along the creeks and streams between the two homes. The days passed congenially, the nights with the usual Indian chants and dirges and occasional bickering over bone games.

Well into June Louisa went out to hoe hills in the warm earth of her vegetable garden. Catherine Maynard had obtained a few cucumber seeds from somewhere and sent them out to the Swale with Dobbins—who'd come for the day to help David build a smokehouse. He'd brought with him his children and Katy. Where Anna was, no one said.

Louisa found that she missed the sounds of the ocean; the quick slap of the water dashing up the beach, the sharp caw of the gulls. But here, in David's Swale, she'd come to appreciate with equal pleasure the new sounds. For here, in the Swale, was a gentle orchestration of field birds trilling, grass rustling in the breeze, mice scurrying about, blue jays scolding. Always, presiding over all, the silent majesty of Mount Rainier—*Tahoma, The Mount That Was God.*

Today, as she worked, she listened contentedly to the music around her; the gay meadowlarks, the playful jabber of her Indian friends who cut and planted potato eyes twenty feet away. Katy, sitting on a grassy slope close by, prattled on about nothing in particular. Gertrude, over by the men— David, Dobbins, and some of the Indians—played hopscotch by herself, lending her own childish strains of singsong as she hopped up and down and tossed her stones. Emily Inez, watching her cousin and trying to imitate, kept getting in the way. Gerty shooed her off with infinite patience far beyond her years.

"You're keeping an eye on those chickens, aren't you, Katy?" Louisa said suddenly, glancing over at her precious cucumber seeds that lay in a saucer beside Katy. Peek-A-Boo and Good Morning were notorious gluttons, forever gobbling up whatever kind of seed they could find.

"How many times are you going to ask me that?" said Katy in a pique.

"Just making sure!" Louisa wiped the perspiration that had gathered along her cheeks and under the rim of her sunbonnet, and began shaping the earth into another small mound, listening now to the men's saws and hammers and their wild guffaws of male laughter. Their animated discussion, she knew, was fueled by the surprise discovery of gold across the mountains. Dobbins had brought them a *Pioneer & Democrat,* heralding the electrifying news.

No one yet knew how much gold was there, but Dobbins reported that hundreds of miners were predicted to start pouring through Seattle, outfitting themselves before striking across the mountains. Fanjoy and Eaton, the two men who owned the mill out by the coal mine, were already gone, selling out to Charles Plummer. Arthur, Dobbins said, was making plans to go to San Francisco to purchase huge quantities of gold-mining supplies. And the King County commissioners, he said, were in emergency council, trying to find ways to open new roads into Seattle and over the pass. "Gold in eastern Washington," he declared in a burst of enthusiasm unusual for Dobbins, "could beat the railroad in putting Seattle on the map!"

Sounds of David's laughter suddenly drifted down from the smokehouse site.

Louisa eased up from her work. David had William—or Wills, as she'd affectionately begun to call her newest nephew—strapped to his back in Emily Inez's old cradleboard, and he was bent over trying to show Emily Inez the right way to jump. He had her under the arms, and was bouncing her up and down. Emily Inez thought it was a different game altogether, and squealed with delight in the springing movement of her father's hands.

Then Louisa noticed the saucer. "Oh no, where are my seeds? My cucumber seeds! They're gone!"

Too late, Katy saw Good Morning already on the run. She leaped to her feet. Hoping to show her aunt how sorry she was to have been derelict in her duty, she took off like a shot, chasing the half-hopping, half-flying chicken all over the yard, wildly, desperately, hoping too that punishing the rooster by tiring him out might make her feel less guilty. Her braids worked loose under her bonnet, tumbled off her head and collected in the calico headpiece at the nape of her neck. In the end, sweating and gasping for breath, she cornered the rooster, and caught him.

Louisa looked grim and determined. Katy knew she wanted those seeds. There were no others to be had in the whole of Puget Sound! This is a fine how-do-you-do, was Louisa's thought, losing my seeds in the craw of a chicken! And Catherine had done her a great favor by bestowing the gift upon her. "Hang onto him," she commanded Katy, "and bring him up to the house." She stormed toward the cabin, with a tearful, frightened Katy following behind. Louisa didn't go for the axe. What was she going to do? wondered Katy.

Still not a word, but a fierce determination showed in Louisa's every move and expression. She disappeared into the house and came out with a handful of formidable implements. David and the other men looked on, puzzled but unconcerned, almost amused.

"Hold him this way!" Louisa ordered. Katy meekly obeyed, too scared to do anything else. "Here! You hold his head! And don't you dare let go, Katy Denny! Stretch his neck!" That was all. Bent on her one purpose, to retrieve her seeds, she took David's razor, found the bulging craw, slashed the neck and the inner skin, while Katy—and Gerty, who, unlike the men, had run over to investigate what all the excitement was about—froze with fear. Though Katy did manage to hold on like grim death, all but choking the life out of the feathered thief.

It took just a minute to force out the seeds, along with the gravel that would have soon pulverized them. Louisa put a silk thread through a needle and tied enough stitches to hold the slits together. "Turn him loose," she told Katy, as though her rooster could live or die for all she cared. Without a word, she bore her seeds to the garden and patted each one lovingly in its place along the short hilly row.

"If that rooster dares come near my cucumbers again," she told Katy with grim satisfaction when Katy finally felt it safe to approach, "I will eat him for supper."

"Auntie, that old rooster will be as tough as a buzzard."

Louisa laughed and pulled Katy into her arms. "Did I scare you?"

"Only a little," Katy lied.

"Guess I wanted those seeds pretty fiercely. I'm sorry."

"Auntie, I think you have company."

Louisa followed Katy's gaze across the meadow. A man was coming in from the road, stooped of shoulder, dragging his left leg a little as if his knee bothered him. The low sun glistened off his hair, making it appear white. Louisa rubbed the palms of her dirty hands down her apron. "Guess I better go see who's coming for supper. Walking in from town he's going to be hungry—"

She stopped so suddenly that Katy turned to look at her aunt. Louisa's hand was at her neck, clutching her throat as if it was torn with pain. Katy could see the veins beneath her pale white skin throbbing.

She's going to faint, thought Katy, reaching out to catch her arm.

But, in an instant, Louisa threw off Katy's hand and was flying across the meadow, skirt streaming behind her. Katy stared after her.

Grandpa? she wondered suddenly. *But of course that's not Grandpa!* Katy decided. *Grandpa wouldn't be strolling across Aunt Louisa's new swale, would he?*

18

June 1855

On one occasion, when bringing in a raft to the mill, John lost a diary which he was keeping and I picked it up on the beach. The last entry it contained read: "June 5, 1855. Started with a raft for Yesler's mill. Fell off into the water." I remember I wrote "and drowned," and returned the book. I don't know how soon afterward John learned from his own book of his death by drowning.

—Henry Yesler, Yesler family files
Museum of History and Industry, Seattle

As in her dream, Louisa knew her trip to James's dying bedside would be interminable. She'd begun packing for Oregon the night Pa arrived—after Dobbins had gone, and after seeing to Pa's every comfort. She wished she could take the pain from Pa's eyes.

James had saved a family from burning to death, Pa told them in a broken voice, but in rescuing the invalid grandmother trapped in an upstairs bedroom, he'd seared his lungs so severely he was near the end of his own time on earth.

"When, Pa? When did it happen?"

He scratched his beard. "Coming back from your brother Wiley's wedding," he said to David across the table. "A month ago, I reckon. Maybe five weeks."

"Wiley's married?" said Louisa, her mind momentarily diverted.

"Yup. A Saturday it was. May 11, now that I'm thinking on it."

The night of her dream. The bittersweet tragedy was too great to bear and Louisa found herself laughing and crying by turns, one moment overjoyed to see Pa, the next in despair over James. "Oh, Pa, oh, Pa, I can't believe you're here!" she'd laugh out loud, giving him a kiss and fussing over him. "Just look at your hair, Pa, white as a daisy!"

"You calling me an old stinkweed?"

"No, no, Pa! But daisies do stink, don't they?"—and suddenly she'd be crying again. James, going into a burning building—It was a wonder he hadn't died, Pa said, in the inferno of falling timbers and stairs cascading in.

And so she laughed and wept in turn, torn inside out. And to think of all those days and weeks she'd known—*for she had known, she had!*—days and weeks spent dillydallying, wasting time, planting silly old things like cucumbers! When she could have been on her way *and even be there by now!*

Was he at peace? she wondered. *Had he forgiven her for marrying David? Had he forgiven David?* She wasted no time in fresh grief over James. She'd known too long, in her own way. Now, there was only to get there in time to say good-bye.

They left in the morning, Sunday, leaving behind their grand new house, their hens and Watch and the growing gardens to the care of Tom, the Bells, and Curley and Madeline at the Indian camp. They left before dawn, bags on their backs and clutched in their hands. Louisa, holding Emily

Inez, shut the door firmly behind them, but not without stopping to breathe the smells of her new home that she liked so well. The fir pitch, the sawdust, the sweet ripe cedar. Would her new-house smells still be here when she returned?

They hurried through the woods as fast they could along the Mercer Road, the sky overhead slowly, slowly lightening. No one spoke, each praying that Charles Terry, pilot of Dr. Webster's *Water Lily* and their own good friend from Seattle's earliest days, had not made a run up the Duwamish for a load of Dr. Webster's coal, but would instead make an immediate return to Olympia. But not too soon! prayed Louisa. Dear God, not too soon. Don't let Charles leave us behind!

Hurry, hurry, hurry. The word banged in her ears. Hurry, hurry, hurry. Squirrels chattered it too. Hurry, hurry, hurry. Somewhere far away a cougar screamed. HURRY!

A smaller crowd this Sunday, noticed Louisa as they came into town. The chorus of "Onward Christian Soldiers" drifted through an open window of the church. *I hate that song!* thought Louisa, her skirts swishing around her ankles as she half ran to keep up with David and Pa—there was a swarm of activity on Plummer's Pier! *Why would Christ lead against the foe, forward into battle? He who restored the soldier's ear in Gethsemane!*

"Louisa needs a pair of man's boots," said Pa a half hour later when they were standing around in the cookhouse. Their tickets to Olympia had been purchased at Plummer & Chase, and Doc Maynard was hustling up to the church to let Arthur and Mary Ann and Dobbins and Anna know they'd be leaving in just minutes. "You got a shoe shop in this stumpy town where we can get her feet shod?" Pa asked, poking his nose out the cookhouse door and squinting across the Sawdust.

"On Sunday, Pa?" asked David.

"Sunday or not, she's got to have them."

Louisa looked down at her feet.

"What do you think?" David asked her. "Think we ought to buy shoes on the Sabbath?"

"What's wrong with my moccasins? George Seattle made these, and I'm partial to them."

"Pa's right though. You need a man's boots to get over the Cowlitz. I'll buy you some, if you think it's fitting."

"Maybe Olympia has a shoe shop," she suggested, "and we can get them tomorrow."

"Good idea," said Pa. "And *I'll* buy the boots. No, Dave—" Pa held up his big, strong hand. "You've been wasting your money again, buying her trinkets, don't think I didn't notice. You best keep what you got. You'll need something to get back home on."

Henry Yesler came over, laughing. He dropped a water-stained book on the table beside Louisa. "While you're waiting, Mrs. Denny, you can look here, see what I found on the beach last week. Go on, take a look inside. Won't bite. It's only John Holgate's diary."

She had no desire to read another man's diary, John's at that, Widow Holgate's twenty-two-year-old son. But at Mr. Yesler's urging, and seeing David and Pa's curiosity aroused, she picked it up. *JOHN HOLGATE, Territory of Washington, County of King, Seattle.* She thumbed through the rumpled pages, wondering what Mr. Yesler thought was so funny. Things looked pretty ordinary to her. *Sunny, no clouds. Cow sick.* Yet here was Mr. Yesler, busting his buttons with suppressed laughter. Impatient, he finally reached over and opened the diary to its last entry, and jabbed a grimy finger at the page. "There!" he said, laughing out loud. "Yessiree, read that, Mrs. Denny!"

"*June 5, 1855. Started with a raft for Yesler's mill. Fell off into the water.*" Two more words had been added in different script. She squinted in the dim light to decipher the scrawl.

"Why, you old scalawag," she said, smiling up at Mr. Yesler despite herself. "Is this you who added *'and drowned'*?"

185

Pa grabbed the book, read it, and roared. He slapped Mr. Yesler across the back the way men do when they like each other.

Mr. Yesler warmed to Pa right away. "How long do you think it'll take the boy," he asked Pa, "to discover he's dead and drowned?"

"You mean to say, sir," said Pa, "that he's got to learn the bad news himself? You're not going to break it to him gentle?"

"Mmm . . . I see what you mean. Soon as he got out of church I was going to give him his book. What do you reckon I ought to do? Tell him, or—"

Pa winked at Louisa. "Think we ought to stick around and see the joke bite Mr. Holgate in the face?"

She said no.

An hour later they were still waiting in the cookhouse, and Emily Inez was fussy. This was Louisa's first inkling the trip would prove as endless as her dream portended. Mary Ann and Arthur, Dobbins and Anna—quiet and aloof, though she said nothing about their row—and all the children came down to say good-bye. Time dragged, all the children got fussy, yet no one wanted to leave until David and Louisa and Pa were gone. They ended up eating lunch at the cookhouse with the millhands; a noisy, rowdy group, telling and retelling the joke on John Holgate who, upon being called inside and given the diary, had merely said, "Thank you, sir. I was wondering where I'd dropped it."

They finally got underway after three o'clock. Immediately a squall blew up. Charles, still new at being a pilot, lost his bearings and they blundered around on the choppy sea, everyone sick and losing their cookhouse lunch. Finally Charles managed to find Steilacoom and put in. Cold, hungry, he and his passengers stumbled up to the village. But the hour was late and the hotel keeper refused to be roused from his bed. David was furious. Pa kicked at the door. Charles rattled again and again at the bell. Nothing.

"The old goat," grumbled Charles. "Let's try the store."

He turned them to the right and banged on a dark window. Minutes later the proprietor, a man with a salt-and-pepper beard, let them in. He kindly let them camp on his floor. He even brought new blankets off the shelves and fed them fresh bread and hot oyster stew from his wife's kitchen. But all night long the rain beat on the roof. Hurry, hurry, hurry. *How can I hurry when I'm still only at Fort Steilacoom?* Louisa fretted, unable to sleep.

"David," she finally whispered, lying as close to him as she dared, knowing Pa had sharp ears. "Will we get there on time?"

David, she discovered, was crying. She didn't care anymore that Pa might hear. She slid into David's arms and he welcomed her with a desperate fierceness.

In the morning, with storm abated, the *Water Lily* churned steadily through the *salt-chuck*, as the Indians called the sea. The side-wheel's steady turning around and around echoed. Hurry, hurry, hurry. *"Stetchas,"* said Charles at last to Louisa, giving her a lopsided grin and pointing straight ahead to the little hamlet of Olympia. *"Stetchas.* Bear's Place."

She held no memory of the Territory's capital. Her eyes were not on the surroundings, but were fixed somewhere ahead to where James lay gasping for every painful breath. Pa had said his lungs were bleeding, and kept filling with infection. Each day it grew harder to get his breath, and more painful. With each passing day he grew weaker too, choking on his own phlegm.

"Pa, why didn't you write? Why didn't you come right away?" she asked while they waited impatiently in Olympia for the mail coach to take them down the Cowlitz Trail to Oregon.

"He wouldn't let us. How's yer shoes, honey? Fit you fine?"

"Yes, fine, Pa."

They were ugly but serviceable boots, bought a half size too big on purpose, and she wore two pairs of men's woollen socks to fill the space. David was worried she'd get blisters. She did anyway, even with the extra padding.

The six-horse team, drawing the mail coach, plunged and floundered over a stumpy, muddy trail that stretched and wound on forever. The road was so bad, the passengers lurched and bounced, tossed side to side. Emily Inez oftentimes screamed in fright. Once Louisa bit her tongue during a particularly rough jouncing. Worse, the wagon sank up to its hubs in black mud, and over and over again everyone had to get out and walk while the men threw off their coats and threw their shoulders to the wheels. How many miles did she walk in that sucking, gooey mud, carrying Emily Inez until she thought her back might break? That night Louisa soaked her blistered feet in a bucket of hot soda water at Ford's Prairie. She'd recognized instantly the side stair to their accommodations. *Hurry, hurry, hurry,* she dreamed all night long.

The mail ride ended three days later at Warbass's Landing. From there, they took a short canoe ride to Monticello. *Wasn't this where Arthur and others had come three years ago, to a convention calling for separation from Oregon?* "Will we never get to Oregon?" she asked.

David said yes. Tomorrow they'd cross the Columbia River. Then they'd be in Oregon.

A tiny steamboat, almost microscopic on the wide water, carried them across the great Columbia River at dawn. Louisa gazed over the sparkling waves. Hurry, hurry, hurry. The little steamer's engines rumbled beneath her feet, vibrated up through her legs, her back, into her skull. Hurry, hurry, hurry.

They spent another night in Portland. A grandfather clock on the other side of the wall ticked off every second and bonged on the hour, every hour, all through the long, dark night. Hurry, hurry, hurry.

An even smaller steamer carried them up the Willamette River in the morning. The noisy little boat wound slowly, torturously, upriver to the falls. Hurry, hurry, hurry.

At the portage, they disembarked, and walked along a narrow plank walk built up one side of the riverbank. It rose higher and higher, around the cascading falls and up to a high, rounded hill. Its noble outline stood dark with giant firs against a vivid blue summer sky. Below was the river, the rushing, silvery flood of the Willamette . . . her banks fringed with wild roses in riotous bloom. But up here was the river too, and they boarded another boat.

They got off at Salem. A man driving a milk wagon gave them a lift as far as the Waldo Hills.

"From here on in, we walk," said Pa when the milkman let them off at a fork in the road. They took the trail all hemmed in by stout oaks and high, waving poplars.

"How long now, Pa?" Louisa asked.

"It won't be long, Sugar Lump. This is the last leg."

Hurry, hurry, hurry.

They stopped at a little creek to eat the bread and cheese Pa had bought in Sublimity. How many hours had they been walking? Louisa wondered when they resumed their way. Emily Inez, riding David's shoulders, fell asleep, her cheek pressed against the top of his head, her arms falling loosely down around his ears.

Will we never finish this walk?

"Now, Pa? Are we nearly there?"

"Yes, daughter, nearly there."

"But you said that hours ago!"

The muscles in her legs cried for rest, and she began to glance about for a place to sit down. But then a horrible thought seized her. *What if James died yesterday? What if he died only an hour ago?*

She pressed on, one foot after the other. Ten minutes, twenty minutes, a half hour, now an hour. Still she kept going.

She didn't know that Pa and David, trying to keep up with her, cast anxious glances between them.

The trail ended abruptly, startling her. There was a house, a little log cabin covered in hollyhock and wisteria and clematis of brilliant hues. Everything aflame with color, alive with perfume. Was she here, then? She stood silently, disbelieving, her legs trembling. Who sat on the porch, under a luscious grape arbor?

Two figures, a woman and a child. The child, seeing Louisa come through the trees, sprang up. "Pa! Pa! You're home! I knew you'd come today! I knew it!" Louisa stared as the child flashed past in a frenzy of excitement, a sweet-looking girl about five years old and dressed in homespun and calico. She passed without a glance, and Louisa turned to watch her throw out her arms and plow straight into Pa. Pa swung her up and smothered her in kisses. *Loretta? Ma and Pa's baby?*

Louisa whirled back around. That had to be *Ma* on the porch!

A tall, erect woman. Dark gray dress. Tightly corseted. A white lace cap on her head.

Louisa ran like wind. Ma too. And then she had Ma in her arms, or Ma had her, she didn't know which. They laughed and they cried, and they held each other's faces. They kissed each other, and kissed again, still laughing, still crying. They stared into each other's eyes, searching for all the changes that had surely taken place in the long years apart.

Ma's hair was still black. *That's good,* thought Louisa. *Mine won't be in any hurry to turn. What an odd thing to think, at a time like this!* "You are fine, Ma? Your arthritis, your hands, are they good?" She took Ma's hands and held them to see.

"I am fine," said her mother in a voice so warmly familiar that Louisa cried all over again to hear it.

"And James? Is he . . . is he—"

Ma's happy face saddened. "I'm afraid you'll find him much altered."

"He's still alive?" Louisa breathed, hardly able to believe she was really here, that she had come in time, that Ma, her own Ma, was standing here.

"Yes, he's been waiting for you—though we thought it best to say nothing of Pa going off to fetch you. He thinks Pa's at Salem, helping with the church raising. But he's been waiting just the same. No, don't cry. No!" said Ma. She fished into her black silk apron for her handkerchief. "Go in, but you must give him a smile. He needs your strength."

"Will he *want* to see me?" Louisa asked abruptly, suddenly frightened that he would not, and she glanced fearfully ahead to the cabin.

"Oh, Liza, he loves you so. And he's been waiting, holding on so long for you to come—I don't know that he can live another twenty-four hours."

Louisa sensed David beside her. Emily Inez was still asleep on his shoulders, slumber heavy in every line of her body. Ma's hands went up to her mouth in joy to see the baby.

"Hello, Ma," said David. He eased Emily Inez off from his shoulders and handed her, still sleeping, over to Ma.

"She looks just like you, Liza, dear," said Ma, "when you were this age."

"She has David's coloring, though, and all his pretty curls."

"Yes, I can see that."

"Are you going in?" David asked her.

"Oh, David, I don't know what I've been thinking all this while. I don't know what to say to him! I don't want to see him dying!"

He smiled a little. "You can warn him that I'm here."

Louisa nodded dully and pushed forward, away from Ma, away from David, toward the beckoning house and James.

19

July 2, 1855

At length the log cabin home was reached . . . Grandmother
was tall and straight, dressed in a plain, dark gown, black silk
apron and lace cap; her hair, coal black, slightly gray on the
temples; her eyes dark, soft and gentle.

—Emily Inez Denny, David and Louisa's daughter
in *Blazing the Way*

Nothing could have prepared Louisa for the sight of
the thin stranger sleeping sitting up, supported by
a half dozen pillows, in Ma and Pa's bed. She stood in agony
at the bedroom door, trying to find James in this gaunt, fever-
ravished skeleton of a man. Even his stillness was odd, for
James was a man of constant motion. The only movement
coming from him now was the tortured rise and fall of his
chest, his lungs struggling to breathe. How could he sleep,
working so hard?

Ma had vases of pretty flowers on the nightstand, on the
dresser, on the windowsill, wherever James might glance.

The window was open. A small breeze played with the curtains. A chair sat close to the bed. Slowly she eased into the room and carefully sat down, keeping her eyes fastened to the face of her stepbrother. Could this really be James?

His wasted hand lay limply on the bed beside him, palm up. She placed hers on top and when he opened his eyes, staring into hers, she knew with a stab of cruel pain this *was* James. No one else had such beautiful blue eyes.

He tried to say her name.

"Shh," she whispered, rising to lean over the bed and kiss him hello. His fiery hot mouth burned her own lips.

"I wondered if you'd come," he said, panting.

"What can I do? What will make it easier for you?" she asked, searching the bed for a new way to support his frail body.

"Did David come?"

"Yes, Emily Inez too. David says to warn you he's outside."

James smiled, and Louisa nearly cried—such a slow, teasing smile he had. "Oh, James, you must tell me what I can do! You look so uncomfortable!"

"Can you get the smoke out of my lungs?" He started to cough, and pitched forward, coughing and choking, gasping, sucking for air. He couldn't breathe! He was choking to death right in front of her!

"Ma! Ma! Come quick!"

Ma came running in and all but flung James back onto the pillows so she could reach her fingers down his throat. Phlegm, blood, and corruption spilled out in curdled lumps, clearing the clogged passages.

"You're going to have to learn how to do this yourself," said Ma as Louisa watched in horror.

For a while it seemed as though he breathed easier, at least she hoped so, but soon his chest was struggling again, his lungs straining to grasp whatever feeble air he could strain through the blocked passages of his nose and throat.

Ma wet a towel and gently bathed his face. "There's some oil, Liza dear, in one of those jars over there. Yes," said Ma when Louisa found the bottle and held it up. "Rub a little onto his mouth while I pull off these soiled sheets."

Louisa rubbed the oil into the blue-gray ridges and fissures of James's swollen fever-cracked lips. "Why is he burning up, Ma?"

"Pneumonia. The doctor said it would happen. That's when Pa went to get you."

His eyelids fluttered open. He lifted his arm and reached for Louisa.

"What is it?" she asked, sitting on the bed beside him and holding his arm close to her.

"Where's David?"

David ducked into the crowded room. "I'm right here."

"Thank you . . ." He was too weak to say anymore.

"You shouldn't have done it, big brother, gone into a burning building like that." David went around to the other side of the bed. "What's that?" he asked, bending over, putting his ear to James's lips. "No, I guess not. And you're welcome, I'm glad to have brought her."

"I'll see about these sheets," said Ma. "Then I'll put on some supper. You two must be starving."

James closed his eyes.

"He needs to sleep," said Ma at the door.

"Should we leave him?" asked Louisa.

Ma didn't answer, and went out.

Louisa looked across the bed to David. They stared forlornly at each other, listening to James breathe, a terrible sound.

When James woke he seemed a little stronger, though every breath he drew intensified the glaze of pain in his eyes. Louisa tore herself away, leaving him with David. This would be their only chance, she realized, to be together before James was gone.

"Is he at peace about dying?" she asked Ma when she finally found Ma in the garden, bent over at the waist and pulling up carrots.

Ma kept pulling carrots. "I think he has his moments when he wishes he never went after that poor old woman upstairs, but those are only moments . . . If he had to do it all over again he'd have done the same, and charged into that blazing house. Because that's the way he is. Was," she added, easing another carrot out of the black earth.

Louisa started to cry.

Ma straightened up. "We wouldn't have him any other way, would we?"

Louisa shook her head.

Ma nodded toward the corn. "Behind there are the radishes."

Louisa dutifully went to pull a few, grateful to Ma for sending her where she could snivel, yet do something useful, while she pulled herself together.

After supper Ma cleared the dishes, Pa sat with his pipe behind his newspaper, and Sam, another of David's brothers, said, "So Arthur didn't come."

"No, couldn't make it," said David. "Not that he didn't want to. But he's running for the legislature again. What day is it? The second?"

"Yup."

"Election's in two days. When he wins that, he's off to San Francisco to get some mining supplies for his store. The miners'll be coming through Seattle before you know it. You heard about the gold in Colville?"

"I heard."

David patted his stomach and let out a gentle burp, then followed his brother outdoors to sit on the front porch. Sam was Louisa's age. Like James, he'd never married, content, apparently, to live under the same roof with Ma and Pa. Someone needed to. They were getting on. "Tell me about

Wiley," said David in reference to the youngest of their brothers. "Did he really go and get himself married? Isn't he only twenty?"

"How old were you when you got married?" said Sam with a fierce grin behind his heavy dark beard.

"Touché," said David, and he laughed. It was good to be with Sam again, though the reason for their visit wasn't good.

"Yup, went and got himself hitched. Living over in the next county now, took on her Pa's farm."

Dusk had begun to wrap gentle arms around Oregon's Waldo Hills, darkening the scrub oaks and blue spruces and the yellow-green aspens and willows. The shadows reached across the yard, embracing the garden, the vine-covered henhouse, and the porch where the two men sat talking.

"Things all right with you and Liza?" Sam suddenly asked, glancing toward the bedroom window.

Louisa had left James's side only the one time. Now she refused to leave at all, not even for supper. They could see her by the bed, her pretty profile softened by the sheer white curtains.

"You used to get awful sore about those two," said Sam.

"I was an idiot," said David sharply. But he was angry with himself, not Sam, and said as much.

Sam guffawed and slapped his thigh. "You were no idiot. James gave you a run for your money!"

"I guess he did, at that," said David with a chuckle, wondering how in the world he'd got on without Sam.

They talked about a lot of things. Arthur and politics in Washington. Pa and politics in Oregon. The Indian unrest everywhere. Sam told David about the Rogue River Uprising, about the miners killed last month. David gave him a rundown on what was happening on the Sound, wondering as he spoke what changes might have taken place since their departure. Nothing fearful, he hoped.

Pa came out to sit in the wicker chair. The reeds creaked under his weight, a comfortable sound in the stillness of the coming night. Frogs croaked from somewhere behind the house.

"When James is gone," said Pa suddenly, talking around his pipe, "I want you to consider staying here, son."

"Me, Pa?" David was as surprised as he could be.

"I've been hearing things. Things up your way sound a might rough."

"If you're talking about the Indians, Pa, Sam's just been telling me it isn't exactly smooth down here. At least we haven't had any Indians attacking white folk yet."

Pa glanced from one son to the other. "Maybe I'm just getting old. Or maybe," he grumped, "a body just gets used to his own danger."

"Well, I got to fetch in the cows." Sam puffed away at his pipe. "Want to come along, Dave? Ma might have that ice cream ready by the time we get back."

"Show me around the place while you're at it. Quite a spread Pa's got here."

"You know Pa." Sam punched Pa in the shoulder and leaped off the porch.

Pa watched them go, and wondered if life could be more bittersweet than it was tonight. One son brought home to him, if only for a few days, while losing another son forever. No, not forever. They'd see James again.

"Pa? Why are you sad?"

"Do I look sad, Loretta?" he asked his youngest child, his only daughter. One girl after eight boys . . .

She nodded in the shadows beside him.

"Then, climb up in your old Pa's lap and we'll sing a happy song. How's that? What shall we sing?" he asked as she climbed up and settled close to his heart.

"Itsy-Bitsy Spider, Pa."

Louisa watched through the open window as Sam and David cut across the yard in the fading light, Sam whistling for their old sheepdog. Jonah came racing around the corner of the cabin, and began barking and leaping at the stick David held ready to throw for him. She could hear Pa and Loretta on the porch, softly singing an old childhood favorite. *All so peaceful,* she thought. *Like the old days in Illinois. Except for James.*

He said very little to her. All his energy was spent trying to breathe. He seemed content, though, to lie and watch *her* talk. She thanked him for her book, and told of all the friends who'd borrowed it. She spoke, too, of the different pioneers in Seattle, some of whom he knew from his visit two years before. She got a smile when she told about Ursula McConaha marrying Lewis Wyckoff.

"That's good . . . Lewis loved her . . ."

"Ursula was married to George when you were there."

"That doesn't stop a man from loving someone else's wife."

There, it was out, the terrible love he had for her.

"Oh, James, I'm sorry! You have suffered so, and it's all my fault!"

"No, no one is to blame." He gave her a weak smile. "And I'm not unhappy, Liza. David is good to you, that's all I can ask. I think in a way, though, I'm glad to die." His eyes went away from her a little. "Because in heaven there is no marriage. We'll be free to love each other in a way we don't yet know. A more perfect kind of love. I'll wait for you there, Liza. And when you come, and when David comes, we'll all be together and it won't matter—none of this will."

The speech had cost him everything and he lay gasping, staring at the ceiling, lost in his pain. She leaned over and ran her fingers through his sweat-dampened hair.

"James," she whispered. He turned to face her, coming back to her through the cloud of his suffering. "Here's some of Ma's gum arabic water. It's time to take some more."

He nodded assent, but in his struggle to rise up enough to take the spoon in his mouth, he started to cough again. He lurched forward so swiftly he all but knocked the medicine out of her hand. She sprang back and screamed for Ma.

"No use . . . I'm drowning," he gasped. "I'm drowning in my own juices."

Ma rushed in. She pulled a wad of clean cloths from her apron pocket and wiped the blood and mucous from James's mouth and beard. Louisa rushed to dampen the towel. Gently she bathed the sticky perspiration from his forehead, full of grief and fright at how so strong a man could be reduced to such weakness. He was as helpless as a child, a baby.

A baby. "Ma! Didn't you once save a baby by sticking a hollowed-out reed down its throat and sucking out the mucous?"

James clutched Ma's sleeve. "No . . ."

Ma started to cry.

"Why, James, why?" Louisa begged him, falling on her knees beside his bed. "If you won't let her help you, let me help you!"

"No . . . stay."

"Please, James, I'll be right back, I promise! I can help you breathe! I can help you get better!"

"Liza, you can't save me," he rasped, the rattle in his chest and throat muffling his words so she could scarcely hear him.

"Oh, James, let me try!" Her eyes glistened, and a tear trickled.

He reached out to touch his finger against the tear, tracing its passage down her cheek to her throat where he wound his finger around a strand of her hair. "Let me go, Liza . . ." He fell back onto his pillows. "Let me go . . ."

Unable to speak, she began to stroke his red hair. He sank even farther back into his pillows, so exhausted he could hardly keep his eyes open. He was so hot! If only it were winter! If only they could wrap him in ice and bring the fever down!

"Remember the night I held you outside Fort Hall?" he panted, looking up at her. "When the Indians—"

She nodded.

"Hold me like that."

199

She climbed into the bed with him.

"Hold me tight, Liza. Like we held each other then."

She wrapped her arms fiercely around him, cradling him, taking on his strangled fight for breath. *Dear God, let me do this for him,* she prayed silently, and for a long time her chest strained, struggling as if to take his burden from him. Then their breathing became one, and together they sank into the darkness of sleep.

When she woke, the moon had risen, filling the strange room with an even stranger light. David had fallen asleep on a stuffed chair on the far side of the bed. Somewhere in the distance she heard an owl call. Closer up, a cow bawled for her calf. There was the sharp croak of frogs in a pond.

She shuddered. Just night sounds, she told herself, glancing around, afraid of the strangeness. Ordinary night sounds, and then she understood. It was not the sounds that had frightened her, that had made her shudder. It was the quiet. The absolute silence that had come while she slept.

She tightened her arms around James, comforted at least by his weight. She would not waken David, not yet. She needed time to cry alone, and to say good-bye.

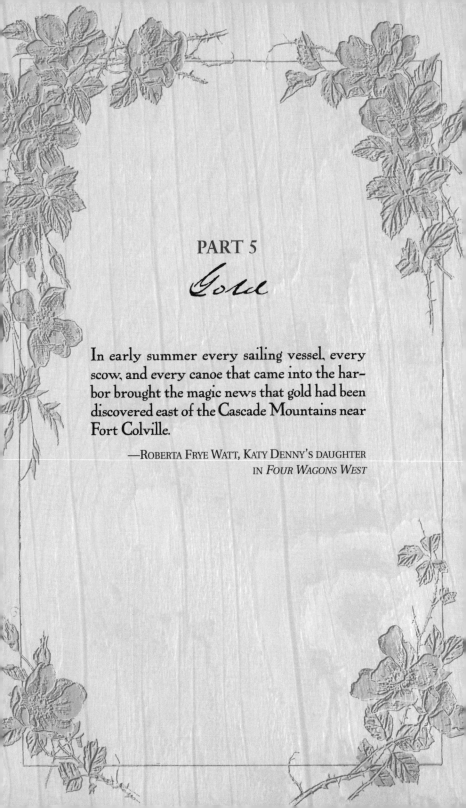

PART 5

Gold

In early summer every sailing vessel, every scow, and every canoe that came into the harbor brought the magic news that gold had been discovered east of the Cascade Mountains near Fort Colville.

—ROBERTA FRYE WATT, KATY DENNY'S DAUGHTER
IN *FOUR WAGONS WEST*

20

Late July, 1855

Fort Colville is a trading post of the Hudson's Bay Company,
situated on the east bank of the Columbia river, a short distance below the junction of Lewis and Clark's river. There are
present three routes by which Fort Colville is accessible from
this region of the country . . .

From Seattle, Steilacoom or Olympia . . .

—*Pioneer & Democrat,* July 20, 1855

The steamer *Traveler* was built in Philadelphia, dis-
mantled the winter of 1855, shipped in sections
aboard ship around Cape Horn, then put together again in
San Francisco where she was purchased by Captain Parker.
Parker had in mind to replace the shipwrecked *Major Tomp-
kins.* Thus it was he who steamed into Portland the end of
July, en route to pick up his first passengers, bound for Puget
Sound of Washington Territory.

Hundreds of Oregonians had gathered in Portland and were bent on getting to Washington. Newspapers had reported the successful conclusion of the Walla Walla Treaty, and in every issue, editors posted Governor Stevens's official notice that the ceded lands were now open for settlement—side by side with updates on Washington's gold. Twenty thousand dollars of Fort Colville gold had come into Portland, and wild rumors circulated that the miners already there were making upward of a hundred dollars a day! The Oregon *Statesman* reported:

> The Willamette Valley, in consequence of the gold furor, is being depopulated with a completeness no one would have believed possible. The price of horses and mules has increased not less than 100 percent on most articles required for an outfit.

The *Standard* bemoaned the consequences:

> We are informed that the farmers of Oregon are finding much difficulty in procuring harvest hands, save at enormous wages—most of them having determined to harvest their grains single handed, assisted only by their families—participated in many instances, by the "mothers and daughters."
>
> Do all the reports from the gold fields, thus far, justify the desertion of so large a portion of the population?

No one knew of Father Ricard's warning to Governor Stevens. No one knew of the truculent conduct of the Yakima, Cayuses, and Walla Wallas at the council. Even if they did, gold had its own allure. Which is why, when David and Louisa boarded Captain Parker's *Traveler* on Saturday, July 27, it was with a crowd of eager Oregon miners.

That same Saturday, July 27, the *Traveler* cleared Astoria, and Washington's newly elected delegate to Congress, Colonel Patton Anderson, left Olympia for an inspection tour of the mines. It was imperative that someone go. The tide of immigration, once strongly set toward Oregon and Washington, now flowed steadily toward California. A whole state had been peopled and a government established in a region little known and rarely mentioned until Mr. Marshall, in 1849, discovered gold in the tail race at Sutter's mill. Oregon and Washington languished for want of interest and attention while California developed rapidly. *But with the discovering of gold in their own country? Was this their opportunity to "go ahead of California"?* Saddled onto Colonel Anderson's mules were mining tools and enough provisions to last six weeks. He and his team of fifteen to twenty men would carefully examine the area, determine the truthfulness of the reports, and then come home with detailed information.

The discovery of gold gave impetus to *every* activity on the Sound. If men weren't crossing the mountains to make their fortunes, they were preparing to profit in other ways. Arthur Denny, after winning—a third time in a row—his old seat in the legislature, had immediately set sail for San Francisco in order to secure an ample inventory of mining equipment to sell in his store. Other Seattle men, determined to make Seattle the logical seaport and supply station for the gold fields, resolved to build the trail through Snoqualmie Pass, fifty miles to the east. Chief Justice Judge Lander, newly moved to Seattle and with a well-equipped team of explorers, guides, surveyors, and builders, left town at the end of the month, vowing not to return until the road was built.

They went out by way of Squak, past the southern sloughs of Sammamish Lake and up through the Cascade foothills to Snoqualmie Falls. Here, the first week in August, they separated. One group took the old Indian path, the other the overgrown Hudson's Bay Company packing trail. They would meet at Lake Keechelus just over the summit and decide the better track.

That same week, the *Traveler,* having steamed due north and around Neah Bay of Washington Territory, turned out of Juan de Fuca Strait down into Puget Sound. No longer at sea but in the arms of the earth, the sheltered water was less turbulent and Louisa, ill with seasickness, found she could actually sit up without feeling nauseous. When they put into Bellingham the following day, a Sunday, their first port of call, she felt well enough to insist on being taken out on deck.

The sunlight was warm, the water a sparkling blue. A blue haze spread over the land, and a welcome breeze, perfumed with the woodsmoke of evergreens, came softly to her face. "We're home," she sighed, sitting farther back in David's steadying arms, feasting her eyes on the scattered cabins of Bellingham and the tumbling waterfall that powered Misters Peabody and Roeder's sawmill.

"I don't look forward to telling Arthur that James is dead," said David quietly, watching Emily Inez run up and down the deck, pushing hard into the wind and then turning around and letting the wind push her.

"But it was a nice funeral, wasn't it?" Louisa asked, tipping her head back to see David's face. "All those people, maybe a hundred, do you think?"

"Everyone likes their postmaster."

"Not everyone likes their schoolteacher."

"I still can't get over all those children, the poem they composed." David swallowed with difficulty, and blinked back sudden tears. "That was a real tribute to my brother—"

"Our brother."

David pulled her tighter into his arms and kissed the top of her head. "Our brother . . ."

The next day at noon, August 5, with the sparkling sea and warm haze as blue and comforting as the day before, they drew near Seattle. David and Louisa stood by the bulwarks amidships, watching the shoreline become familiar and dear even as their daughter played happily between them, pulling on their knees and swinging in circles. Quite suddenly Captain Parker ambled over.

"If it weren't for this haze," David boasted to the approaching captain, "you could see the mountain."

"What mountain?"

"Rainier if you like the British name, sir. *Tahoma,* if you prefer the Indian. Not that it matters. Just call it 'the mountain.' Everyone'll know what you mean."

"What's it like around here?" Captain Parker asked, his keen blue eyes piercing the haze to examine the surrounding headlands. "Is the Sound as marvelous as everyone swears?"

David laughed at the enormity of the question, and Louisa smiled at the white-whiskered captain. "This is the Promised Land, didn't you know that, Captain Parker?"

"Seems someone told me that once," he quipped, returning her smile. "What about the Indians? Those drums I hear from time to time don't sound too friendly."

"Well now," said David. "You might as well ask if the white folk are friendly!"

"Are they?"

David laughed, and Louisa decided she liked Captain Parker. "Oh, Oh!" she cried all of a sudden, pointing, standing up on tiptoe. "There's our little cabin! Do you see it, Captain Parker? That's where we lived when we were first married, and until four months ago. Oh . . . But it looks so forlorn . . ." She dropped back on her heels.

Captain Parker pulled off his hat. "If I might, Mr. Denny, have a word with you?"

Louisa sensed the captain preferred his word with David alone. "If you'll keep your eye on Emily Inez," she told them, "I'll go below and pack our things."

An hour later the *Traveler* inched alongside Yesler's wharf. *Home!* Louisa nearly cried with happiness to see the stumpy village with its clustered cabins and Indian huts, the noisy mill, the steeply rising hills all around. How *good* to be home!

Everyone came rushing down to the beach to see the new steamer. David and Louisa stumbled with rubbery legs off the gangplank onto the wharf, Captain Parker beside them, carrying Emily Inez. Miners pushed and shoved and jostled from every side, but David managed to steer a steady course toward the cookhouse in search of Mr. Yesler. Louisa waved to Ursula, Catherine Maynard, Widow Holgate, though she held tightly to David's arm for fear of getting trampled. She was so very weak, and the rush of the crowd made her dizzy.

"Looks like your purser is giving everyone the tour, Captain," said David, gawking back over his shoulder to watch the crowd surge onto the wharf.

"Free too!" said the captain, puffing out his chest.

Louisa smiled. "Captain Parker, I'll be impressed when you start giving everyone free rides around the Bay."

"Now that," he told her, "is an idea to tuck under my hat."

They found Mr. Yesler perched on a stool outside the cookhouse, his wiry hair springing out of his head like the quills of an annoyed porcupine. As usual, he was whittling. He whittled like some women knit, and was never without his jackknife. Louisa once asked Mrs. Yesler if he slept with it. But Mrs. Yesler had embarrassed her. Mr. Yesler, Mrs. Yesler had said, slept with *nothing!* Approaching him now, Louisa desperately tried to picture the square, boxy man with at least a nightshirt on.

David introduced the captain.

"Pleased to meet you," said Yesler with a big-toothed grin.

David bent over and whispered.

Yesler snapped his jackknife shut. "Well, that is easily arranged, Captain Parker. You go to the mill there, and tell George Frye to have the Indians wood you right up. Take all you want. Help yourself, and pay for it when you feel like it. It's good to have a steamer again. Scranton spoiled us with the *Major Tompkins,* and we've been limping along with the

Water Lily too long. It'll be nice to have regular service again and know when we're getting our mail. Well now, Mrs. Denny," he said in one breath, "you look green around the gills. You better have a sit while your menfolks tend their business." He offered her his chair.

"Thank you, I think I will." She sat gratefully, wondering why she should feel so nauseous now that they were on dry land. Suddenly she remembered the last time she'd seen Mr. Yesler. "Did John Holgate ever find out he drowned?" she asked.

Mr. Yesler chortled, remembering too. He then pulled out his knife and popped open the blade. His broad back pressed against the logs of his cookhouse, he was whittling again. "Arthur won the election," he told her as she watched with interest his big knife blade flash in the sunlight, the scented pine chips raining down onto the ground by their feet. "Yessiree. Denny, Webster, and Phillips. Two Whigs and a Democrat. And Tom Russell's sheriff again. Better warn your husband that Wyckoff went out to assess your new house. He and Tom'll be around shortly, I expect, to collect your new taxes."

"What about the referendum—the Maine Liquor Law?"

Mr. Yesler spat. "Passed in King County. 81 to 44."

"It did?" she looked up at him, amazed.

Mr. Yesler grinned. "Lost in the Territory, though, Mrs. Denny. 650 to 564! We stay wet."

"Oh," she said, dashed. She rested her head against the logs and wished David would hurry. So close, yet still so far from home. Oh, she'd give *anything* to be home right now, to lie down in her own bed!

"Things have changed a bit since you've been gone," Mr. Yesler rattled on. "Charlie Plummer applied for a liquor license. He's selling spirits now in that bowling saloon of his. Even ordered a bar from San Francisco. And he took over Fanjoy's sawmill, out at Mox La Push. When Charles Terry isn't running the *Water Lily* up and down the Duwamish day and night collecting coal for Dr. Webster, he's hauling lumber like there's no tomorrow for Plummer. Going to put me right out of business, that Mr. Plummer. *Yessiree.*"

Louisa sat forward a little looking across the Sawdust. *Was that Mary?* Yes, and her sister seemed terribly upset, pushing, squeezing through the press of people, craning her neck and glancing all around. "Mr. Yesler," she interrupted. "I think my sister is looking for me. Can you fetch her? I don't feel well, and I fear something may be wrong."

Mr. Yesler eased down until he was squatting on his haunches beside her. He rubbed a hand through his prickly hair.

"Mr. Yesler?"

"Something *is* wrong."

She felt the rise of bile in her throat, and knew she was going to be sick.

"She's carrying a heavy load this week, your sister. Arthur's still in San Francisco—gone to get his gold-mining supplies. And your brother's gone. Went with the Judge and some others—Nagle, Matthias, Plummer, never mind who—to explore Snoqualmie Pass and put the road through."

"What's happened?"

"Anna's run off is what's happened."

Louisa whirled to meet his eyes. "Anna? Why? Where would—"

"Seems she was biding her time, waiting for your menfolks to be gone. Near as any can figure, she took the *Franklin Adams* to San Francisco last week. Took the children with her too."

Louisa felt suddenly very cold. "Where did she get that much money?"

Mr. Yesler pinned a steady eye on her.

"Oh," she gasped, like someone just punched her. "The property . . ." And then the memory of their quarrel came flooding back. *What am I up to, you ask! I'M doing some-*

thing? Do you see ME running off? Do I run away whenever I can't stand it anymore?

"I'll fetch Mary Ann for you now, if you like, Mrs. Denny."

"Please." Head reeling, dizzy, Louisa put her head down by her knees, the earth coming up at her in swirling circles. She should have known! She should have known Anna was planning on running off! Of course that was her plan! Why else did she react so defensively, so violently, to such an innocent question? *What are you up to, Anna Boren?*

"Louisa!"

She looked up, saw Mary. The next thing she knew, she was throwing up and then Doc Maynard was there, scooping her up in his arms and jogging across the Sawdust to the nearest house.

21

Thursday, August 29, 1855

How are we to reach the gold fields by the nearest and most practical route? With a view of arriving at a conclusion of that question, a party of 15 or 20, one of whom was Chief Justice Lander, left Seattle a few weeks since with a view of exploring the Snoqualmie Pass of the Cascades. That party has returned. . . . their report is very favorable. Should this prove to be a GOOD ROUTE to the mines we doubt not but that much of the foreign travel to the Colville mines must leave the waters of the Sound. Let our neighbors at Seattle keep the ball in motion and they will accomplish much for the territory.

We repeat, we want for nothing but a good wagon road across the mountains to put life and mettle into all business of this territory.

—*Pioneer & Democrat*, Saturday, August 31, 1855

*B*uoyed by the news from Doc Maynard that sometime in March she would have another baby, Louisa's grief over James and her worry over the breakup of her brother's family ebbed . . . like a heavy tide turning back. And when she got back to the Swale, to her own home, surrounded by everything familiar, she found herself quickly regaining the strength she'd lost on the difficult sea voyage and, with her strength, a new peace of mind.

With death came birth. Sorrow gave way to joy. Life was an evolution and one had to embrace it . . . take the good with the bad. She found herself at home in the cycle, and woke well rested each morning, eager to see what each new day would bring—usually Madeline.

Just about the time Louisa saw David off in the mornings—cutting wild hay these days with Mr. Mercer—Madeline would come waddling up to the house, two sharp sticks and tightly woven baskets on her back. The camas, a bulbous root, was the natives' chief vegetable and August was harvesttime.

Louisa looked forward to digging camas. Emily Inez particularly enjoyed herself, for camas digging meant taking off her shoes and socks, tying her skirts up high between her legs, and then walking barefoot into the warm, boggy marsh. This is what Curley had meant when he said "dig with toes, not hoes." They walked around in the ankle-deep marsh water, enjoying the delicious ooze of the mud, listening to the lovely "squnch," all the while feeling around with their toes for something round and hard. When they touched the round, hard root, they dug their toes down deeper into the goo, beneath the root, the warm mud getting colder, then wiggled their toes until the roots pulled loose. A quick flick of the ankle and the bulb popped up! Bobbing, floating, on the water! Then they would stab it with their stick and toss it over their shoulder into their basket. Emily Inez had her own basket, a little one just her size that Madeline had made for her. The little girl took great pride in that basket, and she raced to fill it faster than either her "Maddy" or her "mama."

While wading around, there were things to see, too. Polliwogs and waterbugs scooted and hid. Purple violets and other swamp things grew in abundance, along with skunk cabbage and the villainous devil's club. Louisa loved nature and taught Emily Inez and Madeline the Latin names for everything. And afterward, their harvest almost too heavy to carry, they piled their baskets together beneath some leaning alder tree and shinnied up to tear away the moss and get the licorice root. It was sticky and sweet and Emily Inez loved it.

The only worry Louisa had these lazy, warm, exciting days was the occasional Indian drums. Kamiakin of the Yakima and some of the Colville Indians had apparently held a big council at Grande Ronde on the other side of the mountains. Ever since, there had been the drums . . . and scores of messengers crossing and recrossing the mountains.

A few of the settlers feared that Kamiakin, angered by the miners rushing pell-mell through his country on their way to the gold mines, was inviting the western Indians to join in a war against the whites. Most of the pioneers, however, resisted the notion. The Yakima chief was up to no good, this much was certain, but the Nisqually—the largest of the disaffected tribes on this side of the mountains—didn't seem to be paying a whole lot of attention. Seattle certainly wasn't. And Leschi had withdrawn to his farm on the Nisqually Flats and was preparing his fields for fall plowing. This did not sound like a man preparing for war. The troubles, whatever they were, were on the other side of the mountains, and the drums, Louisa told herself, were something the governor would address when he got home. As for now? This was fall, a time to harvest, gather, and store. Winter would come in its own good time.

That same afternoon, David's and Tom's scythes lay on the ground beside the creek, near the spot where they'd eaten lunch. Not far away, their rifles leaned against the trunk of a cedar. The afternoon was hot, but the creek made a cool, laughing sound and the heat served to ripen the piercing sweetness of the wild hay. When Tib and Charley moved on to the next shock, the wheels of Tom's big conestoga rolled over a carpet of tiny little bluebells that the scythes had missed, crushing the fragile petals and emitting a gentler, lighter fragrance.

From every direction in the hot, perfumed air came the trill of the meadowlarks. When one sang close to the wagon, Tom and David ceased their labor to listen. There was a trick to the last note that escaped them. They could not, for all their trying, duplicate it. Behind them, silent, was Rainier, a single splash of white against the day's azure sky.

He and Tom made for a good team, thought David with satisfaction. They both knew the importance of birdsong, the snowy vastness of the mountain behind them, the blend of perfumes wafting up from the wagon's wheels. No sound, sight, or scent was lost to them. And they needed these things to brighten the dark note of the drums that sometimes interrupted the peace.

No one knew *exactly* what the drums meant, though it was obvious the gold miners had stirred up something in Yakima country. Yet the Yakima had signed their treaty and, as far as David knew, they weren't unhappy over their reservation assignments.

The afternoon lengthened, Tom pitching the hay up onto the wagon, David building a compact load, tight enough to withstand the long road into town where they would unload and store the hay in Plummer's new livery shed. Tib and Charley would have plenty to eat this winter.

"One more shock and we can call it quits!" hollered up Tom at last. The sun, David saw, hung low in the sky. Louisa would have supper waiting. He held on while Tom took hold of the horses' bridles.

"Git along there, you two!" Tom gave his team a cluck, the wagon lurched forward. The smell of the bluebells being crushed beneath the high wheels rushed up to David in a heady scent.

The last fork of hay was pitched up, David tamped it down while Tom walked all around the wagon, trimming off the loose wisps with his fork. "Looks good to me, Dave!"

David jumped down with a whoop.

Tom gathered up their scythes and the rifles by the creek. Together they washed their faces in the cold bubbling water, then clambered aboard by way of the wagon tongue, David with a fistful of bluebells for Louisa. Blue was Louisa's favorite color . . . and she was with child again.

"Sitting on the nest" was the way Doc Maynard had explained things to him the afternoon they'd arrived home from Oregon three weeks ago. When he'd flown across the Sawdust like a chicken with its head cut off, taking the steps two at a time onto Yesler's front porch. David smiled now, thinking about it. How pleased Louisa had been, hearing the news, as if she'd gotten on the nest all by herself!

He had his own nest, he realized, way up here, on top of the hay, and the view was fine! Spreading before him was a whole sea of yellow waving grass, dotted with islands and headlands of scrub oaks and Christmas-tree pines. Between the islands and headlands a large herd of deer grazed in the shoulder-deep grass. Every once in a while one moved with the slow, high leaps and flashes of white that defined them. This was the way it had always been, from the beginning of time. He understood now, as never before, the Indians' objections to the changes being made by the whites. From the distance came the throb of the drums. And yet . . . yet still the meadowlarks sang.

"Any word on Anna and the children?" Tom asked all of a sudden, the wagon rumbling leisurely across the shorn field.

"No. And until Dobbins gets back from the pass, there's nothing I can do—except keep hoping she sends a letter. Letting us know where she is, at least."

"Is Arthur home?"

"Don't expect him for another week."

Tom shook his head. "Sure hope he doesn't get stuck with a store full of goods no one wants."

"How's that?"

"Doesn't seem so many are going over to the gold mines these days. Especially with those drums . . ." Tom jerked his head to the east. "And all the rumors. Indians picking off the miners when no one's looking."

"You haven't been reading the papers, have you, Tom?"

"Nope," said Tom with a smile. "Never believe anything you read in a newspaper, son, and that's good advice!"

David chuckled. "Well, the men are still going over. More all the time. Someone actually made it back, and said September is when to go. The water will be down enough—"

"Colonel Anderson?"

David gave him a puzzled look.

"Colonel Anderson, our new congressional delegate? Went to the gold mines to see what's what?"

"No. Bennet and Wilber I think their names were."

"Sure is strange where he's disappeared to."

"Who?"

"Anderson."

"Thought Anderson said to give him six weeks before his return. It's only been a month, Tom."

They came to the trail that led over to the Swale.

"You might as well get on down," said Tom, "and get on home to Louisa. When I get into town, I'll get Dexter to help me unload the hay."

"You're sure now?"

"I'll be around first thing in the morning. Now that the haying is done, we can get your timber down to the mill."

"Yesler's backed up. No need to hurry."

"The sooner you get in line, the sooner you get in. And you need the cash."

"I don't want to take advantage of you, Tom!"

Tom laughed. "Who's taking advantage of whom? Giddyup there, Tib and Charley!" he hollered out. "Away you go, that's it!"

Dobbins *had* returned from the pass. When he found Anna gone, he went wild with rage and worry. He stormed out to the Swale in a black fury, his hair standing on end from pulling it out by the roots, his face contorted with grief and wrath. Red sparks of something kindred to malice flashed from his eyes. Louisa, just coming in from the swamp, dumped her basket of camas bulbs on the stoop outside.

"Emily Inez and I are going berry picking," she told Dobbins quickly and in a shaken voice. *Oh, dear poor Dobbins!* she thought, torn between her love for him and needing to take care of her little girl. Yet she couldn't stay and have Emily Inez frightened by her own uncle.

When David got home, Dobbins was no better for the wait. David watched helplessly as the distraught man strode up and down the long front room, swinging his arms, pulling on his beard, pulling on his hair, swinging his arms again.

"I've tried everything I know to make her happy!" Dobbins finally roared. "Everything! I even sold her hundred and sixty acres for a song because she wanted a piano! Do you know how much Maynard got last week for *ten* acres?" He spun around hard on his heel.

"No," said David quietly, gripping the back of Louisa's new rocking chair.

"$2400! For *ten* acres! *One hundred thirty-one lots!* $2400! If that was me, selling at that price? I'd be sitting on $38,400! *$38,400!* But I have NOTHING!" He punched his fist into the log wall. David heard the cruel snap of bones, but Dobbins wasn't done. "She said she wanted a piano!" he bawled, grabbing his wrist to stay the pain. "I let her! I said, *'Go ahead if that'll make you happy, but you know it won't! Nothing makes you happy!'* Did she buy her precious piano? No, because she didn't *want* a piano! She was planning on running away that whole time!" He kicked one of Louisa's footstools. It bounced erratically across the floor. David watched it tumble and finally land upside down. "She robbed me out of thirty-eight thousand, four hundred dollars!" howled Dobbins, and he grabbed his hair with both hands. He leaned into the wall, and over and over he banged his head into the logs. Over and over and over.

David rushed to pull him back. Dobbins threw him off. David came at him again. Next thing he knew they were both on the floor, boxing, pummeling each other, Dobbins crying and beating at him with impotent fury. It was a wonder Dobbins could hit anything with his broken hand, but he was a madman, bent on destruction of something, anything, himself—David if need be. David breathed a prayer for forgiveness, then hauled back and threw everything he had into a cruel punch against Dobbins's temple. Dobbins's head lolled sideways, his eyes rolled up inside his head, and his body went limp. David stared down, panting, and then pushed his forearm against his brow to stop the sweat from running into his eyes.

He brought Dobbins around with a cold compress, then helped him over to the rocking chair.

"Sorry," Dobbins mumbled.

"You really do love her, don't you?"

"*What kind of question is that?*" snarled Dobbins.

"Forget it. What are you going to do?"

"Let her go. She made her decision."

"What about the children?"

"It would kill her if I took them from her."

"It's not going to kill you? It's not going to kill *the rest of us?*"

Dobbins didn't answer.

David went over to the stove. He put on a kettle of water and rummaged around in a cupboard for the medical supplies. Dobbins's head and hand were both bloody and riddled with splinters. Before any broken bones could be set, the abrasions would have to be cleaned.

"You want to do this lying down or sitting up?" David asked, hauling the supplies over to the table.

Dobbins eyed the bandages, the needles, the hydrogen peroxide. He looked at his broken hand. "Guess I can take it sitting up."

While David worked, he talked, telling Dobbins the way it was going to be. "And no use arguing about it," he said at the outset, "because the minute Arthur gets home he'll tell you the same thing."

"Tell me what?" said Dobbins, wincing.

"That you're going to go after Anna, and when you find her, you're going to take her home to Illinois."

"Illinois?"

"Yes, Illinois! It's where she's headed, and it's not safe for a woman to be traveling alone, let alone a woman with a child and a babe in arms! If you do nothing else for her, you'll do this, so long as I have breath in my body. I've watched too long and said nothing. Now I'm saying it. That woman wasn't made for this country and it's twisting her—*and* you—inside out."

"What about Gerty? William?"

"Anna will have to decide. She bore those children, she birthed them. A mother has her rights, it's her choice. But if it helps any, tell her that Liza and I'll take Gerty and Wills— if she lets you bring them back out here. We'll adopt them, if that's what she wants."

"I don't have money to get to Illinois," argued Dobbins.

"I've thought of that, too." Pulling up the footstool and sitting down in front of Dobbins, David gently probed his brother-in-law's hand, trying to determine where he'd broken it. Dobbins bit his lip. Perspiration beaded his forehead. But he said nothing and let David poke and prod.

"You took the blow right here," said David. "Sit tight." He took a firm grip and gave a hard jerk on Dobbins's middle finger. Dobbins went white. He breathed out hard. David gave him a minute. "You got your breath yet? I've got two more to set."

"Go ahead . . ."

While David set the bones and bound Dobbins's hand and fingers with soft blue cloth, cut from the calico that Louisa was saving for her wall border, he told Dobbins how they were going to manage the money. "I'll advance what you need. I'll rent out your house to some new family in town and pocket what comes in. When your advance is met, I'll send the rest to you in Illinois so you've got something to come back on. You can join an emigrant train next summer, or come back around the Horn."

Dobbins sank into the back of the chair. His fury was spent. In his eyes was the cold light of sanity again. David smiled and leaned over, and patted Dobbins's knee affectionately. "Hurry back, brother. We'll miss you something awful while you're gone."

22

Early September, 1855

THE FORT COLVILLE MINES: Both in this territory and in Oregon the excitement seems to be unabated with regard to the reported gold discoveries on the Pend d'Oreille River and its tributaries east of the Cascade mountains. In this territory Anxiety seems to be on tiptoe—large parties are hurrying forward in order to test their reality—all would seem to be life and bustle on the Columbia River—large stock of goods, and miner's supplies, pack animals, etc. have been lodged at The Dalles, and elsewhere along that river, where buildings are being rapidly constructed—new town sites are being laid off, and, from all accounts, everything would seem to bear somewhat the semblance of California in the memorable year of '49.

—*Pioneer & Democrat,* August 1, 1855

*T*he first week of September passed so swiftly the days had the feel of wings. Arthur arrived home at the beginning of the week, and while the cargo on the *Harriet Thompson* was exchanged, import for export, Louisa and

Mary Ann sorted through Anna's house, packing up what they thought she might like to have with her in Illinois. Dobbins would take the crates with him when he departed on the *Harriet Thompson* at the end of the week.

David stayed on at the claim throughout the entire week. He and Tom had taken all his timber into town, and now the salmon were running. Jim and George and Curley had come to help catch, clean, and fillet enough fish to fill his smokehouse.

Arthur all but lived at his store. Dawn to dusk he outfitted the scores of men responding to the latest proclamations in the newspaper. *"The Indians have been perfectly friendly and express a desire to have the whites come and work the mines"* was the way William Bennet and Hiram Wilber reported their experiences. Arthur marked everything up 150 percent, then 200 percent.

"A much easier way to bring home gold," he boasted, staggering in exhausted every night after dark and sitting down to a warmed-up supper. "And safer."

Arthur didn't trust the reports. Bennet and Wilber went too far, he told Louisa and Mary Ann, when they claimed the Indians *wanted* whites to come work the mines. *"Friendly* was stretching things, but *inviting?"* He shook his head. "Do those drums, pounding away every other day, sound like an invite to you? And the rumors of impending war haven't gone away."

He brought the subject up again on Thursday night.

"But you keep selling mining equipment," said Louisa.

"When a man decides he's going to chase gold, there isn't anyone—not even you, Louisa—who's going to change their minds for them. Just this morning Charles Walker and John Avery came in, looking at outfits."

"Charles? and John?" said Mary Ann. "From the Collins Settlement? Weren't they both on Maurer's jury last fall?"

"Yes to both questions." He smiled. "With three of their pals, I might add—newcomers. All wanting the very best stuff too. Now, that's what I mean." He pointed his finger at Louisa. "A man with gold fever is so convinced he's going to make a million there's no telling him different. Walker and Avery are both giving up their farms to get over there. Don't look at me like that. I tried to talk some sense into them. I said, 'Anyone out your way ever hear from Fanjoy and Eaton?' 'They're too busy making money,' is what Walker said. So yes, Louisa, I'll keep selling mining equipment."

"Maybe you should have asked them if they've heard about Colonel Anderson—who's missing," she said. "He didn't go to make money."

Arthur regarded her seriously. "Maybe I should have."

By Friday evening Anna's house was clean and ready to rent. The *Harriet Thompson* was gone, a hundred tons of coal in her hold, Dobbins staring morosely over the stern poop. In the morning Louisa would go home. A sad week . . . she could hardly wait to put it behind her and get back to David.

Tired, she drifted into sleep, lulled by the ticking of a clock Arthur had bought for Mary in California, a rather august grandfather clock with a lovely moon and stars on the face, and with a pleasing chime. But a different sort of noise startled her into alert wakefulness. She sat up on the floor where she was sleeping in the front room. Someone, she was sure, was at the door.

Hastily she got to her feet.

"Denny, Pat Kanim!" *A harsh whisper.* "Let me in!"

Louisa threw a blanket over her shoulders and felt her way across the room, shadowed eerily in thin moonlight. She had hardly lifted the latch when the Snoqualmie chief pushed in. "Where's Denny?" he whispered.

She pointed to the bedroom door.

"Get him."

In 1849 a large band of Snoqualmie warriors had beached their canoes on the Nisqually Flats and strode angrily over to the British fort then in existence. Pat Kanim had learned that a Nisqually chief, Lahalet, was beating his wife; the woman happened to be Pat Kanim's sister. Lahalet, it was reported, had taken sanctuary in the fort and Pat Kanim wanted to speak with him.

To the men inside the fort, though, a hundred warriors to resolve a domestic dispute seemed excessive. Particularly since it was only a year ago that Pat Kanim had driven two settlers off Whidbey Island, declaring he'd tolerate no whites on Puget Sound. Pat Kanim, they decided, had really come to carry out his threat.

The ensuing confrontation erupted in a short burst of gunfire at the fort gate, and when it was over one American and a Skykomish medicine man were dead.

Revenge by the Americans was swift. Two of Pat Kanim's brothers were hung, and in two months' time, a company of American soldiers was putting up their own fort at Steilacoom. This gave Pat Kanim a healthy respect for the swiftness and power of American revenge. On a subsequent trip to San Francisco he saw the sheer numbers of the white race, and realized completely the futility of fueling further animosity, no matter the grudge. He became a loyal *"Boston tillicum"*—friend of the Americans.

"There's going to be trouble," he said now, sitting at the table with Arthur, the two of them looking ghostly in the shadows. "Miners *have* been killed, maybe as many as eight."

Arthur looked startled.

Louisa felt her throat constrict. Mr. Fanjoy, Mr. Eaton! All those miners on the *Traveler!* They'd be east of the mountains, in the heart of Yakima country by now! And what about Mr. Avery and Mr. Walker, who'd just left? And Colonel Anderson, their new delegate to Congress who'd gone out to inspect the mines? *Where was he?*

"There is more," said Pat Kanim. "I have been to Fort Steilacoom to tell the soldiers this. Now I am telling you. Kamiakin and the other tribes have declared war. Kamiakin is ready to fight for five years if he has to—unless he kills all the Bostons sooner. He says the Sound Indians will help. If we don't, he'll treat us like Bostons and kill all the adults, take our children for slaves."

"Is anybody listening to his boasts?" Arthur asked. "What about Seattle? What does he say? Nelson? Leschi? What do they say?"

"I don't know. I'm not waiting to find out. I'm taking my people and going away, where Kamiakin can't find us. I have no wish to fight."

They talked a little more.

"Where will you go?" Louisa heard Arthur ask. Pat Kanim had opened the door, and she shivered in the draft.

"Steilaguamish River. We go there every year to hunt wild mountain sheep. We're safe there."

When he was gone, Louisa sat watching Arthur's thoughtful face in the eery light and shadow.

"Are you determined to go out to the claim tomorrow?" he asked all of a sudden. She nearly jumped out of her skin.

"We still don't know anything. Do we?" she told him.

"No, I guess not."

"He only confirmed what we've all suspected."

He sighed. "All right, I'll see if Yoke-Yakeman can take you out in the morning, I don't want you going by yourself. But promise me"—he got to his feet—"that you'll tell David what's happened. Tell him to come talk to me if he has any ideas about averting catastrophe."

Arthur paused at the bedroom door. "You still have your inside house, you know."

He referred to the house next door, the cabin David had built for them two years earlier during another Indian scare. Suddenly Arthur chuckled softly and said, shaking his head. "Maybe Anna's the only one in our family with any sense. Good night, Liza."

"Good night, Arthur."

226

The next morning Jim and George Seattle, Curley, and David found little enthusiasm for their work. They'd been taking salmon out of the creek all week, the fish so thick it had been shamefully easy. All they'd had to do was scoop in their pitchforks and dump the fish, slithering and flopping, into big tin buckets. The hard part was cleaning them. A week of this, though, and they were bored. Even Watch looked bored, lying on rocks by the stream, nose in his paws. David suggested they go exploring farther up the creek, to see if they could find the spawning ground. Curley said he knew a place where the fish were so thick one could walk across the water on them.

"Wake..." said Jim Seattle scornfully in Chinook.

"Halo!" Yes! argued Curley emphatically. "It's so! So thick you can walk on their backs and not get your feet wet!"

"Are you going to show us how it's done?" Jim insisted, switching back to Duwamish.

"David will," said Curley in Duwamish, leading out. Watch, catching on that they were off on an adventure, lumbered to his feet and gave chase.

Ordinarily the creek was five to six feet wide, at the most a foot deep with just a few inches at the riffles. Not much of a stream for one fish to swim up, let alone thousands. Yet every fall a whole army of them came, swimming upstream, bent on a singular mission. First by tens, then hundreds, and finally thousands, they swam against the current with their bellies full of eggs or milt, crowding the creek banks and each other in a frenzied effort to reach the top. They pushed with their reddish-orange and silver backs out of the water— sometimes everything but their bellies—in their effort to wriggle and slip across the shallow spots. Bears fattened off them; men set their nets or simply scooped them up. Still they charged on, the whole army leaping clean out of the water if necessary to cross fallen trees or leap small waterfalls. They didn't eat. They didn't sleep. They drove themselves up the very same route they'd come down as babies;

nothing would stop them, and every year they came to do just one thing—to give birth and then die where they'd been spawned.

How the salmon knew where to return was an unanswered question. Nevertheless they always found their way, and always it cost them everything. The females, more dead than alive, came to the same dark cold pond where their lives had begun. Here they laid their eggs. The males came after them and left their milt. Male and female then floated downstream, their brilliant color gone, scales torn, fins frayed, tails battered, bloody, most of them blind, every one of them dead or nearly dead.

Not a whole lot in life for a salmon, thought David, watching the amazing fish defy all odds in the stream beside him. Ordeal and death, that was about it. *Is that all life has to offer anyone?* No, there was love. Somewhere in the struggle there was love. *At least for some of us,* he thought sadly, thinking of Dobbins and Anna, and then wondering suddenly if Louisa would come home today. Surely she and Mary Ann would be finished packing up Anna's belongings.

Curley, up ahead, stopped. "Whoa! See! I told you!"

David scampered in closer. The whole front line of the army was battering away at an eight-foot-wide riffle scarcely an inch deep. The determined tangle of salmon made a splashing mess of gray and red and tarnished silver and dull gold in a moving, swirling wet pattern. "Easy to walk on!" grunted Curley, giving David a push.

"Go ahead then," David invited him.

The Indian scowled and pointed back at David.

David threw up both hands. "I'm not doing that!"

George arrived and gave Curley a poke in his britches with the sharp end of his pitchfork. "You talk big, Salmon Bay Curley. Let's see you do it."

David laughed, but Curley was mad. "Fine," he said. "I will do it." He started scrambling over to the riffle.

Seattle's sons and David sat down on some large rocks to watch. Curley stood on the bank's edge, seemingly measuring the distance.

"He's going to jump, then say he walked," said George.

"He can't jump that far, he's too old." Jim squinted.

Curley did jump, right foot first, legs spread far apart. He touched down halfway across, slithered, then shot straight down on his bottom, feet in the air. Fish leaped, thrashed. Water flew. Curley came up like a shot, shaking the water off himself like a dog.

"I slipped," he protested, crashing up the bank.

The rest of them laughed all the way home.

They said good-bye at the trail crossing, everyone heading back to their respective destinations. Curley, to Madeline and his little shack on Salmon Bay. Seattle's sons, out to David's old cabin where their canoes were beached. David, up to the house.

"Good-bye," said George one more time to David, giving him another firm handshake. Jim shook hands again too.

"Thanks for the help!" he called after the brothers, reluctant to see them go.

They both waved. "You're welcome!"

He felt a strange loneliness after they'd gone. Quickly he gathered up the empty buckets left by the creek, stacked them inside each other, then slung them over his back. The pitchforks he clutched in one hand, his fingers stretched around the three handles. "Come on, Watch. Time to go home." His heart lightened a little. Maybe Louisa was back.

They stopped first at the smokehouse to see if he needed to put more green alder on the smoldering fire. He did. And while adding one or two logs of the wet green wood he couldn't help but admire the pinkish-orange fish fillets drying on the racks. They may have played today, but it didn't matter. The racks were nicely filled. Winter was going to be fine, having fresh-smoked salmon anytime they wanted. No more having to wait on some Indian passing through, looking for a trade.

He was coming up to the cabin when Watch stopped.

"What is it, boy?"

Watch started to growl low in his throat.

David quickened his pace, came around the necessary house, and saw the horses. Indians from over the mountains! For a moment David froze, staring at the telltale haircuts of the most vicious band of the Yakima—the Klikitats. Louisa! She was home! In the garden with them! He could see by her short, jerky movements that she was frantically digging potatoes.

23

Late Saturday Afternoon, September 7, 1855

Late that summer of '55 a number of Indians visited the sweetbriar bride and insolently demanded "Klosh mika potlatch wapatoes!" which meant, "Give us some potatoes!" They were so ugly and threatening that she hurried out and dug the potatoes so that they might have no cause for displeasure.

—Roberta Frye Watt, Katy Denny's daughter
in *Four Wagons West*

One of the men pushed Louisa, hard. She stumbled, but reared up, back straight.

"*Icta mika tickey?*" David hollered, shouting at the Klikitats as he ran. "What do you want?" He wasn't afraid, he couldn't afford to be. Watch started to bark.

"*Icta mika tickey?*" he repeated.

There were five of them. A skinny fellow with narrow, hard eyes answered, *"Tickey nesika tslanies!"*

"They're looking for a runaway woman," Louisa told him bravely. "I haven't seen anyone—as if I'd tell them. Then they said to get them potatoes."

"Where's Emily Inez?"

"Inside."

He reached for her hand. "If you want potatoes," he told the men in Chinook, wishing he knew Yakima, "get the potatoes yourself! *Don't make a woman do it for you!*" He started quickly toward the house, hoping to gain entrance and bar the door before any of the insolent blackguards had the sense to realize he and Louisa were gone. Behind him, he heard them laughing at him. "Hurry," he urged Louisa.

From around the corner of the house came two more of the Klikitats. Watch instantly sprang between them and David and Louisa. "Easy, boy," warned David, pushing Louisa inside. "Easy now." He reached out to quiet the dog and the men rushed forward . . . and were inside.

The Klikitats no longer seemed interested in either him or Louisa—or Emily Inez who came flying out from behind the stove to leap into his arms. They were more interested in the furnishings. One kept looking in Louisa's wall mirror, shouting boo at himself, and jumping back. The rest went around picking things up and putting them down again, jabbering back and forth in their own language. Watch growled menacingly at David's side.

Louisa came around on his other side and slipped her arm through his. He felt Emily Inez hide her face in his neck.

The skinny man with the hard, narrow eyes discovered the lockers beneath the bed. He pulled them open, shut them, pulled them open again. *"Hiyu klosh!"* he said with sincere regard.

"Mashi," said David stiffly, accepting the compliment.

Louisa was not pleased; the man had started to go through their things, carelessly, discarding and admiring. He held up Louisa's boots from Pa.

"Do you think they'll take them?" she asked anxiously as he handed the well-worn boots over to the others for inspection.

"No," said David.

The boots, though, were put on the floor, not back in the locker.

Now they held up his red long johns, turning them upside down, inside out. They discovered the drawer in the back. One made a graphic bathroom gesture. The others howled with glee. The long johns were tossed onto the floor next to Louisa's boots.

"I *don't* want them going through our things!"

"Shh . . ."

Next were Louisa's muslin drawers. These elicted a great deal of discussion and Louisa hissed beside him, "They better let well enough alone!"

Someone laughed obscenely, raw and ribald, and it was followed by loud, leering cheers. This was too much for Louisa. One minute she was standing beside David, the next, eyes blazing, flashing, her voice cracking with anger, she was among the Indians.

"Get out! *Klatawa!*" she yelled, pushing at them, first one, then another, backing them across the room, toward the front door. *"KLATAWA!"*

Watch sprang, barking, snarling.

David stood in a daze, Emily Inez rearing up in his arms to stare at her mother, looking on as if none of this was real. Louisa was snatching up their clothing, throwing everything back into the locker. She kicked the locker shut and was back at the Indians, driving them out of her house, Watch biting at their ankles. *"Klatawa! KLATAWA!"* she yelled. She used the word like a flail.

The men felt the skinning. They certainly felt the dog's teeth, shredding clean through their knee-high moccasins. One or two got out the door. Was the invasion over? But then David felt the sharp end of the skinny man's spear in his ribs.

He pushed the spear away from him. *"Icta mika tickey?"* What do you want?

The skinny man pointed to Louisa. *"Tatoosh-klootchman!"*

Yes, she is a brave eagle woman, he agreed.

"Tatoosh-klootchman! Spose mika swap?"

No, he didn't want to swap.

The Indian offered some gold dust out of his pouch.

"No trade!" said David angrily.

"KLATAWA!" Louisa bodily threw herself on the man, pounded on his back, pulled his hair. *"KLATAWA!"*

Watch sprang from across the room. He leapt high, and Louisa staggered backward as Watch carried the man to the floor.

"Down, boy!" David shouted. Quickly he handed Emily Inez over to Louisa. "Down! Down! That's enough!" Watch finally, reluctantly, let go.

The man wasn't hurt. David hauled him to his feet, let him brush his clothes back into place, then started him rudely toward the door.

"Tatoosh-komox! Spose mika swap?"

David all but threw the man out. *"No I don't want to trade my dog!"*

Not until the door was shut and the bar dropped into place did David draw a full breath. He watched through the window as the seven intruders painfully mounted their horses. *What had she been thinking? Going at them like that? She could have gotten the whole family killed!* And Watch hadn't been much better. If he'd been allowed, he would have torn their Indian throats out! When David could no longer hear the hoofbeats drumming the earth, he turned around to find Liza. She was in the bedroom, collapsed on the edge of the bed with her legs and feet splayed out in front of her. She was very white, and very still. He sat down carefully next to her, easing Emily Inez onto his knee, jiggling her up and down to keep her quietly amused, amazed that she showed no outward fear.

"Are they gone?" Louisa stared at the wall.

"Yes."

"I could have gotten us all killed," she whispered.

A moment ago he wanted to yell at her. Now he wanted only to protect her.

"I was only doing what you told me to," she continued, still staring at the wall. "Never show fear, you said, or it's all over. But I got so busy *not* being scared, I wasn't scared, and the next thing I knew, I was mad. Madder than a bee stuck in a bonnet!"

He started to laugh. He couldn't help it. The relief was too much, and she did look pathetic sitting there like that.

Gathering herself up, she whirled around. "You don't know, David! You don't know what's happened!"

He stopped laughing.

"Eight miners were killed at the coal mines! Pat Kanim came to tell Arthur—" But then she saw Emily Inez's face. She got up and hurried out of the room.

When he followed after her, she said very calmly, "Wait until Emily Inez is in bed."

Four hours later, supper done, their little girl asleep and a game of checkers going between them, David listened to the story. "Do we know who the miners were?" he asked.

"No, but I'm scared for Mr. Fanjoy and Mr. Eaton. And Mr. Walker and Mr. Avery. Oh yes, we know one man. Henry Mattice. Pat Kanim says he was the first."

"I know Henry. He's from Olympia."

"He assaulted a Yakima chief's daughter."

"Sounds like Mattice."

"The tribe killed him for it, and then Qualchin, a nephew of Kamiakin's, attacked two other groups of miners. Pat Kanim doesn't know who."

"But eight doesn't sound too bad," said David thoughtfully. "Not when you consider the hundreds that are over there. When the Oregon Indians get their dander up they polish off twenty-five men at a time."

"But what about *our* Indians, David? What will *they* do? Will they listen to Kamiakin? Pat Kanim says Kamiakin will kill them if they don't!"

For the first time he noticed furrows between her brows. "No . . ." he told her. "They'll do the same as Pat Kanim. Disappear for a while." He regarded her tired, weary face and said, "Liza, since when have the Sound Indians ever taken their orders from the Plains Indians?"

"Maybe since we started hearing those drums?"

He smiled and reached across the checkerboard to rub her chin. "I know some of the Indians here are upset—"

She pushed away his hand. "Yes, and so why *shouldn't* they join Kamiakin?"

"Because I just spent a whole week with Jim and George. The Muckleshoots, Puyallups, Nisqually . . . they're all waiting for the governor to get back. Hopefully we can get the boundaries remapped. Nothing's going to happen, at least not until then."

"Do you honestly think Governor Stevens, when he gets here—*if* he gets here—will do that?"

He didn't answer.

"*I* don't think so. And I can hardly blame Leschi or any of the others for joining Kamiakin. Surely it's less painful to die by the knife than slow starvation."

"But, Liza, I'm telling you"—he reached for her chin again, to cup her face firmly and force her to meet his eyes—"right *now* our only worry is these marauding Klikitat."

"Oh, David, I could have gotten us all killed. . . ." she repeated, whimpering.

"No," he said softly, withdrawing his hand. "I've been thinking about that. If those wretches wanted to kill us, they'd have done it right off. They only wanted to give us a scare,

236

throw their weight around a little, maybe show the Sound Indians how tough they are and how easy we spook. But *some* white folk don't spook." He gave her a grin. "You did good, Mrs. Denny."

"David." The color drained completely out of her face, and for the second time in one day, David froze.

"The Klikitat," she said, voice breaking, "are back."

The hair on the nape of his neck stood straight up. Watch, by the fire, growled and pushed back his ears.

But then suddenly her face relaxed into a smile. *"It's Suwalth!"*

He whirled around.

Suwalth was beckoning through the window. *What is he doing way out here?* David leaped for the door.

Suwalth shot through. "Quick! Turn out your lamps! NOW!"

24

Saturday Night, September 7, 1855

[My parents] forsook their cabin in the wilderness and spent
anxious night at the home of William Bell, which was a mile
or more from the settlement.

—Emily Inez Denny, David and Louisa's daughter
in *Blazing the Way*

*L*ouisa hurtled through the house, blowing out first
one lamp, then another. David and Suwalth spoke
in hurried, hushed tones.

"Louisa, get Emily Inez," said David briskly even as the
house plunged into darkness. "Don't dress her, we haven't
time. Just wrap her in a blanket. You better wear Pa's boots.
We have to try and get into town."

"Tonight? Why? Oh, what's happened?" *Have the Klikitat
come back?*

"Liza, hurry!"

She stumbled toward the bedroom. David felt along the mantel for his rifles, then his ammunition pouch. A minute later, standing at the door, ready to go, Suwalth said something more to David. David nodded and let Suwalth out. Louisa tried desperately to read David's face in the dark. Where was the danger? How bad was it? But his face was a mask. He was listening for something.

Two owl hoots.

She shuddered. David said, "Coast is clear." He seized her arm and pushed her outdoors into the black night. Rain was moving in, clouds covered the moon and stars. "You too," he whispered. "Come on, Watch."

"I can't see where I'm going!"

"Just follow me. *Shh!*"

He moved them across the dark swale into the even darker shadows of the trees.

"Where's Suwalth?"

He reached out and put his finger against her mouth. Two more owl hoots. David took her arm again and they darted forward, toward the road, toward the sound of the owl. Emily Inez started to whimper. Louisa held her close and crooned, "You must be a very quiet girl. . . ."

When they came to the road, they didn't walk in the open. David tucked both his rifles up under one arm and guided Louisa with the other, moving them swiftly but carefully over the uneven ground along the road's edge. Louisa got the feeling he'd yank her right off her feet into the underbrush if need be. Someone was after them, and not just to scare them either!

Was Suwalth the owl? He must be. Guiding them along in this terrifying stop-and-start flight. How had he known they were in danger? What *was* the danger?

Everything in her wanted to ask the questions, but she knew it was pointless. There was only to follow . . . and pray for their safety. *Thank God for Suwalth!*

Mr. Mercer's road started into town on more or less a straight line south from Lake Union. After a while, though, the road angled southwest, toward the Sound, skirting Denny Hill, a high cone-shaped hill between Arthur's and Mr. Bell's claims. At the Bells' house the road turned south again, running along the bank into town. Louisa, shivering with cold and fear, felt herself give way to tears when they angled southwest behind the hill. Such a long way to go yet! If David would just tell her what was happening!

She felt the first sprinkle of rain on her nose. A minute later David shrugged out of his coat and wrapped it around Emily Inez. More weight to carry, but Emily Inez would stay drier. Another five minutes and the rain was coming down so hard all she could see of David's face was the dimmest blur. He had to be soaking wet, and it wouldn't be long before she and Emily Inez were too . . . despite their coats.

The sound of the owl became hard to hear. Once, standing in the stillness and pouring rain, Watch panting beside them, Louisa wondered if something had happened to Suwalth. David did too. She could feel his fear, as if it were something she could reach out and touch. But then blessedly, faintly, two hoots.

Then the rain really let go. It fell in sheets down through the three-hundred-foot trees. Soaked, Louisa had thought a body couldn't get wetter. A body could. The rain cut through her clothes, through her skin, into her bones. Emily Inez started to cry and Louisa was helpless to stop her. The sound of the rain, at least, muffled her cries.

No wind, only the rain, a storm of its own. It came at them like a hurricane, slashing, trying to drive them off the road. The road ran with water. The side of the road grew slick with mud. The three of them became half drowned as they ran in short spurts along the road's edge; running and panting, then stopping, breathlessly listening. *Where, where was Suwalth?*

They stood holding each other, Emily Inez crying between them, in the black rain. Had they lost him? Suddenly, right beside them, ten feet away, two short hoots.

"Suwalth!" yelped David, jumping with fright.

They all jumped, even Suwalth. They'd been so close! Suwalth ran over, laughing with relief. At least Louisa *thought* he was laughing. His whole body was shaking.

They started on again, heads bent in submission to the rain. If she hadn't paused to shift Emily Inez in her arms and been forced to look up, she would have missed the light coming from the Bells' cabin. She reached out and grabbed David's shirtsleeve.

Gratefully, David and Suwalth agreed to stop at the Bells'. Five minutes later Mr. Bell answered the door, and was stunned to find three dripping-wet figures staring numbly out of the rain at him, a baby too. Watch didn't wait for recognition, he burst through the door and headed straight for the hearth. He shook himself furiously, water flying everywhere.

"Can we come in?" asked David.

Mr. Bell stepped back, still too stunned to speak. But as the apparitions tripped over themselves and stumbled over the threshold, he came to himself.

"By all means! Here, let me get the fire going!" He crossed the room in a hurry, shooed Watch from the hearth, and started throwing on new logs. "Laura!" he hollered up the loft. "Come down and take the baby! She looks like a drowned kitten, and mewing like one too!" Laura, thirteen years old, the eldest of the Bells' five children, rattled down the ladder and took over Emily Inez, letting Louisa clumsily tear off her own soaking clothes. Suwalth and David followed suit, everyone else in the cabin politely turning their backs until they got themselves wrapped in scratchy, but dry, blankets. Mrs. Bell was at the stove, her head over a steaming bucket, breathing a bitter-smelling herbal concoction Dr. Smith had prescribed for her consumption. She hastily patted her damp face dry and put the kettle on. The other girls—Olive, Virginia, and Alvina—one by one peered groggily down from their beds in the loft. Austin, the baby, in his trundle bed in one of the back corners, slept through the babel of voices and exclamations of surprise.

Louisa, sitting before the fire and unable to get warm, heard the story, along with the Bells. Suwalth, David said, had been pretending friendship with the Klikitats and other Yakima all summer long in order to keep abreast of their movements. This afternoon when the Klikitats came in from the Swale, they said they weren't going to wait for the Sound Indians to help them anymore. They were going to start killing every outlying settler that night.

"Oh, my," gasped Sally Bell, the red spots on her cheeks growing redder against her paling skin. "Are we safe staying here?"

"We don't have much choice," David told her. "The rain would kill you, Sally. Bill, you're a good shot with a gun. Can you keep a post all night? I've got to go back out there with Suwalth and see that Mercer is warned."

"Of course," said Bill gravely.

"Oh, but you can't!" wailed Sally, beseeching David.

David looked to Louisa.

Had the war come? Was it here? she wondered, searching his strained, worried face. *Is it too late to warn Mr. Mercer and the girls?* And what of them? How were they to manage here? All these children and only Mr. Bell to protect them against bloodthirsty savages?

She swallowed down the ache in her throat. "You do have to go. But we'll be all right," she whispered painfully. *David, oh, David, don't go back out there!*

Sally started to cry. The girls up in the loft started to cry too. Louisa, alarmed at the turn in affairs, sat up straight. "Let's try to find the rainbow," she said firmly, surprised to hear Ma's strong voice in her own. "If we forget our blessings we'll scare ourselves silly. Right off, I'd say our first blessing is Suwalth. In fact, if we had a short word of prayer, right now, we could thank God for Suwalth and his timely intervention. There's no use in worrying over what *might* happen, better to be grateful for the salvation we know *has* happened."

"I agree," said Mr. Bell before she had time to realize her forwardness. "We have more to be thankful for than to be frightened of. Girls, come on down, all of you, come sit on my knee. Laura, see that Emily Inez stays warm. And if no one minds," he said, three little girls piling into his lap, "I'd like to say the prayer."

No one minded. They all bowed their heads where they were, everyone gathered around the warming fire, and Louisa, holding David's hand, listened to Mr. Bell's steady, quiet voice as he spoke to God in their hour of peril. Suddenly, in a warm rush of gratitude, she thought how good, how wonderful, to have these friends! Here, in the middle of a godforsaken wilderness, they were nonetheless surrounded by Christian families . . . and dear, kind, brave natives like Suwalth!

And was Suwalth their only friend? A thousand times no! There was Jim! George! Seattle! Curley! Yoke-Yakeman! Klapki-latchi! Lachuse! Pat Kanim! Names and faces flashed before her like a whole army calling muster.

How could they fear, protected as they were by so many of God's angels?

PART 6

War Drums

Although the real plotting that was going on among the Indians was not discovered by the settlers, there were hints of it and even warnings all through the summer. But the pioneers had grown used to this undercurrent of fear and that was one reason why they were not more alert to the imminent danger at this time.

This sense of danger had become a part of the very life on the frontier—a nameless dread of something unseen and lurking in the shadows. Referring to the hardships of that period, the sweetbriar bride said in after years, "I wouldn't go through it again if you were to give me the whole state of Washington."

—Roberta Frye Watt, Katy Denny's daughter
in *Four Wagons West*

25

Saturday, September 14, 1855

The five [miners] were met by Indians, who pretended to be friendly, and deceived the whites into believing they were on the wrong trail. Jamieson and Walker went ahead to be shown the route . . .

—Clarence Bagley
in *History of Seattle*

Walker, Avery, Jamieson, Merilet, and Barier had little trouble following the widened road over Snoqualmie Pass, but when they reached the Yakima River they found that the rumors they'd heard of having to cross it seventy-two times were likely to prove correct.

At first they merely pulled off their shoes and stockings to wade across. But as they descended, the river swelled both in depth and width, and they had to take off their pants in order to get over without getting completely soaked. This had to be done so many times and with such a loss of time

247

in dressing and undressing that they finally decided to remain on the north bank and cross only when compelled. On foot, they could hug the bank more closely, they figured, than a train of horses. And if they lost the road? Avery was an old navigator. He'd taken the bearings of Fort Colville from the maps before starting out. He was confident so long as he could see the sun by day, or the moon, North Star, and Aldebaran by night that they had no fear of getting lost.

They left the river several days later and pressed on in a northeasterly direction, soon coming to a large, well-traveled road, all the tracks going one way. Had the tracks run both ways they would have followed one way or the other until meeting someone, but as the tracks went only the one direction, *farthest from their course,* they resolved to cross over the road and keep to their own.

They traveled all afternoon, the ground rising rapidly beneath their feet, but it was bare prairie ground and so they had little trouble traversing the terrain. That night, however, away from the river, they suffered terribly for want of water; their bread and salt pork had produced a terrible thirst. They pushed on through the dark, staggering with fatigue and desperate misery, in hopes of finding water. Exhaustion eventually forced them to stop.

At daylight they hastened on, their thirst driving them forward without waiting for breakfast. Three hours later, wondering if they might expire from prostration, they finally espied some small timber and bushes. Girding their wits, they pushed on, finding not only water, but a trail. They stayed here for some time. But when rested—and their enthusiasm regained—they decided to take this new trail; it ran nearly the direction they wanted to go. They would, they agreed, see where it might take them.

By late afternoon they reached the edge of an almost-perpendicular precipice. Before them, a thousand feet down, they saw one of the loveliest panoramas the human eye could hope to behold. As far as the eye could see was a lush green field, level as a floor. A river, like a silver ribbon, extended north to south in beautiful curves and appeared no larger from where they stood than a man could jump across. The Columbia!

"I will remember this day the rest of my life," said Jamieson with great content, taking in the beauty with hungry eyes. "What day is it, anyway?"

"Saturday," someone answered.

"No, the *date*."

"Fourteenth, I think."

"Have you ever seen anything prettier?" sighed Jamieson. "Something to write home about, ain't it? Saturday, September 14, 1855, Dear Ma . . ."

While gazing on the scene, they spotted some objects close to the river. Walker, who had the best eyes, squinted across the distance of ten miles and said they were Indian houses. The moving objects, he said, were horses grazing on the plain.

So far, danger from the Indians had not troubled their thoughts. Since leaving the other side of the mountains, eight or ten days previous, they'd not seen a single human being, Indian or white. Now here was evidence of life, and whether they were to meet friend or foe was a pivotal question.

Their provisions were getting low; yet if they had reason to think their lives were in danger, they had enough food to retrace their steps back to Seattle. They'd heard the rumors, of course, before leaving, but as there was no verified information, they'd determined to come. To go home now, after having come so far—and with no further information to sway them—would indeed seem foolish.

Leading down from the precipice was a switchback trail. "Shall we?" asked Jamieson, hefting his pack.

"Might as well meet our fate," agreed Avery. With that they began the descent.

At the bottom they could see nothing of the river, nor the Indian village. They struck out toward the east, figuring they'd sooner or later come across both. An hour later they saw an Indian on horseback. On seeing them, the Indian rode up. They couldn't understand each other, though, and the Indian galloped away.

"What do you think?" asked Walker, curiously watching the green grass spring back up, leaving no trace of horse or rider.

"Didn't seem like such a bad fellow to me," remarked Jamieson.

"Shall we go on?"

Avery took a step forward. The others fell in line. Within minutes, the gallop of horses could be heard, and over the horizon rode their new friend, with several others. Two had guns.

"We're at their mercy," said Charles Walker steadily. "Our safety depends on showing we have perfect confidence in them and fear no danger."

One of the Indians spoke Chinook. They were on the wrong trail, he bluntly told the miners. To get to Fort Colville they had to cross the river, and the best place to cross was downriver, at an Indian camp. There they could get a scout to guide them part of the way back up the Columbia. They would need a guide, he said, for a long section of the trail had no water. Where there *was* water, it couldn't be found without a guide. "If you want," he volunteered, "we'll show you back to the other trail."

Jamieson and Walker, being the faster walkers and more able to keep up with the horses, soon left Barier, Merilet, and Avery far behind. Back across the grass they all traipsed, back up the zigzagging trail, up, up the high, steep precipice.

"How far are we going to have to go?" lamented Barier when they got to the top. The only evidence of Jamieson and Walker along the dusty trail ahead were footprints intermingled with Indian pony hoofprints.

Avery mopped the sweat off his face. In an hour, he knew, dusk would be upon them. They'd be cold enough then.

Merilet grumped, "We probably have to go all the way back to where we found water this morning."

Night had all but closed in when they finally came into the small timber. Soon they passed a familiar patch of hazel brush. "Like I said, right back where we started," grumped Merilet.

"Maybe Jamieson and Walker had enough sense to stop at our watering hole," said Avery. "I hope so. We can find the other trail in the morning."

"Ah, maybe they have supper cooking!" fantasized Barier. "Maybe they caught a rabbit or two and we eat good tonight!"

They came to another clump of hazel brush, very close to their earlier campsite. They passed on around, and nearly tripped over Jamieson's lifeless body on the trail.

But no, he wasn't dead! Avery, Barier, and Merilet dropped to their knees beside him.

"Boys," gasped Jamieson. "Look out for yourselves. I've been shot; Walker is dead." Avery quickly lifted their comrade, hoping to ease his breathing. But blood gushed out of his mouth and he went limp.

"He's dead too," said Avery.

David, Louisa, and other settlers who'd come hastily into town the night of September 7 wondered over the next few days if they'd "jumped the gun." One day passed, two . . . yet nothing untoward happened. Mr. Bell and David, having snuck out once to their claims to check on things, felt brave enough the second day to take out Tom's wagon and begin hauling back some of the important items; Louisa's chickens, the Bells' two cows, their basic food stuffs, flour, sugar, other items their wives needed from the house.

Mr. Mercer went home. He said someone had to keep the fire burning in David's smokehouse or the whole town would be smelling like rotten fish when the wind blew from that direction. Henry left, too, leaving his mother with Ellender at the mansion. He worried about his apples. Any day now they'd be ripe; he didn't want them falling onto the ground and getting bruised.

The farmers along the Duwamish River went home as well: Luther and Diane Collins, the Buckleys, Henry Van Asselt, Bennet Johns and his six children, Eli Maple, Mr. Lewis, Dr. Grow, Tim Grow, George Holt, August Hogrove. No one could afford to lose a year's crops—except Charles Walker and John Avery, who'd already abandoned everything to go to the gold mines.

Abbie Jane and Ed Hanford, though, did not return to their claim south of the Point. They moved their four boys into a little house up on Fourth and James, not far from Widow Holgate. She was Abbie Jane's mother, and the closer proximity of their two families suited them all just now. The Bells stayed put too, handily moving into Dobbins and Anna's house. David and Louisa tried to view this as a holiday and swept out their "inside" house. Everyone struggled to adjust, and everyone, those who stayed as well as those who went back, wondered if they'd done the right thing.

The week passed on and slipped into the next, summer fading warmly into another colorful Indian summer. The "inside" settlers, those who lived permanently in town, went about their business: working the mill, minding their stores, onloading or offloading cargos of oceangoing ships. The "outside" settlers who'd gone back to their claims kept busy, dawn to dusk. The virgin soil, fed for thousands of years by primeval forests, coupled with the long hot summer, had produced crops of such size it was scarcely believable.

Luther Collins had cabbages weighing in at forty-two pounds. Turnips came in at twenty-nine pounds. Beets were twenty-nine pounds as well, apples were four pounds, onions two pounds. His apples and peaches measured sixteen inches in circumference and he had over 200,000 apple, peach, pear, and cherry trees for sale in his nursery. Vegetables, of all varieties, he shipped out to all points around the Sound, along with chickens and eggs, pigs, dairy products, and beef cattle. Captain Parker's *Traveler* logged many miles, transporting a lot of peas and potatoes.

David and Louisa tried not to think about their empty house and abandoned gardens, though they did what they could. Each morning, David took Watch and went out to the claim to pick produce and do some weeding—and monitor his smokehouse. Louisa faithfully canned what he could bring in until pretty soon she had close to five dozen jars of green beans, yellow beans, peas, carrots, chard, beets, tomatoes. The lettuce and radishes and what was left of August's strawberries they ate fresh each day as he brought them.

"This strikes me as going about things the hard way," he told her one night during supper. They sat at their little table, overlooking the Sound.

"*Sum-muckle* and enjoy the view," she said.

He laughed and reached over to tug her ear. "You're a pickle, Louisa Denny, telling your husband to shut up."

"Pickles! I almost forgot, that's what you have to get me tomorrow. Cucumbers! Mary Ann says Mr. Williamson got some dill weed in yesterday and if you give me two cents I can get some."

"Dill pickles this winter?" His eyes lit up.

"Yes. Bring me everything that's ripe, and I'll have Catherine Maynard and Mary help me. We're going to split three ways."

"Did Parker get in today with the mail?" he asked suddenly.

"Yes. But nothing for us. I was hoping we'd hear from Dobbins."

"You know I don't like you going down to Plummer & Chase . . . now that they serve liquor."

"How else am I going to get our mail?"

"I told you, let me do it."

"Oh pooey, you sound like Arthur."

"Oh *pooey*, probably because we both have strong views on the subject."

253

"David," she said pointedly, "the drinking is downstairs. The post office is upstairs. If you want, when I go past the stairs, I won't look. How's that? I'll even plug my ears, if you wish. That way I won't hear things a lady shouldn't."

He gave up. "How about a paper? Did we get one?"

"Yes. We even got the latest issue, the one that came out last Saturday." She sat up a little and pulled out the September 14 issue of the *Pioneer & Democrat*.

"You were sitting on it?"

"Where else was I supposed to put it? It's so crowded in here!"

He laughed. "You're going to get newsprint ink on your bottom!" He took the paper. "Any word on Colonel Anderson or any of the other miners?"

"No, and the editors say Colonel Anderson was due back a fortnight ago."

"What about Europe?"

"The Allies gained the Sea of Azoff, they captured four Russian steamers and 240 of their supply vessels."

"Maybe this is the beginning of the end?" he asked.

"I hope so. Should we take our peaches and cream down to the beach?"

This was Emily Inez's clue she could join the conversation. "Mama 'n my built playhouse, Papa!"

"Yes, out of the driftwood," said Louisa.

"We had tea! With Angemeen!"

"Did you have sugar?" he asked her.

"My have two, Papa!"

"Two! And *who* is spoiling *you?*"

A few minutes later, straddling a high log and listening to the waves, David spooned Luther Collins's sliced peaches into Emily Inez's open mouth. Louisa had already finished her dessert and was walking along the beach, looking for baby crabs under the tidal rocks. How pleasant to be on the water again, he thought to himself. The salt air was so strong tonight he could taste it. But how long could they go on like this, he wondered, living in town when so much needed to be done on the claim? Maybe Tom was right. The Klikitat seemed to have retreated. Foiled, had they gone back to their own kind? To lend what trouble they could on the other side of the mountains? Maybe he and Louisa should go back to the claim. But then again, she was expecting, and he didn't want her to risk any further night flights into town. One had been bad enough.

Down toward town, past the clutter of Indian shacks—and floating just offshore—was his last winter's timber. Still waiting to be cut. He and Tom had made a big raft to keep everything from going out with the tide, linking the stoutest of logs together with rope and light boom-chains, making a circle, or "fence." Inside the fence the rest of his timber floated. A rather primitive log boom, to be sure, and he wished Yesler would hurry up or he and Louisa stood a good chance of losing their whole season's work.

It had happened before. Strickler, Carr, Ross, and McNatt out at Salmon Bay had lost everything, their boom some-how coming apart while rafting down the shoreline to the mill. Their logs had been washing up all summer long, in Seattle, over at Alki, across the Sound, clear down at Olympia.

"Katy!" chirped Emily Inez all of a sudden. Arthur's children had discovered them and were scrambling down the clay embankment. Emily Inez, no longer interested in her peaches, climbed down and ran off to play. David finished the peaches and set the empty bowl aside, content to be alone in the late summer stillness and watch the children. Watch and Moreover romped in and out of the water, carry-ing back the sticks the older girls tossed out for them to catch.

"Hey, there!"

He turned a little, to watch Arthur come down from their houses.

"What do you think of going out next Sunday to check on the wagon road? See if there's a way we can improve it?"

"Are you out of your mind?"

255

"I don't think so," said Arthur, sitting down on the log carefully and leaning forward, elbows on his knees.

"If I go anywhere," David told him, "it'll be back home. *Not* the mountains . . ."

"No harm in asking. Some of us have decided to do it."

"Who?"

"Lander and Butler. We're going to meet Bigelow at Black River."

"You're *all* crazy."

"That's what Mary says," said Arthur, sighing. "But nothing seems to be happening, at least not around here. Quiet as a church mouse, with the Klikitat gone. And I didn't get to go on the first trip. I want to see what they did, what more can be done."

"You're crazy," David repeated.

"We leave Sunday. You're sure you don't want to come along? It's not like you're doing anything here."

That made him angry. "You're crazy," he said.

26

Monday, September 23, 1855

Notwithstanding the evidences of savage unrest, the rumor of pending war, the settlers of Puget Sound were enterprising and ambitious. In the summer of 1855 Judge Edward Lander, A. A. Denny, and Hillory Butler left Seattle to inspect the wagon road over the Cascade Mountains, hoping to find ways of improving it.

—Dr. Edmond Meany
in *History of the State of Washington*

Monday morning, September 23, proved to be exasperating. Louisa had decided to roast some green beans to make coffee, and since Katy and Nora loved the aroma they'd come over to help.

She put them to work beating the egg whites while she stirred the beans constantly, to prevent their burning. When they were nicely browned she mixed in the egg whites. Katy and Nora crowded in close, sniffing, searching for the first hint of the rich scent to come. The browned beans sizzled a little and Louisa gave them another stir, then set them aside to cool.

"You can take turns doing the grinding," she told the girls, "*after* we clean the lamp chimneys."

In the excitement, Katy somehow managed to break a chimney, then Nora spilled dogfish oil all over her dress. These minor catastrophes Louisa dealt with. But then the girls managed to tilt the small coffee grinder while singing "Ainery mainery, Dibberty Dick, Deedy Didey, Domonick, Howchy powchy, High Pon Towch" at the top of their lungs. The precious drawer of ground beans all spilled onto their laps and down onto the floor. This was too much! Louisa snapped, "I swear, I need the patience of Job this morning! What is the matter with you girls?"

"Oh, Auntie, it smells SO good," said Nora, unbothered.

"Here." Louisa handed them both a sheet of newspaper. "Dump what you have in your skirts onto the paper, then see what you can save from the floor."

Katy, appalled, stared down at the earthen floor. "You can't mean that!" she said.

"A little dirt," said Louisa crossly, "never hurt anyone—"

"Wait until I tell Mother, she will be perfectly astonished at you, Aunt Louisa!"

"Oh, Mrs. Denny, oh, Mrs. Denny!"

Louisa hurried to the open door. Mrs. Butler was coming up the trail from Mary Ann's house, her Southern skirts swaying like an upside-down flower, her silly little parasol bobbing over her head.

"Oh, Mrs. Denny, oh, Mrs. Denny, you *are* home!" cried Mrs. Butler, her voice screeching up the path ahead of her. Louisa dashed out to see what was the matter. "Oh, Mrs. Denny," the Virginian woman gasped, taking hold of Louisa's arm, panting hard. "The worst thing—you can't imagine! Just the worst!"

"You better come inside."

"Oh, but I can't walk, I can't walk another step! I've run all the way!"

Somehow the woman did manage a few more steps, and Louisa got her into a chair, wondering what could be worse than the bad news already received this last week. Colonel Anderson had returned, but joy over his safe arrival had been short-lived; Henry Mattice *was* dead. So were upwards of seventy-five other miners, not eight—all ambushed and brutally murdered. Friday last, acting governor Mason had ordered Yakima Indian Agent Mr. Bolon up from The Dalles to investigate. Agent Bolon set off for St. Joseph Mission on the Yakima River, close to where Kamiakin lived. This morning, rumor had it that Agent Bolon stupidly went into Yakima country alone.

Katy, still brushing the coffee beans stuck to her skirt onto the paper, took one look at Mrs. Butler and said, "Should we take Emily Inez down to the beach, Auntie?"

"Yes, if you would. Now, Mrs. Butler," said Louisa just as soon as the girls were gone. "What is it? Whatever has happened?" She pulled up a chair and sat down opposite the distraught woman, taking both her hands.

"It's just so frightening, I don't know where to start," blubbered Mrs. Butler, retrieving her hands to fish down inside her bosom for her handkerchief. "Your sister isn't home—"

"No . . . she took the boys over to Abbie Jane's."

"Though I don't know why I came to tell her! She can't do anything, except get all worked up like me! But someone's got to go after our husbands! Someone has to, I tell you! The Indians are on the warpath! Three miners—" She choked back a sob. "Mr. Avery, that nice man from the Collins Settlement, do you know him?"

Louisa nodded.

"He just came in, him and two others I never heard of— in worse shape than I ever saw a human being. Skeletons! Walking skeletons! Ten days without food, covered with scratches, sores so bad you can scarce see their faces! Doc Maynard's got them now, down at his house. I suppose—"

"Mrs. Butler," said Louisa quietly, "there were four other miners with Mr. Avery when they left. Where are the other two? *Where's Mr. Walker?*"

"You don't know? No, of course you don't know!" and Mrs. Butler started to bawl again, tears flooding her eyes and running down her cheeks. "*That's what I came to tell you!* The Indians killed them, that's what, and Mr. Avery and the others had to escape for their lives! They've been hiding in the woods by day, creeping through the woods by night. Ten days and ten nights! It makes my heart faint just to think what they've been through, and now my husband is walking right into the same thing! Him and Arthur Denny and Mr. Lander, I mean Judge Lander—Do you see? I'm so upset I can't even keep names straight—"

A shadow fell across the table and Louisa sprang up. "Oh, David, did you hear?"

"Yes. Hello, Mrs. Butler." He came in and helped himself to a slice of bread. "You've got nothing to worry about, Mrs. Butler," he said calmly. "They left yesterday, and can't have gone far. They were to stay the night with Henry Van Asselt, then go on down to Black River to meet Dr. Bigelow. I'll send Yoke-Yakeman and Klap-ki-latchi after them."

"Oh, dear," said Mrs. Butler breathlessly, wringing her hands. "But can we trust *Indians?*"

"It's a trying time," David told her gently. "But if you can look past a man's skin to his heart . . ."

"Oh, Mr. Denny, I'm sorry, I keep forgetting how fond you are of them. But to me they seem no different than darkies. They ain't even human, I don't think—" and she was off crying again.

David went around the table, squatted down beside her, and took her hand. "Mrs. Butler, don't you think they're human enough when they're willing to go after fools who should have known better than to take off in these perilous times?"

She sniffed. "Yes, I suppose you are right, Mr. Denny."

"I am right. Now, if you'll excuse me, I better go see what can be done."

"Yes, of course," she sniffed.

When he was gone she dried her eyes, only to start weeping immediately, holding her hanky over her face. "Oh, Mrs. Denny, I'm so ashamed! A body feels positively heathen alongside your husband!"

Louisa picked up the papers off the floor and began to dump the coffee grounds the girls had collected into a bowl. *September 21, 1855 . . . last Saturday's paper. Just another report on the dead miners. And Colonel Anderson's report on the mines. A lot of gold dust, but no quartz bearing gold. Very little slate.*

All that enthusiasm, high hopes, and yet such a vexation to the Indians, she thought. All for nothing.

27

Monday Noon, September 23, 1855

After the escape of the three miners to Seattle in early September, events occurred in rapid and tragic succession. Sinister rumblings like slow approaches of a storm now burst into decided bolts of thunder and flashes of treacherous lightning.

—Roberta Frye Watt, Katy Denny's daughter
in *Four Wagons West*

oke-Yakeman and Klap-ki-latchi, loyal and hardworking employees of Arthur, figured they could get to Black River before tomorrow's dawn. They paddled steadily, with practiced strokes, up the Duwamish to the junction of the White and Black Rivers, keeping a sharp eye peeled for trouble. Even if it meant their lives, they would bring Arthur back to David. There was no point, though, in being blindsided by one of Kamiakin's secret scouts.

At the same time, on the far side of the Cascade Mountain range, pocketed in the folds of the Simcoe Mountains of Yakima country, Agent Bolon was eating his lunch. A small stream meandered past his campsite.

He was annoyed. Yesterday he'd reached St. Joseph Mission near where Kamiakin had his camp, but had found no sign of the head Yakima chief. He hung around for a day, talking with everyone he could. When all efforts failed to locate the old man, he started back this morning for The Dalles. He'd barely traveled a half day and was just sitting down to gnaw on some hardtack when here came Skloom and Qualchin, Kamiakin's chief lieutenant and his nephew. Obviously Kamiakin had no wish to explain himself, yet desired that Bolon do so.

He did. He explained very clearly and in no uncertain terms that he'd come to find out who had murdered Henry Mattice. Also, who else had been killed? And who were the responsible parties?

Skloom skirted the questions. He questioned the agent instead as to why white men were in Yakima country when the land had not yet been paid for, and he told Bolon that Henry Mattice had been killed for defiling Chief Teias's daughter. This was happening too much, Skloom went on, and at the last council, held in Grande Ronde, the Yakima, the Walla Walla, the Cayuses, the Colville, and the Pend d'Oreille Indians had all discussed ways to defend themselves against such intrusions by the whites. "I, myself," Skloom explained, "counseled against war, but most everyone else present was in favor."

"You surely know," said Bolon, sharing his lunch with the two men, "that if war is begun you will be defeated. You also know that the miners are not going into your country to remain but are merely passing through on their way to the far-away gold mines. Near the Pend d'Oreille."

"They have no right to come through our land," repeated Skloom.

"The attacks must stop," Bolon answered firmly. "If they don't, it is fair to warn you that the soldiers will be sent into the valley and war *will* begin. It will also begin if you don't name the murderers and turn them in."

Skloom got to his feet. "Kamiakin says to make sure you get back to The Dalles safely. We will escort you; this is dangerous country for a white man." He glanced over to Qualchin, who stood to his feet.

"Very well. I thank you," said Bolon. He fit his hat down over his red hair, brushed the crumbs off his stomach, then went over to his horse to saddle up. He and Skloom led out, Qualchin behind, and in this way they proceeded in silence for some distance. Suddenly a shot rang out. Bolon felt the bullet hit his back, heard the shattering of bone, then saw the ground rush up to catch his fall. He landed on his face, confused as to what had happened.

Skloom flipped him over. He lay facing up at the sky, a gray sky. Suddenly Qualchin's face appeared over his, upside down. He seized Bolon by the hair, jerked his head back so that his chin pointed straight up. The last thing Bolon saw was the knife. The last thing he heard was the war cry. The last thing he felt was the cold, almost painless slash through his neck, and then the hot rush of his blood jetting God knew where. The last thing he thought was God forgive the poor ignorant savages.

Kamiakin's boast—"BOLON IS DEAD!"—swept through the mountain passes like a cold wind; an icy draft on the heels of Arthur Denny, Judge Lander, Dr. Bigelow, and Hillory Butler as the four men raced back into town, accompanied by Yoke-Yakeman and Klap-ki-latchi. When they arrived, the whole village came out to welcome them, weeping and laughing by turns with relief. Fear soon replaced relief, however, when Kamiakin's boast became known. "BOLON IS DEAD!"

With the boast came rumors of gigantic proportion. When the gruesome details of Bolon's murder were revealed, his throat slit, his body and even his horse burned beyond recognition and left to smoke in a rubble of blackened bones in the Simcoe Mountains, some of the whites in the territory panicked. Mixing rumor with fact, they soon convinced themselves of a massive "general uprising" involving Indians from southern Oregon to Puget Sound. Fifty thousand savages! Marshalling forces! Only a few thousand defenseless whites!

The people in Seattle remained levelheaded; nonetheless the leading citizens quickly divided in response to the obvious presence of the traumatized miners in their midst and the terrifying news of Indians boasting the murder of their own agent. A few insisted there was little need for alarm, not in Seattle. The Klikitats were gone. The only Indians—they could see—were Suwalth's Duwamish. Docile. Dependent upon Mr. Yesler for their livelihood and sustenance.

Yet when "docile" Suwalth—supported by most of the old-timers—recommended precaution, the "do nothings" —mostly newcomers—pointed out it was Suwalth who'd sounded the alarm—*over nothing*—two and a half weeks before.

"Yet if he hadn't gotten us in a flap," Arthur insisted quietly, "something *would* have happened."

Hasty, frequent meetings at the cookhouse continued— until finally a consensus was reached on two courses of action. First, they would request soldiers be sent from Fort Steilacoom into the vicinity of the mountains to protect the scattered settlers along the White River. Second, they would build a blockhouse to protect themselves.

Misters Woodin and Wetmore, leaders of the "do nothings," went back to their tannery and shoe shop uphill on Yesler's "skid road," laughing at David Denny for volunteering his whole season's timber to build an unnecessary fort. Louisa bristled at the ridicule and promptly put them in their place with the tart observation, "People scoffed at Noah when he built the ark!"

Ed Hanford donated the use of his oxen, and supervised the cumbersome task of hauling David's timber up from the water onto the high bluff at the foot of Cherry Street. There, many willing hands put the perfectly hewn logs into place, two stories high, the joints made close. Plans called for a thick shingle roof and two bastions, made of sawn boards from the mill.

"Soon as we finish," said an exhausted David to Louisa on Friday night, September 27, "I'm going to build you another house, closer to the blockhouse. I don't want you and Emily Inez way out here, running—"

"Way out here?" Louisa sat up in bed. "Cherry is only two blocks away, downhill!"

"Two blocks too far," he said, hands behind his neck, staring at the ceiling.

"Don't be a goose. Where are you going to get the money?"

When he didn't answer, she flopped back down beside him on the cedar bough mattress he'd made. "You gave away a whole year's income to build the fort—"

"You'd rather I didn't?" he interrupted, surprised.

"I'm not criticizing—"

"Doc Maynard gave away all those blankets! We each have to do what we can, Liza," he pleaded with her.

"I'm not criticizing; I'm just stating the facts. You gave away a whole year's income, several hundred dollars. We're in debt up to our ears from our trip to Oregon. The house in the Swale, I hate to think what that cost us, *is* costing us. And it's not like Dobbins owns the land near the fort anymore. Judge Lander and Charles Terry—"

"Why don't you let me worry about the money?"

"I can't help it. I *am* worried."

"We have enough worries to trouble us. But I'm not going to let worry over money stop me from doing what's best."

"Maybe that's what I don't understand," she persisted. "Why is it best for us to live next to the blockhouse? We're only two blocks away. Two blocks isn't far."

He sighed. "You're on the nest, *remember?*"

Oh . . . so that was it. Louisa shyly reached over to touch her husband's face. He was remembering her awful run up-hill when Luther Collins hung Masachie Jim, when she was expecting Emily Inez. He was scared something would happen again. He *did* have a lot of things to worry about.

He seized her hand and held it to his mouth. "I'll build you a real floor in the new house," he cajoled, kissing each of her fingers.

She laughed, giving in. "A *real* floor?" she teased him. "*Just when I was getting used to dirt again?*"

"You want dirt? I'll put in a dirt floor Widow Holgate will be proud of."

Widow Holgate had the nicest, coziest little cabin in town. Louisa laughed again and rolled over on top of David. "Oh, I suppose," she said, covering his face with kisses, "that if you're going to go to all that trouble you might as well put in real boards, Mr. Denny."

Kate Blaine, sick with her first pregnancy and unable to sleep, got up out of bed, lit the table lamp, and sat down to write her mother in Syracuse, New York. *Dear Mother,* she scratched onto the waxy blue paper she'd saved from inside the sugar barrel. Her lamp flickered, holding back the shadows.

You will doubtless see by the papers' accounts of more Indian troubles in this territory, but do not give yourself any uneasiness about us. Four men who had started from this place for the gold mines were murdered by the Indians about 150 miles from here. Our Indians, to all appearances, are as friendly as ever, but lest they may be treacherous, they will be watched closely. The people here have sent to Steilacoom for soldiers to protect the scattering settlers in the vicinity of the mountains, across which the Indians lived who committed the murders, in case they should make any hostile demonstrations. We think, however, they know the strength of our people so well they will make no attack on the settlements, but only wish to be cautious and provide against any emergency.

When she reread her letter, Kate knew she was trying to allay *her* fears, not her mother's.

Sixty miles south, in Olympia, Acting Governor Mason, his own night oil burning, sealed two dispatches. He had on his desk a letter from Seattle and a large map of the territory. Circled in ink were the Simcoe Mountains, Yakima country. "Make all haste," Mason told his scouts, handing over the two dispatches. One was to Major Haller at The Dalles, ordering him to march his command north into Yakima country. The other was to Major Maloney of Fort Steilacoom, ordering him to march his forces east into Yakima country. The armies would rendezvous, and their mission was to punish the Indians responsible for Agent Bolon's and Mattice's deaths, and to protect all whites still in the area. "May God go with you," Mason said quietly to the two scouts as they headed out the door. "And may he guide our governor home," he added when they were gone.

East of Olympia, up in the foothills of the Cascade Mountains fifty miles away, on the Sound side of Naches Pass, Alan Porter knew he'd be the first to be molested when the Indians came through: His ranch was situated near the headwaters of White River, in a picturesque valley called Porter's Prairie. Below him, stretching sixteen miles downriver, were sixteen other claims, clear down to Mox La Push where the Black and White Rivers converged to form the Duwamish. When Porter had learned the fate of poor Walker and Jamieson, he'd known then the fate of his downriver neighbors Fanjoy and Eaton. He took to looking over his shoulder wherever he went, and he started sleeping with two loaded guns beside his bed. But when the news came of Agent Bolon's grisly death, Porter could no longer content himself with a wary eye and ready fire. He took to sleeping outdoors, away from his cabin. He did not want his throat slit while sound asleep.

Friday night on the twenty-seventh, he came in late from his fields, having gone out in search of missing cattle. The night was quiet, an autumn chill hung heavy in the air. The moon held little light and he thought to himself that he really ought to start carrying a compass. But not to worry, not tonight, there was his house, the roofline a stark silhouette.

Suddenly he saw movement around his cabin. *Visitors? At this hour?* He hurried forward, wondering who had come to visit his humble ranch at such an ungodly hour. Perhaps they needed shelter. He was cutting across the back field, coming up alongside the barn when it came to him that these were no ordinary visitors. These men were stationing themselves around the house!

Crouching low, he darted forward, gun in hand. Dart and duck, dart and duck. Finally he reached the dark shadow of his barn. Catching his breath, for it came in short, suppressed gusts, he edged up to the far corner and peered around, keeping his body well hidden.

Indians!

He pulled up straight, heart pounding, back pressed tightly against the wall. Indians . . . they were here . . . at his house . . . everything he'd feared. Somewhere in all his fears, though, he hadn't thought about what to do when it happened. *What* do *I do?* he wondered in panic.

There was only one thing. He had to abandon his ranch and head downriver, warning his neighbors as he went. *Like Paul Revere of the Revolution eighty years ago,* he thought grimly.

Without waiting further, he retraced his steps, away from the house, the barn, back out through the trees. He took the long way down to the river, then had to furtively creep back up along the riverbank, up past his house, to where his canoe lay upside down on a sandy shore. He got it flipped over and into the water. He pushed off; trembling, he eased himself down flat along the boat's narrow bottom. If spotted, he wanted the Indians to think this was just another canoe slipped from her mooring.

He started to count to twenty, the river bouncing him quickly along. At twenty he would sit up and start paddling. At the count of ten he heard an owl. At fifteen another owl. At eighteen he bolted straight up, heart in his throat, a knee-jerk reaction to the bloodcurdling cry ripping through the night, stopping his heart and nearly wrenching his ears clean off. He scrambled to his knees, canoe tipping, grabbed his paddle and dug in. Jim Riley! He had to get to Jim's place, he had to warn him!

All night long down the river. First Riley, then Corcoran, then David Neely and family. Robert Beatty. John Thomas and bride. Henry Adams. Joseph Lake. Arnold Lake. Sam Russell and family. William Cox and family. Moses Kirkland and family. Enos Cooper. Harvey Jones and family. George King and family. Will and Elizabeth Brannan and baby. At Mox La Push he let Charles Brownell take over. Brownell knew the Duwamish River settlers better.

He was too tired, too tired to get in and out of his canoe anymore, too tired to stumble up to yet another darkened house, too tired to rasp out one more time, "The Indians are coming! The Indians are coming!" He was too tired to keep his head up as he paddled down the Duwamish.

He must have slept, the current carrying him. Because when he woke, the canoe was bobbing gently in the mouth of the Duwamish. In the distance, five miles across the bay to the northeast, was Seattle.

The sky, a pale splash of beckoning pink, had just begun to lighten behind the still-dark trees. Smoke from the mill spoke of habitation, of solidity, of safety. He was here, he'd made it! He seized his paddle with new energy, and a half hour later Alan Porter slid the nose of his canoe onto the beach even as the sun burst forth upon the day, a startling blood red. Mr. Yesler, sitting outside his cookhouse, paused his whittling to gape.

28

Saturday, September 28, 1855

. . . on the night of September 27, 1855, he saw some men stop at his house. Thinking they were white men needing shelter he hurried forward, and was nearly on them when he discovered that they were Indians. It did not take him long to realize that they had come to murder him. Not finding him, they attacked his house.

Then, like Paul Revere, he hurried down the river, his steed a swift canoe, warning the settlers as he fled toward Seattle. All of them soon followed and came into the village, frightened refugees, forced to leave their homes and gardens, all the fruit of their toil to the Indians. It was sickening news to the settlers in Seattle.

—Roberta Frye Watt, Katy Denny's daughter
in *Four Wagons West*

Fifteen families from White River, plus another eight from the Duwamish, flooded into Seattle all day Saturday. Panic-stricken, their only thought being to reach the safety of their own kind, they abandoned everything to hurry down the rivers, traveling by foot or by canoe. When the *Water Lily* arrived from Olympia, Captain Terry heard the news and immediately reversed engines, steamed back across the Bay to head up the Duwamish River to pick up any stragglers.

The Felker House filled first. Then the Latimer Boardinghouse. Pioneers quickly opened their homes. The Butlers' southern hospitality accommodated three families. Arthur and Mary Ann took in the Neelys. David and Louisa welcomed Will and Elizabeth Brannan and their one-year-old baby girl.

Elizabeth could not stop weeping. David said he was sorry, but he had to leave them and get back to the blockhouse. Will said he'd lend a hand. "I really am sorry, Liza," David whispered, kissing her good-bye, glancing one more time to the bed where the terrified English woman cowered under the covers with her baby. "But we still have to get the rafters up, the roof—"

"Don't worry. We'll be all right."

Louisa let Elizabeth cry; it was all she could do for the distraught woman. She kept herself busy by baking. If they had to go to the cookhouse tonight—the cookhouse being the emergency plan until the blockhouse was completed—they would at least go with some bread. She also packed an emergency basket, filling it with bandages, herbs, a sharp knife, scissors, a needle and thread. In another basket she packed a spare set of clothes for both families. David's shirts would be too big for Will. But better too big than too small. Into Emily Inez's tiny basket she packed her daughter's most precious toys: her wooden blocks, her rag doll, a whistle. Suddenly Elizabeth sat up.

"I will kill Doris before I let the Indians have her!"

Louisa dropped what she was doing. Emily Inez, playing under the sink, looked up.

"I will!" declared Elizabeth fiercely, hugging her baby to her breast and staring at Louisa with eyes swollen almost shut by exhaustion and tears.

Louisa quietly sat on the bed. "Is that what you call her?" she asked, holding out her arms to take the frightened child. But Elizabeth shrank back, away from Louisa.

"Elizabeth," said Louisa gently, "let me take Doris for a little time. You're exhausted. You need to sleep."

"I can't sleep! The Indians are coming!" screamed Elizabeth, shrinking farther back and scrambling up against the head of the bed.

Dear Lord, what am I going to do with her?

"I will kill anyone who tries to touch her, I will kill myself, I will kill us both first, but I won't let them have her!" sobbed Elizabeth in her clipped accent.

Louisa got up and fetched David's extra gun off the mantel. She laid it on the table next to her rising bread. "Elizabeth," she said, "I won't let them get Doris. You go to sleep. If need be, I'll shoot the first Indian to cross my door."

She could see Elizabeth thinking it through.

"Can you shoot?" she asked.

"If I don't have to shoot far, I can."

"You promise?" pleaded Elizabeth.

"Would I let harm come to my own child?"

Elizabeth looked over to the sink. Emily Inez pounded two pots together and smiled.

"Your baby is soaking wet," said Louisa. "Let me change her diapers. She's getting you wet, and she's getting my bed wet."

"Oh! I beg your pardon," said Elizabeth, starting to come around.

"Never mind that. I just want to make your baby more comfortable. I'm surprised she hasn't brought the roof down by now, in holy protest."

She hardly had Doris's wet nightgown off before Elizabeth, eyes finally closing, was fast asleep. Poor dear frightened woman, thought Louisa, covering her friend with blankets and tucking them in. It must have been a horrifying night, even worse than when she and David had fled for town. At least they'd had Suwalth, and only two miles to go. Not twenty.

"So your name is Doris," she said, looking down with a smile at the little girl who stared up with solemn blue eyes. A tiny little thing, and so sweet. "Emily Inez, come see the baby."

Emily Inez toddled over and stood up on her toes to see over the edge of the bed.

"I'm going to give her a bath," said Louisa. "Can she play with your duck, Emily Inez?"

"No," said Emily Inez, happily diving under the bed to fetch from her toy box said wooden duck, whittled by Mr. Yesler.

An hour later, Louisa sat on her front stoop with both babies, showing them how to draw circles in the dirt with some sticks she'd given them. Anything to keep them occupied while she rested a minute. This was hard work, having two children underfoot. But not nearly so hard, she realized, as trying *not* to think about the danger closing in.

For now that she had time to think, fear began to gnaw at her heart. Their situation was perilous, and growing more so all the time. They were woefully unguarded. Behind them was the forest, possibly hiding any numbers of hostile Indians. In front was the Bay, cutting off escape. And there were so few of them; scarcely two hundred souls even with today's influx. And how many thousands of Indians?

Two blocks away, the men worked feverishly on the blockhouse. She could hear their hammers, their shouted instructions, their saws whining through the thick boards from Mr. Yesler's mill. Had Mr. Wetmore and Mr. Woodin decided to help? She hoped so. For though the men worked rapidly, it was obvious to her they had a long way to go before the fort would be anywhere near done.

She tried to think back to the last big Indian scare; when Mr. Collins hung his third Indian. But that scare was nothing next to this! *Even so, how had she seen it through? Where had she gotten her courage? Her strength?* Ahead lay the Olympic Mountains, their jagged white peaks easily visible in today's clear sky.

. . . I will lift up mine eyes unto the hills, from whence cometh my help? My help comes from the Lord, who made heaven and earth. Unbidden, Psalm 121 came back to her. *He will not let your foot be moved, he who keeps you will not slumber. Behold, he who keeps Israel, will neither slumber nor sleep—*

"Hello, Mrs. Denny."

Louisa started up. "Widow Holgate!"

"I scared you, I'm sorry."

"I'm a little jumpy today."

"We all are."

"You caught me thinking of an old psalm. My mind was a million miles away."

"Oh, which one?" asked Seattle's only Baptist.

"Psalm 121."

"My favorite!" declared Widow Holgate, and she clapped her hands together under her chin.

Louisa scooted over on the stair to make room. "I'm not sure I understand it," she confessed as the widow sat down. "Bad things, terrible things, happen to people, Christian people. Like the Ward party on the Snake River last fall. Those poor women and children, tortured to death by the Indians. But for some reason, when I dwell on the passage I'm comforted. *Do you think me foolish?*"

"Not at all," said Widow Holgate, patting Louisa's knee. "Do you think Jesus understood Psalm 121 very well when he was hanging on his cross?"

"I hadn't looked at it that way before. But no, I don't suppose he did."

"We don't have to understand, my dear, to be comforted. The peace of God passeth all understanding, that's what the Good Book tells us."

"Mighty good thing too," said Louisa, looking out to the mountains again.

"Louisa, my dear, I just came to invite you and Elizabeth to my house tonight for prayer and Bible study. I'm inviting all the ladies. We'll meet again in the morning—if we're still alive."

Louisa turned to look at her.

"I've decided to do this *every* morning . . . until God should send us help."

"Widow Holgate, what a wonderful idea!"

"You must bring Emily Inez, if it's not past her bedtime. The children can learn right along with the rest of us how God intends to do this thing."

"Oh, *thank you*, Widow Holgate. Thank you! What time?"

"Seven."

While the men worked round the clock on the blockhouse and the women prayed, Major Haller on the far side of the territory readied his men to march out. Finally, Thursday morning, October 3, they were ready to go: 107 officers and men, mounted; a pack train, with enough provisions for a month; a howitzer. They marched northward out of The Dalles, toward the Simcoe Mountains of Yakima country.

From Fort Steilacoom that same day, October 3, Major Lieutenant Slaughter was working his way up White River with a detachment of forty soldiers.

In Seattle, that night, a shot rang out.

The whole village ran pell-mell from their houses into the dark, in all manner of undress—nightshirts, pants, blankets. With shoes, without shoes. Mr. Butler threw on his wife's red petticoat. Some ran for the cookhouse, others for the incomplete blockhouse.

David and Louisa, Will, Elizabeth, Arthur and Mary Ann, the whole Neely family—they ran down First Street in a frenzied panic, tripping over each other in their frantic effort to keep track of the children lest one get lost or left behind. When Arthur finally pushed them all into the blockhouse, Louisa looked up and saw the stars. She knew then it was over. This was how they would die.

For a few minutes she listened to the harsh, frightened breathing of the pioneers, whose faces she could barely discern in the starlight, and the soft whimpering of the children crowding up against their parents. Waves lapped the beach below. Everything else seemed strangely silent. Louisa suddenly wondered if they'd run out here for nothing. Where was the gunfire? The war cries?

As the minutes passed, others began to wonder the same thing. One by one the men got up to peer out the door.

"Maybe it was a false alarm," suggested David. "What do you say if I sneak down to the cookhouse? See what everyone down there thinks?"

"Oh, David, be careful!" cried Louisa, grabbing the tail of his nightshirt.

"I will."

How long they sat shivering in the night air waiting for David to return, not knowing whether to be scared or relieved, Louisa could only guess. Finally she asked Arthur how long it had been.

"Five minutes," he whispered, Orion asleep on his shoulder. How blessed to be a child!

"Five minutes? That's *all?*" She settled back against the cold logs and waited some more. She'd forgotten her emergency bags. They were at home, by the door. *Where was David?* Had he been ambushed? Was he lying on the Sawdust, his throat slit?

Suddenly, she heard, *"Watchman, tell us of the night, What its signs of promise are—"*

"It's David!" She scrambled to her feet and flew to the door. "Everything must be all right! He's singing!"

"*—Aught for joy or hope foretell? Traveler, yes, it brings the day, Promised*—Hello, folks," said David cheerfully, coming through the doorway and plucking Emily Inez out of Louisa's arms. "We can all go home, false alarm. Plummer was just cleaning his pistols and one went off."

Mr. Bell helped Sally to her feet. "I think I'm going to shoot Mr. Plummer," he said.

It was funny, but no one laughed. Everyone crept home, wondering when the call would be real.

"David, remind me the next time," said Louisa when they were back under the bedcovers and trying to get warm, "to take our bags."

29

Friday Morning, October 4, 1855

Abbie Jane Holgate Hanford told how a little group of pioneer mothers gathered together after Porter's alarm and prayed together that the Lord would send them protection.

—Roberta Frye Watt, Katy Denny's daughter
in *Four Wagons West*

don't know how much longer I can take this," cried Sally Bell the next morning at prayer meeting. "Sometimes I wish the Indians would just hurry up and get it over with. What are they waiting for?"

"Sally Bell, I declare, what kind of thinking is that?" demanded Ursula, horrified.

"I don't know, I just want—" Sally sniffed, and dabbed at her teary eyes and runny nose with her damp hanky. "I just want to get this over with. All this waiting, this wondering..."

"I know what she means," said Abbie Jane. "We're so help-less. We don't know where the Indians are, what they're doing . . ."

Louisa looked around at their small group. Last night's scare had left every one of them with taut nerves. Dark circles ringed their eyes. *We're wearing out from the strain,* thought Louisa. *The babies are too.* One or two of the babies, like Emily Inez, played happily at their feet. But the others sensed the tension and were fretful. In Olivia's room, a small lean-to added behind the back wall, Louisa could hear the older children. Olivia, seventeen years old and the Sunday school teacher at Reverend Blaine's church, was helping them cut pictures from old magazines and paste them into a scrapbook. They, too, were subdued and anxious.

"Whose turn to read our Bible passage today?" asked Kate Blaine.

"Mine." Louisa took a deep breath and looked over to Sally. "Do you remember, Sally, when we first met? That night on the Snake River when my family stumbled onto your campsite?"

"Yes."

"We'd been running all day from some renegades?"

"Yes, I surely do, and a wonder none of you were killed!"

"Do you remember, Mary?" Louisa asked her sister. Mary Ann shuddered, just thinking of it.

"Arrows whizzed right through the canvas," Mary told the others. "If so much as a wagon linchpin had broken, we'd be dead."

"Last night after the scare, I couldn't sleep," Louisa went on. "I got to thinking about that day, then for some reason I got to thinking about Daniel."

"In the lions' den?" asked Kate.

"Probably because right now I can't imagine which is worse—lions or Indians."

A few of the women smiled thinly.

"So I thought we'd read from Daniel," said Louisa. "Maybe we can find some encouragement."

And so while Olivia kindly entertained the children and the mothers each did what they could for their babies, Louisa read. The story was a long one but the women weren't in a hurry. Just being with each other gave them strength. Louisa neared the end.

"Then the king arose very early in the morning, and went in haste unto the den of lions. And when he came to the den, he cried with a lamentable voice unto Daniel, 'O Daniel, servant of the living God, is thy God, whom thou servest continually, able to deliver thee from the lions?'

"'Then said Daniel unto the king, 'O king, live for ever. My God hath sent his angel, and hath shut the lions' mouths, that they have not hurt me: forasmuch as before him innocency was found in me; and also before thee, O king, have I done no hurt.'

"Then was the king exceeding glad for him, and commanded that they should take Daniel up out of the den. So Daniel was taken up out of the den, and no manner of hurt was found upon him, because he believed in his God."

"And no manner of hurt was found upon him, because he believed in his God," echoed Sally.

"We must keep believing," said Abbie Jane. "We can't give in to discouragement."

"We must keep praying," said her mother.

Out on the water, a ship sailed into the Bay before a fair breeze. It was Kate Blaine's turn to pray when the ship backed her yards off Yesler's wharf. Louisa was praying when the crew leaped down and tied off. Abbie Jane, bouncing her baby on her foot, had just begun to pray when the ship fired off her guns, sixteen thirty-two-pounders. The thunderous reverberations rolled up the hill. The women looked up, startled. Ursula ran to the window.

Mary Ann was already there, tears pouring down her face.

"A sloop of war..." Ursula was incredulous. "I declare, an honest to goodness sloop of war!"

Mary Ann smiled, and through her tears she whispered, "Louisa, come look. Our prayers have been answered. We have been saved!"

Before night set in, the blockhouse was finished and armed with two nine-pound cannons, courtesy of Captain Sterrett of the sloop of war *Decatur*. And when night did come, dark and without stars, the soldiers went out on patrol, pacing the woods, circling the Point. At each house they paused and called out, "All's well," and went on. To the pioneers getting ready for bed in their crowded cabins this was unbelievable comfort. They would sleep without fear for the first time in a week.

David and Louisa settled on the floor before their fire, a heavy rug beneath them, blankets on top. After a week of sleeping like this, they were used to it, and they were looking forward to a few minutes together before saying good night. The lamps were out, and their guests were in bed and asleep. The babies were asleep. Watch was dozing, one ear cocked.

"I love you, Liza," David whispered, adjusting their pillows, drawing her into his arms.

"I know you love me."

"Do you love *me?*"

She angled her face to meet his, and smiled.

"Why did you marry a boy?" he asked, bending his face to meet hers.

She answered the way she always did when he asked. "Because there were no men about."

Watch whined.

David groaned. "He always does this," he said as Watch lumbered to his feet and padded over to the door. "Who's going to let him out? You or me?"

"You."

283

He stirred, and she eased out of his arms.

When he opened the door, she noticed the hats. Six of them—hers, Elizabeth's, Will's, David's, the babies'—four sunbonnets and two caps all jammed together on two hooks. Amazingly, none had fallen.

She heard Watch whine again. The door creaked open. Watch padded in. David kicked the door shut with an unnecessary slam and seconds later he was back, slithering in under the covers with a shiver.

"Why did you marry me?" he asked again as she snuggled into his cold arms.

"Because there was no man about?"

"No, you married me because you love me, Liza."

"Because I love you," and she cupped his face with her hands.

Out in the night, two soldiers paused and sang out, "All's well."

He stroked her cheek. "We may live to old age yet, Liza."

"We'll have a whole lifetime of loving each other."

David smiled. Outside the footsteps faded away while inside, jostled by his kick at the door and still swinging, were all six hats—four sunbonnets and two caps.

Epilogue

*Friday,
October 4, 1855*

[I] landed on the 4th of October, in such a position as to command the town. Seattle is the nearest point on the Sound to incursions of Indians far beyond the mountains. I considered it my duty to remain at that place until the citizens could organize some means of defense, as they were almost destitute of arms and entirely without organization. They had commenced a blockhouse, which I caused to be completed and armed with 2 nine-pounders . . .

—Captain Isaac S. Sterrett
U.S. Sloop of War *Decatur*

CAPTAIN Sterrett—ordered from the Sandwich Islands to "cruise the coast between Oregon and California for the protection of the settlers"—had interpreted his orders broadly when he chose to put in to Puget Sound of Washington in the fall of 1855.

A few of the settlers thought it pretty lucky he had.

The others knew better. God had answered the women's prayers.

Bibliography

Bagley, Clarence. *History of Seattle: From the Earliest Settlement to the Present Time.* 3 vols. Chicago: S. J. Clarke, 1916.

Bass, Sophie Frye. *Pig-Tail Days in Old Seattle.* Florenz Clark, artist. Portland, Ore.: Binfords & Mort, 1937.

———. *When Seattle Was a Village.* Florenz Clark, artist. Seattle: Lowman & Hanford, 1947.

Bennet, Robert A., ed. *A Small World of Our Own.* Walla Walla, Wash.: Pioneer Press, 1985.

———. *We'll All Go Home in the Spring.* Walla Walla, Wash.: Pioneer Press, 1984.

Binns, Archie. *Northwest Gateway: The Story of the Port of Seattle.* Portland, Ore.: Binfords & Mort, 1941.

Cleveland High School. *The Duwamish Diary.* Seattle: Seattle Public Schools, 1949.

Denny, Arthur A. *Pioneer Days on Puget Sound.* Seattle: C. B. Bagley, 1883.

Dorpat, Paul. *494 More Glimpses of Historic Seattle.* Seattle: Mother Wit Press, 1982.

———. *Seattle Now and Then.* Seattle: Tartu Publications, 1984.

Downie, Ralph Earnest. *A Pictorial History of the State of Washington.* Seattle: Lowman & Hanford, 1937.

Dryden, Cecil. *Dryden's History of Washington.* Portland, Ore.: Binfords & Mort, 1968.

Eckrom, J. A. *Remembered Drums: A History of the Puget Sound Indian War.* Walla Walla, Wash.: Pioneer Press, 1989.

Glassley, Ray H. *Indian Wars of the Pacific Northwest.* Portland, Ore.: Binfords & Mort, 1972.

Guie, Dean H. *Bugles in the Valley.* Yakima, Wash.: Republic Press, 1956.

Hanford, Cornelius. *Seattle and Environs*. 3 vols. Seattle: Pioneer Historical Publishing, 1924.

Jones, Nard. *Seattle*. New York: Doubleday, 1972.

Karolevitz, Bob. "Seattle Transit." *Seattle Times,* 24 May 1964.

Leighton, George R. *America's Growing Pains*. New York: Harper & Brothers, 1939.

Litteer, Loren K. *Bleeding Kansas*. Kansas: Champion Publishing, 1987.

MacDonald, Norbert. *Distant Neighbors: A Comparative History of Seattle and Vancouver*. Lincoln: University of Nebraska Press, 1987.

MacDonald, Robert. "Railroading in Seattle." *Seattle Sunday Times,* 31 December 1944.

———. "Seattle's Mayors." Bellingham Public Library vertical file: Seattle History.

McDonald, Lucille. "Seattlites Recall Cable Car Days." *Seattle Times,* 19 September 1965.

———. *Washington's Yesterdays*. Portland, Ore.: Binfords & Mort, 1953.

Meany, Edmond S. *History of the State of Washington*. New York: Macmillan, 1950.

Meeker, Ezra. *Pioneer Reminiscences of Puget Sound*. Seattle: Lowman & Hanford, 1905.

———. *Seventy Years of Progress in Washington*. Tacoma: Allstrum Printing, 1921.

Metcalf, James Vernon. *Chief Seattle*. Seattle: Catholic NW Progress, n.d.

Monaghan, Jay. *Civil War on the Western Border*. Lincoln: University of Nebraska Press, 1855.

Morgan, Murray. *Skid Road: An Informal Portrait of Seattle*. Seattle: University of Washington Press, 1951.

Museum of History and Industry. Manuscript files:

    "Battle of Seattle."

    Denny, A. A. Memorial album.

    Denny, Emily Inez. "By the Blazing Shore."

    ———. Biography of Princess Angeline.

    Denny, John. Biography.

    Denny, Louisa Boren. Manuscripts.

    ———. Interviews.

    Denny, Sarah Latimer. *Bass Collection*.

    Graham, Susan Mercer. "Fort at Seattle."

    Kellogg, David. Manuscript.

    Russell, Alonzo. Memoirs.

    Smith, D. H. "Early Seattle."

    Wyckoff, Eugenia McConaha.

    Wyckoff, George McConaha Jr. Letter to mother.

    Yesler, Henry. Letters.

    Yesler, Sarah. Letters.

Nelson, Gerald B. *Seattle: The Life and Times of an American City.* New York: Alfred A. Knopf, 1977.

Newell, Gordon. *Totem Tales of Old Seattle.* Seattle: Superior Publishing, 1956.

———. *Westward to Alki.* Seattle: Superior Publishing, 1977.

Oates, Stephen B. *To Purge This Land with Blood.* Amherst, Mass.: University of Massachusetts Press, 1970.

Pacific Telephone & Telegraph Co. *Growing Together.* Bellingham Public Library vertical file: Seattle History. July 1958.

Peltier, Jerome. *Warbonnets and Epaulets.* Compiled by B. C. Payette. Montreal: Payette Radio, n.d.

Phelps, T. S. *Reminiscences of Seattle: Indian War of 1855–1856.* Seattle: The Alice Harriman Co., 1980.

Pierce, Frank Richardson. "The Bell Rang Nine Times." *Seattle Times,* 9 September 1962.

Pioneer & Democrat, 1854–1855. Suzalo Library, University of Washington.

Prosch, Thomas W. *David S. Maynard and Catherine T. Maynard.* Seattle: Lowman & Hanford, 1906.

Raymond, Steve. "Remember When Seattle Had Cable." *Seattle Times,* 8 August 1965.

Records of King County Clerk: Third Territorial District Court 1852–1889. RBD Washington State Archives, Regional Depository at Bellingham.

Richards, Kent D. *Isaac I. Stevens: Young Man in a Hurry.* Pullman, Wash.: Washington State University Press, 1993.

Rucker, Helen. *Cargo of Brides.* Boston: Little, Brown, 1956.

Sale, Roger. *Seattle: Past to Present.* Seattle: University of Washington Press, 1976.

Snowden, Clinton A. *History of Washington.* New York: The Century History Co., 1909.

Speidel, William. *Doc Maynard: The Man Who Invented Seattle.* Seattle: Nettle Creek Publishing, 1978.

———. *Sons of the Profits.* Seattle: Nettle Creek Publishing, 1967.

Warren, James. *King County and Its Queen City: Seattle.* Historical Society of Seattle and King County. Woodland Hills, Calif.: Windsor Publications, 1981.

We Were Not Summer Soldiers: The Indian War Diary of Plympton J. Kelly, 1855–1856. Tacoma: Washington State Historical Society, 1976.